THE LEGACY OF SUNSET COVE

HARBOR
SECRETS

BOOK ONE

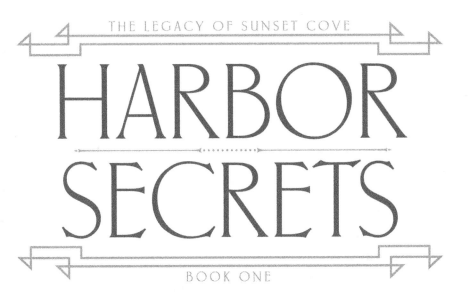

THE LEGACY OF SUNSET COVE

HARBOR SECRETS

BOOK ONE

MELODY CARLSON

WhiteFire
Publishing

This is a work of fiction. All characters and events portrayed in this novel are either fictitious or used fictitiously.

HARBOR SECRETS

WhiteFire Publishing
13607 Bedford Rd NE
Cumberland, MD 21502

ISBN: 978-1-946531-32-2 (print)
    978-1-946531-01-8 (digital)

CHAPTER 1

Early June 1916

Anna McDowell hadn't been home since the previous century. In fact, she'd never planned to return to Sunset Cove at all. Not until she received the telegram last week regarding her father's serious condition. But now that she and her daughter were almost there, Anna had serious misgivings. Perhaps it wasn't too late to change her mind. They could get off at the next station, catch the northbound train back to Portland, and forget all about Sunset Cove and Mac McDowell.

It wouldn't be easy to swallow her pride and beg for her job back, but that was what came from burning one's bridges prematurely. Anna should've known better. Still, there'd been some satisfaction in telling her stodgy old boss what she really thought of him and his prehistoric attitude toward women journalists, even getting him to admit he'd never heard of Nellie Bly.

"Why are you scowling like that?" Katy asked as the train slowed down for a station.

Anna looked out to see the Dalton Springs sign. Their

final destination was less than twenty minutes away now. "Scowling?" Anna forced a smile for her sixteen-year-old daughter, watching as an elderly couple made their way through the coach car.

Katy's forehead creased, obviously mimicking her mother's. "Yes, *scowling*. You were jazzed about this trip, Mother. You said you *missed* Sunset Cove."

"That's true." Anna nervously tugged at a kidskin glove. "Mostly true."

"Really, Mother, I'm the one who should be steamed. I had to leave my friends and the city behind—for the whole summer!"

"Oh, Katy, you should embrace this as a great, new adventure." Anna reached over to tuck an escaped curl back under Katy's wide-brimmed straw hat. This was just one more piece of the McDowell legacy—wild, untamable auburn curls. Anna's father had passed them down to Anna. And then poor Katy, who longed for sleek, bobbed black hair, had been similarly "blessed."

"Visiting a rinky-dink town on the Oregon Coast does not sound like a great, new adventure to me." Katy's lower lip jutted out. "It sounds more like a great big mistake—and not at all like I'd planned to spend my summer."

"Sometimes life requires more of us." Anna feigned confidence as the train's brakes hissed and it slowly chugged out of the station. "My father may be dying, Katy. We have been estranged for too long and—"

"I know, I know." Katy waved an impatient hand. "Your father is a tyrant who never forgave you for marrying when you were only seventeen. You've told me all this before. If you ask me, the old bully deserves to be estranged. I don't see why you'd want to go back...to *that*."

Anna pondered her daughter's words as she gazed out

the window, watching as green trees, a bubbling creek, occasional farms, and milk cows passed by in a blur. Before long they would catch a whiff of sea air...and then Sunset Cove would appear. Little had changed in the past seventeen years. Well, except for her. She turned to look at her daughter. "I didn't tell you *everything*, Katy...."

"What do you mean?" Katy's brown eyes widened with interest.

Anna pursed her lips. This was a story she'd planned on telling her daughter eventually...in adulthood. Katy was only sixteen but already proving herself to be a strong and capable young woman. And, to be fair, Anna had only been a year older than Katy when this story began.

"What is it, Mother?" Katy's countenance softened. "Please tell me."

Anna estimated she had about fifteen minutes to get this story out, and so she jumped in. "As you know, I met your father when he was a traveling salesman. Darrell passed through Sunset Cove in late 1899. He seemed like such a modern man, so full of exciting dreams and fresh ideas... Well, I was only seventeen and I got rather swept away by all of it."

"And he was very handsome," Katy added. "I've seen your wedding photograph. You made a striking couple."

"Yes. Your father was extremely handsome. And I was extremely naïve. Oh, I thought I was rather grown-up at the time, but looking back, well, I see it differently."

"So you got married and moved to the city and—"

"Hold on, Katy. I'm the one telling the story. The part you haven't heard is that your grandfather took an instant disliking to Darrell. For some reason, Mac completely disapproved of my beau."

"Who in the world is Mac?"

"Mac is my father."

"You called your father by his first name?"

"Well, I got into the habit while working at the newspaper. Everyone called him Mac. It just made life simpler. And he didn't mind."

"Oh, I see. So Mac didn't like Darrell. Why not?"

"To be honest, I didn't really know why at the time. But Mac was convinced that Darrell was, well, a bit of a scallywag." That was an understatement, for sure, but Anna wanted to respect that she was talking about Katy's father... and it was unkind to speak ill of the dead. Still, she wanted to be as truthful as possible. Katy deserved honesty.

"*Was* he a scallywag?" Katy's head tipped to one side.

Anna sighed. "I'm afraid he was. Oh, Darrell had a sweet, endearing side to him too. He was well spoken and intelligent. Truly, most people were quite taken with him, and he was a persuasive salesman. My goodness, that man could charm the stripes off a snake. But, truth be told, he had a very dark side as well."

"How so?" Her brow creased.

"It was fueled by his fondness of drink. Of course, this was well before Oregon outlawed alcohol last year." Anna weighed her words, trying to decide how much to say. "What you don't know, Katy, but what you may find out someday...is that your father got involved in some serious legal problems. He was arrested for fraud. And when he passed away, back when you were still a baby, he was incarcerated."

Katy looked genuinely shocked.

Anna reached for her hand and clasped it in her own. "I never planned to tell you this...not until you were grown-up. I didn't want you to think your father's mistakes were any sort of reflection on you. In many ways, your father was a fine man."

"But...but he was a criminal?" Katy's voice had a slight tremor.

"He got caught up in some criminal schemes. He wanted to get rich quickly...he lacked discernment, Katy. And it backfired on him."

"Did you know he was like that, Mother? When you married him, did you know?"

"No, no, not at all. As they say, *love is blind.* I certainly was. I thought Darrell Devlin was my Prince Charming. It seemed he'd come to rescue me from the tiny town that I felt certain I'd outgrown. But somehow your grandfather saw right through Darrell. I'm not even sure how, but he did. Unfortunately, I refused to listen to Mac." Anna smiled sadly. "And yet, I'm glad that I didn't. Otherwise, I wouldn't have you, darling. That makes up for everything."

Katy looked confused. "You just said my father's name was Darrell *Devlin.* But our last name is *McDowell.*"

"After your father was sentenced to prison, I returned to my maiden name. I had it legally changed for both of us. It seemed the prudent thing to do at the time...to separate ourselves from a name associated with crime. I felt we needed a fresh start."

Katy's eyes grew misty. "I don't know what to say, Mother. I feel like my whole life has been a complete lie." She pulled a handkerchief from her skirt pocket.

"No, it hasn't been a lie, Katy. It's just that I didn't think you were ready to know the whole truth before. If we weren't going to see your grandfather now, I probably wouldn't have told you today. I realize how shocking it must be. I'm sorry."

"So is that why you never went back to see your father? Because of—"

"My father was a stubborn man. He told me he would disown me if I married Darrell. I said a few things too... things I've come to regret. But Darrell and I ignored Mac's warning. We snuck away in the middle of the night and eloped. Then when it turned out that my father was right, I was too proud—and like him, too stubborn—to go home and admit failure. It grew even harder as the years passed by."

"Does your father even know about me?"

"I haven't spoken to him since I was seventeen, Katy. Not since I left."

"How did he know how to reach you?"

"It was his doctor who actually sent the telegram." Knowing they were now just minutes from Sunset Cove, Anna quickly explained how her father ran the *Sunset Times*. "As a newsman, he'd always read the *Oregonian*. I suspect he observed my byline...and probably mentioned it to his doctor."

"But everyone assumes A.R. McDowell is a man," Katy reminded her.

"I'm sure Mac could put two and two together. The telegram was delivered to the newspaper office." Anna still had regrets about giving up her job...especially after working her way from lowly secretary to society writer to her recent promotion to an editorial position, albeit under the pretense of writing as a male. Anna was well aware that her begrudged promotion was greatly due to the war in Europe. Although the United States was not involved, some eager young men were already joining the military with the expectation that it was right around the corner. Most members of the press believed it was inevitable, and a few adventuresome reporters had recently vacated jobs at the

Oregonian to do "their duty." So, like her boss had warned, Anna would likely be demoted in the event the U.S. avoided the war...or at the latest, when it ended.

"Are you nervous about seeing your father again?" Katy peered curiously into Anna's eyes.

Anna simply nodded.

Now Katy took Anna's hand. "I'll stand by you, Mother."

Anna smiled. "Thanks, darling. And, like I said, if we both decide that we really hate it in Sunset Cove, we are free to leave whenever we like. But I just can't bear the idea of Mac dying without repairing our relationship and without having met his only grandchild."

"What about your mother?" Katy's brows arched. "Will she be there too?"

"My mother...oh, she left us years ago."

"She died?"

Anna shook her head. "No, my mother packed her bags and went away. I was only six and had no idea why she left or where she'd gone. Later on I heard rumors that she hated small town life, and I suspect it was true. She came from San Francisco. I remember her as being very flamboyant and colorful—completely unlike the other women in Sunset Cove."

"Why did she move there, then?"

Anna got a glimpse of the ocean as the train went over a small rise, which reminded her that Sunset Cove was only a mile away. "My father inherited the newspaper from his father but wanted to modernize it, so he went down to San Francisco to pick up a new printing press. That's where he met my mother. She was quite a beauty, but somehow he swept her off her feet. They married down there, and he brought her home along with the press."

"That sounds rather romantic."

"Unfortunately, it didn't turn out romantic for either of them. I eventually learned that my mother got a divorce and remarried in San Francisco." Anna had heard that her mother's new husband was a much older man—and according to the scuttlebutt, quite wealthy.

"Did your father ever marry again?"

Anna stood as the train slowed for the station and retrieved her small bag from the overhead rack. "Not that I know of, but it's been seventeen years. Anything could've happened."

"Maybe this will be an adventure after all." Katy's brows arched as she stood. "Anyway, you've piqued my curiosity."

As the train stopped, Anna realized that she'd aroused her own curiosity as well. What would they find in Sunset Cove? Had her father remarried? And what about the newspaper? Was it even still there? Thanks to the popularity and increased distribution of large papers, like the *Oregonian*, many small-town papers had failed in recent years.

Anna's biggest questions were regarding her father's health. All she knew from the telegram was that he'd been incapacitated after suffering some sort of stroke—and that was more than a week ago. Was he even alive? And if so, how would he react to seeing her again? Would he even allow her into his home? Did he live in the same house? And why hadn't she sent a telegram to inform him she was coming? What if a surprise like this proved too much for him? What if the shock brought on another stroke...and he died? Then what? Anna closed her eyes, silently praying that her father was still alive...and that he would survive their visit.

CHAPTER 2

Mac McDowell had always been a stubborn man. He'd never been one to give up on anything, but this morning he felt like giving up on everything. As he pushed his barely touched breakfast tray aside, he decided to remain in bed. In fact, he had no intention of getting up again...ever. He vaguely wondered how long it would take to die from starvation or thirst. And, really, would anyone care? With each passing day, he'd reached the conclusion that his life no longer mattered. Maybe it never had.

Somehow he needed to come up with a workable plan to put an end to it—the sooner the better. Too bad he hadn't taken the time to write his own obituary. He'd promised himself to do that for his sixtieth birthday, but that wasn't until next winter.

He knew that writing an *honest* obituary would've been painful. So much brokenness, so much loss, so many mistakes...and what did he truly have to show for all his years? A newspaper that barely covered expenses? A drafty old house with too many empty rooms? And now his bad health on top of everything else. His right arm was useless, he could barely walk, and his memory was a mess.

Mac thought about friends who were his age. They always seemed happy. Lately some of them had been making retirement plans, looking forward to leisure. Harvey Rollins had recently gotten a new boat and planned to do some serious fishing when he quit the police force. And Wally and his wife were planning to drive their new car down the beach road, camping along the way until they reached the California redwood forest. But Mac was an invalid, stuck in bed, and feeling like there was nothing left to live for. Why prolong his demise?

"Come on, Mac," his housekeeper urged as she entered the bedroom. "The doctor said you need to get up and keep moving if you want to get well."

"Don'...feel...li'e..." He hated how incoherent his words had become since his stroke—babbling like a baby. For a man known to have a silver tongue, it was humiliating. Turning his head to the wall, Mac made a low growling sound. Hopefully that would send Bernice the message—*leave me alone!*

"Well, then let's at least open this place up." Bernice jerked on the cord on the drapes, flooding the bedroom with blindingly bright light. "Not everyone has an ocean view out their bedroom window like—"

"Ge' ou' here!" He tried to swear, but the words jumbled. "Lea' me 'lone!"

Bernice just chuckled, talking cheerily to herself as she bustled about the room in her usual, energetic way, picking up and straightening things as if he hadn't just blasted her—or attempted to. Bernice and her husband, Mickey, had been Mac's live-in helpers for nearly forty years, the closest thing to family he had—and he felt bad for treating her like this. But he just couldn't seem to help himself. Why couldn't they all just leave him alone?

With his eyes adjusting to the light, he gazed over the ocean—a sight that used to bring him pleasure...back when he'd been whole. But as he looked at the white topped waves rolling toward the shore, he wondered...

Perhaps the ocean held his answer—a quick and easy way out.

"Dr. Hollister will be here at eleven thirty." Bernice picked up his breakfast tray, then frowned. "You sure didn't eat much, Mac. Can't get well without good food."

He made a sour expression, narrowing his eyes. "Go... 'way."

Ignoring him, she set the tray aside, then laid his dressing robe at the foot of his bed. "Don't want the good doctor thinking we live like a bunch of pigs 'round here." She chuckled as if amused. "Come on, Mac. Time to rise and shine." She leaned forward, peering into his face. "You need me to help you sit up?"

"*No!*" Irritated at her helpfulness, Mac labored to push himself up in bed with his left hand. His right arm remained useless, hanging lifelessly against his side. A bit of strength had returned to his right leg, but he was still clumsy and awkward and couldn't get around without a cane. Even then it was a challenge. As if to add insult to injury, he knew the right side of his face still drooped like a deformed monster...and, of course, he stumbled over words like a drunkard. Why should he want to keep living like this?

"Mickey's on his way to help you dress." Bernice picked up the tray again, watching with what Mac knew was pity as he struggled to sit upright.

Mac considered protesting Mickey's help but knew it was pointless. Besides, it would go better with the doctor if Mac was showered and shaved and dressed. Mac didn't need another lecture. Doc Hollister had some peculiar ideas about stroke recovery—and they did not include languishing in bed, no matter how listless the patient felt. Instead, the young doctor had prescribed a salt-free diet which made food taste like paste, daily doses of Bayer Aspirin, and silly exercises with rubber balls and strings and things.

But Mac was sick and tired of being treated like a child. Why couldn't they all just leave him be...let him die in peace? He looked out over the ocean again... Yes, it could work. When the timing was right, he would do it.

Feeling motivated by his evolving plan, Mac slowly dragged himself out of bed and was nearly into his dressing robe by the time Mickey arrived. Mac had been home from the hospital for more than a week now, and Mickey had a well-established yet merciless routine for putting him through his paces each morning. He'd help Mac just enough to get him moving and then he'd step back and let him struggle on his own. Only intervening when absolutely necessary. Another part of the young doctor's "treatment."

First, there was getting into the shower where Mickey had set a wooden bench for Mac to sit upon. Mac wasn't overly concerned with his hygiene these days, but he tried to humor Mickey, who usually enjoyed a smoke while Mac sat in the shower's spray, attempting to get clean, and then dried with one clumsy hand. But left-handed shaving was still tricky, and when Mickey eventually stepped in to help, Mac didn't protest. Eventually, Mac managed to get himself mostly dressed.

As usual, Mickey was a man of few words. And for this, Mac was grateful.

"Than' you," Mac mumbled as Mickey helped him to button his shirt.

"Glad to help." Mickey straightened his collar. "You're

doing better, Mac. Didn't take nearly as long as a few days ago."

"Tired." Mac reached for his cane and, limping and wobbling, slowly made his way through his bedroom and into the attached sitting room. It felt like hours before he finally reached the easy chair by the window, but he eventually sank into it.

"You rest." Mickey tucked a pillow behind Mac's head. "I'll tell Bernice to bring you some coffee. And I smell something good in the oven too."

"Than' you." Mac used his left hand to lift his right arm, laying the lifeless appendage across his lap with a weary sigh.

It wasn't long before Bernice reappeared with the tray again. This time it was coffee and sweet rolls. Obviously, her attempt to get him to eat something. And now that he was clean and dressed...and not planning to die from starvation...he decided to comply. It was easier, and less likely to arouse her suspicion.

Mac was just finishing his coffee when Bernice announced that Dr. Hollister had arrived.

"Good morning, Mr. McDowell," the doctor smiled as he entered the room.

"Mor'ing," Mac mumbled back.

Bernice pointed to the tray, explaining to the doctor that she'd brought plenty for him, but he just thanked her as he set his doctor's bag on a side table. Then, after pulling a straight-backed chair over, he sat down across from Mac. "How are you feeling today?"

Mac grimaced. If he could get the words out, he'd give the good doctor a cynical answer. Instead, he just scowled.

"I'm sorry. Did you say something?" Dr. Hollister's dark

eyes twinkled as if he found amusement in tormenting Mac into talking.

"I am...fine," Mac mumbled sourly. "Jus' fine."

"Good. I'm glad to see you're working on your language skills." Now he pulled out his stethoscope and began going through the usual steps of his examination—poking, prodding, listening, and looking. Appearing satisfied at last, the doctor began putting Mac through his rehabilitation paces with the rubber balls and strings and whatnot, until Mac couldn't stand one more minute.

With a sorry attempt at a swear word, Mac threw the disgusting rubber ball across the room, hostilely glaring at the doctor. "No more!"

Dr. Hollister simply nodded. "I know this is hard on you, Mr. McDowell, but—"

"Ma—ac!" he insisted. "Call me *Mac.*"

"Good, good." The doctor smiled. "Mac. Let's work on forming some words and sounds that are—"

"No!" Mac firmly shook his head. "No more."

Of course, this was the good doctor's invitation to lecture Mac, explaining how some stroke victims showed great improvement with modern rehabilitation therapy. He explained about how he'd been reading up on the latest treatments and how important it was to keep moving and trying, never to give up.

If only he knew, Mac thought, glaring daggers at the optimistic doctor. Not only did Mac intend to give up, he was currently making plans for his own demise. He glanced out the window toward the ocean again, imagining his permanent getaway. His house was situated high on the bluff...and as soon as the tide came fully in, Mac would limp outside, go across the terrace, toss aside his cane, and take what would hopefully look like an accidental stumble that would plunge him over the edge of the cliff. He would fall into the sea, where the ocean would finish him off. It would be an easy exit and a welcome escape from a disappointing life. And, truly, who would care?

CHAPTER 3

After Anna made arrangements for their bags to be held at the train station, she led Katy down Main Street, pointing out the "sights" of Sunset Cove. "I know it's just my imagination, but the town seems even smaller than I remembered," she confessed to Katy as they walked past the barbershop.

"Maybe it's because you're used to Portland," Katy suggested.

"Your grandfather's newspaper office is still here." She pointed to the two-story, boxlike building across the street. "And since there are lights on inside, I assume the paper is still running."

"Do you want to go take a look?" Katy asked.

"No, not yet." Anna stopped in front of the Sunset Cove Hotel and Restaurant. "Why don't we get some lunch here, and I'll see if there are any rooms available."

"I thought we were going to stay at your father's house."

"Well, that would be better for our finances, but I'm not sure we'll be welcome there. Best to have a backup plan." Anna led the way into the hotel, and, after being assured of room vacancies, they were seated by the window in the restaurant. After making her selection from the limited menu, Anna glanced around at the other diners but observed no one she recognized.

They had just placed their orders when Anna noticed a strikingly familiar face. He had just entered the restaurant and was checking his hat. Anna gasped in surprise, then turned her attention to Katy, making what she knew sounded like idle chatter and keeping her eyes downward.

"What is it, Mother?" Katy sounded alarmed. "You look like you just saw a ghost."

Anna smiled stiffly. "Just someone from my past."

"Why don't you say hello?" Katy looked curiously around and fixated on something...or someone.

"Don't stare, Katy." Anna pretended to be amused by a pair of young women walking past the window.

"I'm not staring," Katy hissed back at her. "But he is."

"Who is?" Anna feigned nonchalance.

"That man—he's headed straight for our table."

Anna glanced up in time to see Randall Douglas stride directly toward them.

"Anna McDowell," he declared. "I would've known you anywhere." He stuck out his hand and grasped hers with a wide smile. "What are you doing back in Sunset Cove?"

"Randall Douglas," she said politely. "So nice to see you again." She paused to introduce him to Katy, trying to get her bearings.

"Now, it's Rand. You know only my mother calls me Randall. I can hardly believe you have a full-grown daughter, Anna." Rand shook his head as he grasped Katy's hand, smiling down at her. "But you are the image of your mother as a girl."

"Rand is an old school friend." Anna tried to sound casual.

"Oh, don't let your mother fool you," Rand winked at Katy. "I was once your mother's beau."

Katy's brows arched. "Interesting."

"Well, that was a lifetime ago." Anna forced a smile for Rand. "It's a pleasure to see you, but we don't want to keep you from anyone—"

"No worries. I'm dining alone."

"Then why don't you join us?" Katy offered.

"I'd love to." Rand was already pulling out a chair. "Thank you." He turned to Anna. "I heard about your dad's illness. I assume that's why you're here."

"Yes." Anna nodded. "Do you know how he's doing?"

"I just spoke to Virginia Proctor yesterday. Do you remember her?"

"Of course. She was my father's receptionist and secretary. Is she still with the newspaper?"

"Yes. According to Virginia, your dad's been out of the hospital for about a week now. He's recovering at home."

"Does he still live in the same house?" Anna asked eagerly.

Rand nodded. "And it sounds like he'll be unable to return to work for a while...or maybe not at all. Virginia sounded a bit concerned about the future of the newspaper."

"Maybe you can run it," Katy suggested to Anna.

"Well, I—"

"Mom is an editor for the *Oregonian*," Katy bragged.

"*Was* an editor," Anna corrected.

"So you really are A.R. McDowell?" Rand asked with interest. "I saw that byline recently and wondered." He frowned. "But I thought your last name was Devlin."

"It *was*," Anna explained. "My husband passed away quite some time ago. I used McDowell as my pen name." She nodded toward Katy. "We both go by McDowell."

"I'm sorry for your loss. For both of you." Rand paused as the waiter returned to their table, now taking Rand's order.

"So, Rand, have you been in Sunset Cove all this time?" Anna was eager to divert their conversation away from her deceased husband. "And do your folks still run the mercantile?"

"I've only been back here three years," he told her. "I went to law school, then practiced in Salem for a few years. But my father passed away, and my mother needed help. So..." He held up his hands. "Here I am."

"Do you have other family?" Katy asked. "Wife? Children?"

"No...I've been accused of being married to my career." He shrugged. "But I just never found the right woman." He glanced at Anna. "Or maybe I let her get away."

Anna cleared her throat. "How do you like living here? Was it difficult to come back?"

"I'll admit it took some adjusting. But truth be told, I'd gotten a little weary of the way of life in Salem. I did a lot of capital work. Both for the senate and congress. It was good experience, but rather demanding...long hours and not much time off."

"I don't imagine law practice is too demanding here in Sunset Cove." Anna glanced around the sleepy dining room.

"That's true, but I don't really mind the slower pace. My office is next to the mercantile, and, if I'm not too busy, I help Mom out at the store. And sometimes I even go fishing or just shoot the breeze with the good ol' boys." He grinned. "Can't complain. I guess you can take the boy out of the small town, but you can't take the small town out of the boy."

"I wonder if that's true about a city girl," Katy mused.

"Katy hasn't been overly excited about coming here," Anna confessed.

"How long do you plan to stay?" he asked.

"I honestly don't know. My father isn't aware that we're coming." She sighed.

"I see...." He slowly nodded, then lowered his voice. "I remember how upset Mac was after you left town, Anna. In fact, a lot of people were concerned for your welfare. But Mac seemed to take it especially hard. Did you ever patch things up with him?"

Anna simply shook her head. "It's partly why I'm here."

"Well, I'm sure he'll be glad to see you."

"I hope so, but..." Anna paused as the waiter set down their orders.

"Mother is worried that my grandfather will throw us out on our ears," Katy said quietly after the waiter left.

Rand just laughed. "I hardly think so. If you ask me, Mac is lonely, rattling around in that big, old house of his."

"I wonder if Mickey and Bernice are still with him," Anna mused.

"They're still there. I saw Bernice at the store a few weeks ago—before your father got ill. She seemed just fine."

"So my father never remarried?"

"No, no...but maybe now that your mother is back in town—"

"What?" Anna dropped her soup spoon with such a loud clang that the few people present turned to look. "You can't be serious."

"It's true. My mother mentioned that Lucille McDowell came into the mercantile a couple days ago. It's been the talk of the town. I just assumed you already knew. According to Mom, she's staying right here in the hotel. You mean you haven't seen her yet?"

"No...." Anna tried to act natural. "I didn't know she was here."

"Oh, Mother," Katy exclaimed. "Isn't that wonderful news? You were just talking about your mother. This really is going to be an adventure."

Anna just nodded, numbly dipping her spoon into the cream of asparagus soup, but her appetite had completely vanished at the thought of her mother being so nearby. In fact, she felt rather light-headed and dizzy at the thought of Lucille McDowell suddenly walking into the restaurant. What on earth would Anna say or do? And why was her mother here in Sunset Cove anyway? The possible answers to these questions made Anna's head throb. Oh, what had she gotten herself into? And was it too late to get out?

CHAPTER 4

To Anna's huge relief, they were able to finish their meal, which she simply pretended to eat, and escape the hotel restaurant without bumping into Lucille McDowell. Anna was so eager to get away from there that she didn't even argue when Rand insisted on paying their luncheon bill. Besides, she reasoned, that was the gentlemanly thing to do after intruding on them like that—not to mention sharing such startling news.

"Come on," she urged Katy as she led her down a side street. "Let's hurry."

"What's the rush?" Katy peered curiously at her. "You told me we were going to see the sights of Sunset Cove before paying your father a visit."

"You've seen enough sights." Anna glanced nervously around.

"You're just afraid you're going to see your mother, aren't you?" Katy's tone was slightly teasing. "What about all your talk of a great adventure, Mother? Wouldn't it be great to—"

"*Please!*" Anna hooked her arm into Katy's. "Don't

torment me. This is difficult enough without thinking about her."

"I'm sorry." Katy actually sounded contrite. "But wasn't your friend Mr. Douglas rather nice?"

"I suppose he's nice enough."

"He seemed to think you were nice too."

"Oh, Katy." Anna let out an exasperated sigh.

"He seemed quite fond of you, Mother. And you never told me you had beaux before marrying my father." Katy elbowed Anna. "In fact, you never told me much of anything about your previous life."

"Apparently, you are learning all about it now." Anna pointed to the tall stone structure up ahead, the largest home on Shore Avenue, perhaps in all of Sunset Cove. At least it used to be. "*That* is your grandfather's house."

"Oh my. You didn't tell me we came from such grandeur."

"Yes, well, my grandfather built this house in the late 1860s, back when my father was just a youth."

"Was your grandfather wealthy?"

"He had a small shipping line." She pointed to the top of the house. "Thus, the widow's watch. Apparently my grandmother wanted that so she could watch when the ships came and went." She stood in front of the iron gate, just staring up at the old stone house. In some ways it seemed a foreign place...in other ways it seemed like home.

"This really is an adventure." Katy opened the gate, waving Anna in ahead of her. "Come on, Mother. Let's see if anyone's home."

With her heart in her throat, Anna led Katy up to the house. She raised the big, tarnished brass knocker on the door and let it fall with a loud clang. "I remember how that noise used to make me jump."

"A doorbell might be more practical."

"Your grandfather is a bit old-fashioned. He only agreed to have a telephone because of the newspaper, and, although I noticed wires in town, I would be greatly surprised if he has electricity here."

"Maybe no one's home." Katy lifted the knocker, letting it fall again.

They waited a couple more minutes, then Anna decided to try the door. Not surprisingly, it was unlocked. "Hello?" she called as she stepped inside. "Anyone home?"

"I hear some noise over that way." Katy pointed in the kitchen's direction.

"That's right. Monday was always Bernice's washday," Anna whispered. "She hated being interrupted while in the middle of it. And it's so lovely outside, I suspect Mickey is working on the grounds today."

"Where do you think your dad might be?"

Anna tipped her head toward the hallway. "His bedroom and sitting room are down there."

"Let's go find him," Katy urged.

"Maybe I should get Bernice first."

"Why bother the poor woman if she's up to her elbows in soapsuds?" Katy tugged on Anna's arm. "Come on."

Anna went reluctantly, tapping gingerly on her father's sitting room door when they reached it. She doubted he'd be in here. Based on what Rand had said, and the doctor's telegram, she expected to find him in bed. Perhaps he had a nurse to help care for him.

"Anyone here?" Katy called out as she opened the door wider, stepping inside and looking around curiously. "This is a nice room." She picked up a bronze sculpture of an Indian maid and smiled. "Pretty piece."

"Don't be such a snoop—" Anna stopped in mid-sentence. Outside was an elderly man with white hair, weaving back and forth as he walked dangerously close to the edge of the terrace. "Oh no."

"What?" Katy turned to look.

"My father—outside." Anna rushed to the glass doors that opened onto the terrace. "He's about to fall."

"Hurry!" Katy yelled.

Anna sprang outside in time to see him toss his cane aside and teeter. His back was toward her as she raced to him, but she could see he was off balance, wobbling precariously close to the low stone wall—the only thing that separated him from a sheer drop-off to the ocean.

"*Mac!*" she shrieked as she grabbed for him with both hands, catching him by his sleeves. She jerked him toward her in the nick of time, plummeting them both down onto the terrace stones with a hard thud.

"Are you okay?" Katy hovered over the two of them, peering down with frightened eyes.

"Wha'—wha'?" Mac turned at Anna with disbelief. "Wha'?"

"Mac. It's me. Anna." She disentangled herself from him and then slowly stood. Dusting off her gray traveling skirt, she tried to align her scattered thoughts. What had just transpired...and what should she do now?

"Come on, Grandpa." Katy's tone was surprisingly cheery. "Let's help you up."

Then Anna and Katy both reached down and, grasping his hands in theirs, pulled him to his feet, but he was clearly unstable. Anna suddenly remembered the doctor's telegram—saying how her father's stroke had left him disabled. Worried he might take another tumble, Anna continued to support him while Katy went to fetch the discarded cane.

Mac looked at her with troubled eyes that used to be a

clear sea blue but now seemed faded. In fact, everything about him looked washed out, pale and old. Nothing like the robust and ruddy redheaded man from her childhood. When had this happened?

"Wha'—wha'—you here for?" He stumbled over his words like a small child—not like the loquacious father she remembered.

"Mac," she said gently. "I'm sorry we startled you like this." She frowned at the low rock wall, something he'd often warned her about as a child. "But what were you doing out here?"

Katy handed him his cane. "Looked to me like you were about to take a dip in the ocean just now." She peered over the edge of the stone wall and then gasped. "Oh my word! That is quite a drop-off."

"This is Katy," Anna told Mac. "Your granddaughter."

"Wha'—wha'?" Mac looked thoroughly confused now—and although it wasn't cold out here, he seemed to be trembling.

"Come inside," she urged. Still holding to his limp arm, she slowly led him back into the sitting room, waiting as he struggled with each step. She helped ease him down into his worn easy chair, silently praying for wisdom...and grace.

"I'm sorry to take you by surprise." She paused to gaze out the window, replaying the strange scene they'd just witnessed. "But it seems to me we got here just in time. What on earth were you doing out there?"

He looked down at his lap, as if embarrassed.

"Mac?" she persisted. "Why did you toss your cane like that? It looked like you planned to go right over that wall—intentionally."

He looked up with teary eyes and slowly nodded. He seemed truly defeated as tears streaked down his wrinkled cheeks. Anna felt shocked. She'd never seen her father cry before. Oh, she'd seen him yell and swear and throw some horrible fits, but she'd never seen him cry real tears. And she'd never seen him this frail—part of his face actually appeared to be sagging.

"Oh, Mac." Kneeling down by his chair, Anna wrapped her arms around his neck and held him tightly. "I'm so sorry. I'm so, so sorry."

"I...sor—sor'...too." He gasped out the broken words. "So sor'."

"You were right about everything," she continued, still holding on to him. "I didn't listen to you. But you were right. And I'm truly sorry, Mac. I'm sorry I was so stubborn—and that I stayed away so long. I hope you can forgive me." She pulled back, looking into his weathered face. "Can you?"

"Done." He nodded, reaching up to touch her cheek with his left hand. "You too? For...gi'...me?"

"Yes, of course, I forgive you."

He looked over her shoulder, taking in Katy with a quizzical expression. "You?"

"This is your granddaughter, Katy," Anna repeated herself. She took Katy's hand, pulling her closer. "Her full name is Kathleen Rebecca McDowell—just like your mother—my grandmother."

His eyes lit up at the mention of his mother, but then his brow furrowed in confusion. "Mc...Dow—ell?" he struggled over his own name, but his question was clear.

"Yes, Mac." Anna nodded somberly. "After Darrell died...I returned to my maiden name. Katy and I both go by McDowell."

He frowned, even more confused. "Darrell...*dead*?"

Anna looked at Katy, unsure of how much her daughter could take, but Katy just nodded, continuing for her. "My father died when I was a baby," Katy somberly told Mac. "In prison."

Mac turned to Anna with wide eyes. "Wha'? How?"

And so, for the second time that day, Anna told the condensed story of how Darrell had tried to cheat the system and gotten caught, but because Katy seemed to be handling it relatively well, Anna told a bit more. "At first I was told Darrell died of influenza in prison." She glanced at Katy. "But I later learned that he might've been killed by an inmate—in retribution from one of his criminal connections." Anna looked back to Mac. "You were right about him. I should've listened to you." She reached for Katy's hand. "Except that if I had listened, I wouldn't have Katy."

"Kay...tee." He nodded at his granddaughter with what seemed like approval and then reached for her hand. "Pray... tee gal. Pray...tee Kay...tee."

Katy smiled. "Thanks, Grandpa. I'm glad I finally got to meet you."

"Holy smokes!" Bernice came into the room and grabbed onto the back of a chair as if to keep from falling over. "Blow me down."

"Bernice!" Anna hopped up to embrace the old woman. "It's so good to see you again."

"Well, I never." Bernice hugged her back. "I just never ever never—"

"Come meet my daughter, Katy." Anna pulled Bernice over to where Katy was sitting next to Mac, still holding his hand.

"Well, I'll be." Bernice just shook her head. "Wait'll Mickey hears about this."

As Bernice ran off to get her husband, Anna watched her father with interest. He no longer seemed as frail and elderly as before. With his eyes fixed on Katy, his face—at least half of it—was beaming. He truly seemed glad to see them. But still she wondered...had he really intended to end his life just moments ago? And if so, why? Was it related to his stroke? Or something more?

But her most worrisome question—and one she wasn't quite ready to face just yet—was did her father know that Lucille was in town?

CHAPTER 5

After a happy reunion with Mickey and Bernice, Anna and Katy took turns talking to Mac over a tempting tea tray. Although it was hard to fully understand his words, they both seemed to comprehend their meaning. He wanted to know more about them, what they'd been doing, where they'd been living, and so on. To Anna's relief, Katy seemed comfortable taking the lead in the conversation, but after an hour or so, Anna could see her father was tiring.

"I'm sorry to interrupt." Bernice picked up the tea tray. "But the doctor insists that Mac get his afternoon nap." Mac started to protest, but Bernice cut him off. "I'm sure you'll want to dine with Anna and Katy this evening." She winked at Anna and then turned back to Mac. "But you'll need your strength to join them in the dining room."

"And I need to make arrangements for our trunks." Anna stood. "We left our things at the train station."

"I'll ask Mickey to take care of that," Bernice told her.

"Can I help you to your bedroom, Grandpa?" Katy offered. Mac rewarded her with a half-smile, taking her arm, and Anna exited the room with Bernice.

"Oh my." Bernice's eyes lit up. "That sweet girl is good

medicine for Mac. Already he is acting more like his old self."

"I'm so glad we came." Anna followed Bernice out through the front room and into the kitchen, noticing how little had changed in the house.

"You're both just what the doctor ordered." Bernice set down the tray. "I just know Mac will get better now."

"Speaking of the doctor, I'd like to speak to him. I want to know about my father's treatment and if there's anything Katy and I can do to help."

"Dr. Hollister's office is next to the hardware store. Or I can give you his telephone number."

"It's such a lovely afternoon, I wouldn't mind strolling through town."

"That's a fine idea." Bernice nodded.

"I thought I heard voices back here." Katy came into the kitchen. "Grandpa is resting now."

"Thank you, darling girl." Bernice patted Katy's shoulder. "I was just telling your mother that having you here will be so good for Mac."

"So are we staying here?" Katy glanced at Anna. "Not the hotel?"

"Of course you're staying here," Bernice insisted. "You're family. And Mickey will arrange for your trunks to be delivered as soon as possible." She looked at Anna. "How about if we put you in the guest suite and Katy in your old room?"

Anna liked the idea of occupying the spacious guest suite. "That sounds perfect. Thank you." She turned to Katy. "I think you'll like my old bedroom. It's twice the size of your room in Portland and overlooks the ocean."

"I can't wait to see it." Katy looked at Bernice. "In fact, I'd love to explore this whole house. Would anyone mind if—"

"You just make yourself at home, darling."

"And I'll be careful not to disturb my grandfather," Katy promised.

"And you might be surprised to discover that we have indoor plumbing upstairs," Bernice proudly declared. "Mac got it installed last year. He said it was because he planned to sell the house when he retired. But I'm sure you young ladies will appreciate having it."

"What luxuries," Anna exclaimed.

"I'm going to go investigate," Katy told them. But before she went, Anna explained her plan to visit Mac's doctor, inviting Katy to join her, but Katy declined.

"I really want to see this wonderful house, and I'd love to go down on the beach, if there's access." Katy tugged on a glove.

Bernice explained where to go to find the beach steps, warning how they could be slippery when it was wet. "But we haven't had rain for a few days."

"It all sounds delightful." Katy hugged Anna. "You were right, Mother. This is feeling like an adventure after all. Almost like a vacation."

After Katy scurried off, Anna let out a relieved sigh. "Katy had been so reluctant to come here...I'm so glad she's happy." Anna suddenly remembered Lucille. "Uh, Bernice...I meant to ask...have you heard anything about my mother?"

Bernice frowned. "No, dear, not for years."

Anna quickly explained what Rand had told her at lunch. "He says she's been staying at the hotel the past couple days."

Bernice's eyebrows shot up. "Good heavens!"

"I have no idea why she's here. Is it possible that Mac contacted her?"

"No, I doubt that. Mac has never mentioned her name—

not since she left." Bernice frowned. "For a while he got letters that were postmarked from San Francisco. I had wondered if they were from her, but the name on the return address was unfamiliar, and Mac never said a word about them. After a while, they quit coming." Bernice fed a couple pieces of wood into the old cookstove and then turned to peer at Anna. "You don't think she came here to see Mac, do you? I can't even imagine how he would react to that sort of shock. Poor fellow, it might finish him off for good."

"Well, perhaps I should pay a little visit to the hotel too." Anna grimaced to think how that would go. "I could warn her to stay away."

"Yes, dear, please do that." Bernice checked on a covered pot, then pointed to the clock. "If you'll excuse me, there's much to be done, and dinner will be at six thirty."

Anna thanked her and then went upstairs to freshen up. The guest suite was a bit smaller than she recalled, due to the addition of a comfortable-looking bathroom, but the bedroom was still spacious and inviting and, like her old bedroom, overlooked the sea. She remembered how Grandmother always wanted this room to look its best, using it for honored guests. As Anna pinned her hat back into place, she had to agree with Katy. Staying here was starting to feel like a vacation. Except for the unfortunate chore she had yet to face—meeting her mother...and telling her to keep her distance.

Anna got her black leather traveling purse and pulled on her gloves in preparation to walk back to town. If her trunk had arrived, it might've been fun to change into one of her summery frocks, but her plain gray traveling suit might be more effective at garnering respect. Both from the doctor and her mother. Anna had learned long ago, working in a man's world, that sometimes severity in dress encouraged others to take her more seriously.

Her first stop was the doctor's office. She realized that the doctor might be busy or making calls, but she was prepared to leave a message, if necessary. "Do you have an appointment?" the brunette at the desk asked with a curious expression. She wore a nurse's uniform.

Anna studied her for a moment, thinking she looked familiar...then recognized her. "Norma Reece?"

"That was my maiden name. I'm Norma Barrows now... widowed." The woman frowned, then blinked. "Oh, I know who you are—Anna McDowell."

"Yes. Dr. Hollister has been treating my father, and I'd hoped—"

"Is that Mac's daughter?" A fair-haired man stuck his head around the corner. He didn't appear to be much older than Anna and seemed too casual to be the actual doctor.

Anna smiled. "Yes, Mac is my father. I'm looking for Dr. Hollister."

He came out extending his hand. "It's a pleasure to meet you, uh, Miss McDowell? Or is that simply your pen name?" He cocked his head to one side. "You see, I've read what I assumed were your pieces in the *Oregonian*. That's why I took a chance in sending you that telegram."

"So you *are* Dr. Hollister?"

He grinned. "Guilty as charged."

"I am Anna McDowell, and I thank you for sending me the telegram about my father."

"Come into my office." He waved her toward a small room with book-lined walls and a large desk. "Have a seat." He nodded to a leather chair and then leaned back onto his oversized and cluttered desk. "I'm so glad you decided to come by. I've been quite worried about your father." He explained how Mac had been dragging his heels regarding his treatment and therapy. "I suspect he might be able to recover, at least partially, if he would simply cooperate with my prescribed treatment. But your father is a stubborn man."

"That's one reason I came to see you. I hoped you could tell me how my daughter and I might help with his recovery." She reluctantly explained how they'd found Mac on the terrace. "I fear he was considering going over, but we interrupted him."

"Oh dear. That's not good." He moved around to the other side of his desk, rubbing his chin. "Although I'm certainly glad you got there in time to intervene."

"But then, after he got over the shock of seeing us, he seemed genuinely heartened by our visit. He got along so well with my daughter, Katy.... Well, it was encouraging, at the very least."

"Do you think he's in any danger of making an attempt like that again?" His frown seemed quite concerned.

"No, I honestly don't think so. Even his housekeeper believes he's already taken a turn for the better. She feels Katy is good medicine."

His grin looked amused. "I will try not to feel replaced."

"No, of course not. It's just that I'd like to do anything we can to help him recover."

Dr. Hollister reached for a book and, opening it, brought it over to show Anna the diagrams and explanations about some new modern therapeutic exercises. "If you could only get him to do these things, he might improve his mobility and muscle function. As for his memory issues...only time will tell."

"His memory?" Anna frowned. "I didn't notice anything. I mean, he definitely knew who I was."

"I believe it's more of his recent memory. When I first questioned him, he didn't know what year it was and several other things to suggest the stroke has impaired him a bit. That's not to say his brain isn't as sharp as ever, but there might be a few gaps."

"I see."

"Perhaps the best thing that you and your daughter can do is to simply converse with Mac. And when you do, encourage him to speak clearly, even if it means repeating words. Get him to use full sentences, or at least try. The more he works on these verbal skills, the better his chance at regaining his speech, which might even help with his memory."

"Of course, we'll be happy to do that. My daughter Katy is sixteen and quite loquacious." Anna chuckled. "I often tease her that she's got the gift of gab."

"That gift could help your father immensely."

"So do you really believe he'll recover?"

"It's my hope that he will improve significantly, but it will take time and work and patience. And I must warn you, it's doubtful that he'll make a full recovery—back to how he was before the stroke. I haven't told him as much, but I don't expect he'll ever be able to return to work. But I also know he was looking forward to retirement. He mentioned that to me at his examination last year."

"I wonder what he'd planned for the newspaper...?"

"You're a newspaperwoman. Perhaps you can step in, Miss—uh, or is it Mrs. McDowell?"

She pursed her lips. "That's a fair question. You see, in Portland, I went by *Mrs.* McDowell. I returned to my maiden name after I was widowed, but because I had a child, it was necessary to go by Mrs. And you're right, I have used A. R.

McDowell as my pen name. But here in Sunset Cove, that may be confusing for some."

The doctor looked slightly confused as well.

"Why don't you simply call me Anna?" she suggested.

His eyes brightened. "Only if you call me Daniel."

She nodded. "It's a deal."

He handed her the book. "How about if you borrow this? Study it and see what you can do to keep Mac on track."

"Thank you—and thank you for your time." She stood, then remembered something. "I have another question...a rather prickly question, actually."

His fair brows arched with curiosity. "Yes?"

She quickly explained the situation with her parents, how her mother left so long ago and how hard it had been on Mac. "But I just heard she's back in town. I'm afraid she must be here to see my father—and to be honest, I'm afraid the shock could be too much for him. Is there any chance something like this could bring on another stroke?"

His expression grew grim. "Yes, that is a very real possibility. As I told Bernice, Mac needs to avoid excitement and overstimulation."

"I see." She twisted her purse strap. "So...perhaps I should go and warn my mother to stay away from him?"

"That would be most prudent, Miss—I mean, Anna."

"Yes, well, then I should take care of this now." She frowned and started to leave, but he placed a hand on her arm to stop her.

"I know this must be difficult for you," he said. "If it would help, I could accompany you to meet your mother... to help her understand our concerns."

She considered this but then shook her head. "I sincerely appreciate the offer, but I think this is something I need to do alone."

"Then be sure to tell her that your father's physician has sent this warning. If she has any questions, you tell her to come and speak directly to me. I am glad to set her straight."

"Oh, thank you!" Anna nodded gratefully. "That would be most helpful."

As Anna left the doctor's office, she felt like she'd just gained an important friend and ally. But like she'd told the good doctor, this was a task that she needed to face alone. *God, help me,* she silently prayed as she marched to the hotel. *Or even better, let my mother have already returned to San Francisco.*

Chapter 6

The minute Anna entered the lobby, she knew the stylish woman coming down the stairs was her mother—and yet, it seemed impossible. Lucille would be fifty-three by now...but the woman in the lilac dress with a three-tiered skirt didn't look much older than Anna. Perhaps Anna was simply imagining things. Resisting the urge to blink her eyes and openly gape, she headed for the reception desk instead. But she immediately realized she didn't know who to ask for. What was her mother's last name?

"Can I help you?" the desk clerk asked.

"I, uh, I want to inquire regarding a guest." She glanced over her shoulder to see the woman also approaching the front desk. "My name is Anna McDowell," she declared loudly enough for anyone nearby to hear. "I'd like to ask about—"

"Anna?" The woman grasped Anna by the arm, spinning her around. "I can't believe it! Is it really you?"

"Please, excuse us," Anna hastily told the clerk. Then, feeling conspicuous and confused, she led her mother over to a quiet corner of the lobby. "Are you—are you Lucille—"

"Of course I am, dear." Lucille nodded eagerly. "I'm your mother."

With trembling knees, Anna sank into a chair, staring speechlessly as Lucille gracefully eased down onto the adjacent settee. Smiling prettily, Lucille leaned a lilac parasol against her knee and daintily folded her hands in her lap. "Anna Rebecca McDowell...I hardly know what to say." She shook her head with an expression of wonder. "My goodness, it's wonderful to see you. I think I would've recognized you anywhere with that auburn hair. You're a bit like your grandmother and a lot like me."

Anna was too shocked to respond, actually grasping the chair's arms as if to ground herself and finding it difficult to breathe.

"So, tell me, my dear girl—how have you been?"

"What are you doing here?" Anna demanded.

"Goodness, dear. Whatever became of common courtesy?"

"*Courtesy?*" Anna bristled even more. How dare this woman—the mother who abandoned her at such a young age—question Anna's manners?

"I'm sure you're surprised, dear. Naturally, we both are. But there's no reason we can't have a civilized conversation."

"You're absolutely right." Anna slowly nodded, trying to contain her feelings. She normally didn't consider herself an overly emotional person, but right now she felt like screaming or crying or throwing a childish tantrum. "I'm sorry." She took in a deep breath. "But it's important for me to understand why you're here." She almost used the word *mother* but knew she couldn't say it without sounding scornful.

"Why I'm here in this hotel? Well, that's—"

"No. I mean why you're here in Sunset Cove."

"Oh, well, that's easy. I heard about your father's illness—"

"Who told you?"

"My old friend, Fern Layton. We've stayed in touch over the years."

Anna scowled. For as long as Anna could remember, Fern Layton had been the town gossip. "That still doesn't explain why you came."

"I felt it was time I returned." Lucille's expression grew more serious. "To repair my burnt bridges."

"With Mac?"

"Is that what you call your father—*Mac*?"

"As a matter of fact, it is, and he has never minded." Anna considered explaining but decided against it.

"Oh, then...I suppose you'll want to call me Lucille."

"Or Mrs.—What is your last name?"

"It's Tyler, but—"

"Fine, Mrs. Tyler. I need to make you—"

"Please, I would prefer you call me Lucille."

"Yes, well, you need to understand that Mac is in no condition to receive visitors. I just spoke to his doctor, and he made it clear that Mac cannot see you. If you have any questions, you may contact Dr. Hollister, and he will explain why you must stay away."

Lucille waved a hand. "Oh, I'm well aware of that."

"You are?"

"Yes. I stopped by the newspaper yesterday. I spoke to Virginia, and the old biddy told me—in no uncertain terms— that Mac wasn't well enough to see me...yet."

Anna wanted to cheer for Virginia. "But you are still here in Sunset Cove."

"Is there any reason I shouldn't be here? I thought this was a free country and people could come and go as they pleased. It was a long trip from San Francisco, I've only been here two days, and I'm still fairly exhausted." Lucille tugged a lace handkerchief from her little purple velvet purse and dabbed her nose. A touching act, but Anna was not buying it.

"Well, that's understandable." Anna reached for her handbag. "And I won't keep you any longer. If you're so tired, perhaps you should take a nap."

"I just had a little rest, thank you." Lucille's forehead creased. "I would much rather stay here and visit with my long-lost daughter." She motioned toward the restaurant. "Please join me for tea or an early dinner."

"Thank you, but I already had tea with Mac. And I already have dinner plans." Anna removed her pocket watch. "Goodness, it's later than I thought."

Lucille pointed to the small gold watch and delicate chain. "Where did you get that?"

Anna tucked the watch back into her vest pocket. "Mac gave it to me for my sixteenth birthday. It belonged to his mother."

"I know." Lucille frowned. "Where are you staying?"

"With my father." Anna prepared to stand, ready to leave.

"But you said he was to have no visitors."

"I'm not a visitor, Lucille. I'm his daughter."

"But Fern told me that Mac had disowned you—after you eloped with some city man." She smiled impishly. "Like mother, like daughter."

"That was long ago. I'm a widow now." Anna stood.

"As am I." Lucille stood too, placing a hand on Anna's arm as if to keep her. "See, my dear, we have much in common."

"Excuse me for disagreeing, but I think we have very little in common."

"Fern also told me that you'd never returned to Sunset Cove."

"It seems she was wrong about that. Now, if you'll please excuse me, I need to go home."

"Home?" Lucille's brows arched. "I suppose it's nice to feel that one has a home."

Anna decided not to respond to that. "Excuse me, but I must be on my way. Have a good evening." And without waiting for Lucille to protest, Anna hurried out of the hotel lobby. But by the time she reached the sidewalk, her knees grew weak and she felt slightly sick to her stomach. Seeing the door to Douglas Mercantile open, she decided to stop for a moment and compose herself. Also, she could get Mac some peppermints, like she used to do as a girl.

"Why, if it isn't Anna McDowell," Mrs. Douglas exclaimed. "Randall told me you were back in town—and that you have a nearly full-grown daughter—but I almost didn't believe him."

"Good afternoon, Mrs. Douglas." Anna forced a smile.

"Oh, you're an adult, Anna." Mrs. Douglas waved her hand. "Please, call me Marjorie. All of Randall's friends do."

"Yes, well, thank you." Anna pointed to the candy counter. "I wanted to get my father some peppermints. I'll take two bits' worth."

"How is Mac doing?" Marjorie weighed the candies and poured them into the paper sack.

"Hopefully he's on the cusp of getting better." Anna explained how his spirits had lifted. "Having his family here seems to help."

"And your mother too?" Her dark brows arched as she turned down the top of the sack. "Is she staying at the house?"

"No, no, of course not." Anna sighed as she set down a quarter. "She's at the hotel. I was just with her."

"I spoke to her yesterday." Marjorie handed Anna the bag with a curious expression. "I was surprised to see how well she looks...for a woman her age."

"Well, I was just thinking the same about you, Marjorie." Anna felt a little guilty for stretching the truth. "I don't believe you've aged a bit since I last saw you."

Marjorie laughed. "Oh, go on with you."

Anna thanked her and, not eager to bump into anyone else from her past, hurried toward home. This day had been a lot more trying than she'd imagined possible when they'd departed from Portland this morning. Although, after the shock of rescuing Mac, their reunion had gone surprisingly well. That was something to be grateful for.

And at least the unpleasant encounter with Lucille was behind her now. Hopefully Lucille would take the warning to stay away from Mac seriously. It was reassuring to hear that Virginia had told her the same thing. The idea of Mac being confronted by Lucille was truly disturbing. Who knew what might happen—it could be a death blow. From what Anna could see, Lucille was selfish and shallow. And it wasn't much of a leap to speculate on the real reason she was in town. Anna didn't like being judgmental, but she didn't trust her mother. Even if Lucille had come here to resolve old differences, Mac did not need that sort of emotional strain in his life. For that matter, neither did Anna.

CHAPTER 7

Although Mac had been reluctant to rest—certain he'd be too excited to sleep a wink—he didn't wake up until nearly five o'clock. And as he groggily pulled himself to the edge of his bed, he questioned whether this afternoon's strange episode was only a wishful dream. But then he noticed Katy's straw hat on the chair by the window, right where she'd placed it before helping him to his bed, and he knew it was real. Anna and her daughter, Katy, were truly here!

"Mick—ey!" he hollered as he reached for his cane and then clumsily hobbled toward his closet. "Mick—ey, where... you?"

"What on earth?" Bernice rushed into his bedroom with an armload of linens and an anxious expression.

"I...nee' Mick—ey. Hel' me dress...dinner."

Bernice's eyes lit up. "I'll let him know."

Mac suddenly felt worried. What if Anna and Katy had gone to stay in the hotel or gone away completely? "Anna... still...here?"

"Of course." She held her bundle of towels like evidence. "That's why I'm fetching these clean linens, and why I'm fixing a nice dinner and doing a dozen other things. It's been a busy afternoon, Mac. I've been getting their rooms all aired out and ready. Even put in some fresh flowers. Mickey cut me some irises and roses. And Katy just got back from a nice walk on the beach. She found some real pretty seashells. Anna has been running errands in town. Right now, they're both freshening up—and that's why they need these linens. So unless you're in dire—"

"Go...go on. I...fine. Jus' nee' Mickey."

"I'll let him know." Bernice scurried from the room.

As Mac balanced himself against the wall, struggling to open the closet door, he despised his helplessness. He hated his dependence on others for the smallest of things. Even more, he hated how his words came out stilted and slurred. But his worst beef was probably his inability to return to work. He had things to do...but no way to do them. Mac felt like an old man trapped in a toddler's world.

And yet, for the first time since his stroke—perhaps the first time in recent memory—Mac was determined to dress for dinner. He knew his trousers were wrinkled from his nap, and his shirt wasn't only rumpled, it had food stains from lunch. He wanted to look respectable for his daughter and granddaughter tonight. But he knew he couldn't manage this feat without Mickey's help.

Mac fought discouragement as he stared into his closet. The trousers, jackets, vests, shirts, ties, suspenders, shoes... all looked like a messy jigsaw puzzle he would never be able to assemble. Why did everyday tasks have to be so cumbersome and overwhelming? But he would not surrender to despair anymore. He now had a daughter and granddaughter to consider. He didn't want them to see him like this. It was one thing to feel as helpless as a child and another thing to act like one. Mac was determined to do better.

"Bernice said you needed me." Mickey came into the bedroom. Still wearing his overalls, he removed his garden gloves.

Mac nodded toward his opened closet. "Dress...for... dinner," he muttered. "Hel'...me." He attempted a smile for Mickey, the first one he'd offered his faithful servant since suffering his stroke. "Plea'."

Mickey laid down his gloves and then removed one of Mac's everyday work shirts from the closet, holding it up. "How 'bout this?"

Mac shook his head. "No."

Mickey retrieved a nice white dress shirt.

"Ye'...goo—d." Mac nodded eagerly. And after a while, with Mickey's patient help, selecting various items according to Mac's yea or nay, Mac was eventually outfitted for dinner. And, as Mac surveyed their wardrobe choices in front of his cheval glass, he felt that he looked fairly distinguished.

"Than' you," he told Mickey after he was finally seated in his easy chair in the sitting room. He had a real sense of victory, but the dressing process had worn him out some.

"Want me to tell the ladies they can find you in here?" Mickey offered.

"Plea' do. Than' you."

Mickey smiled. "You're most welcome, Mac. Glad to see you're feeling better."

As Mickey left, Mac realized that he *did* feel better. Oh, he still had the same frustrating challenges, but he felt a glimmer of hope. And that was something he hadn't experienced in a long time...even before his stroke. He thought about Anna and Katy, how they were both so young and bright and energetic, so pretty and intelligent—

like a breath of fresh air had blown through his musty old house. Although he knew Anna was in her mid-thirties, she still looked very much like the young girl he remembered. And it hurt him to realize how many years they'd lost...all because of his mule-headed pride. How many times he'd almost reached out to contact her but then stopped himself, stubbornly resolved that she should come crawling back to him, convinced that she should beg him for forgiveness.

What an old fool he'd been. But he would get a second chance now. At least he hoped so. Because Mac knew how much he needed her now. He needed both of them. And yet, he wasn't sure he could admit that out loud. Mac McDowell had spent most of his life acting like he didn't need anyone. Or that was what he'd always wanted everyone to think, anyway.

"Grandpa!" Katy rushed into the room, looking as fresh and sweet as a summer garden in a pretty pink dress. "I love your beach." She proudly held up a sand dollar. "I found seven of these. Aren't they beautiful?"

He nodded. "Yeah."

"My, don't you look smart, Grandpa." She nodded with approval. "And I must tell you how much I adore your house. My room is perfectly delightful." She set the sand dollar on the windowsill and pointed to the nearby chess table. "That is a very handsome chess set. Do you play?"

He frowned, wondering if he could still strategize. "I use' to," he mumbled.

"Great." She moved the table next to his chair. "I'm not as good as Mother, but I'm trying to improve. I'll be white." Just like that, they were playing, and Mac was pleasantly surprised to discover that, even though he was making the moves with his left hand, his brain seemed to function normally. And although Katy wasn't bad for a beginner, he could see that he was winning.

"Grandpa!" she exclaimed when his bishop took her queen. "Have mercy."

He firmly shook his head as he removed the queen. It wasn't long until he backed her king into a corner and, chuckling victoriously, declared, "Che'ma'."

"Grandpa, you are even more mercenary than my mother."

"You're calling me mercenary?" Anna teased as she entered the room.

"Grandpa is quite the chess player," Katy told Anna.

"He taught me to play." Anna sat down on the other side of Mac. "But I rarely won a game."

"You should play him, Mother."

"I would love to." Anna pointed to the mantel clock. "But it's nearly time for dinner."

"After dinner, then," Katy suggested.

"If Mac is willing." Anna smiled at him.

"Yeah." He nodded. "We...play."

Then, with Katy on one side and Anna on the other, the three of them slowly made their way to the dining room. And despite his shuffling steps, Mac felt a lightness in his feet.

Anna knew that Mac was uncomfortable with his affected speech. And she tried to conceal it, she probably felt nearly as uncomfortable. She was well aware that her father had always been an opinionated and outspoken man. But he'd also been a gifted conversationalist, able to engage with almost anyone on any given topic. He was well-read and intelligent and had always provided lively and entertaining banter around a dinner table. But not tonight.

Seeing Mac's struggle over every word, trying so hard to string them along into complete sentences…well, it was painful. Thankfully, Katy hardly seemed to notice. Like her grandfather, she too had the gift of gab. And having Mac for her audience seemed to bring out the chatterbox in her. For most of the meal, Katy dominated the conversation. And neither Mac nor Anna tried to stop her.

"I will finish high school next year," Katy was telling him as they ate their chocolate cream pie for dessert. "And I would like to attend college in Portland. I know most girls don't want to continue their education, but I am not like most girls." She smiled at Anna. "I suppose I take after Mother. Although I don't care for a career in journalism. My interest is art." She paused to take a sip of tea.

"Tha's goo'." Mac nodded. "School…art…ver' goo'."

"Mac went to college," Anna told Katy.

"Jus'…one…year," Mac clarified.

"Still, it was the first year the school was established," Anna explained. This had been something Mac used to boast about to friends. And Anna had even hoped to go to the same school when she heard it was coed. But Darrell had derailed those plans.

"Wha' school…you wan' go to?" Mac asked Katy.

"Museum Art School," Katy answered. "It's connected with the Portland Art Museum." She sighed. "I remember the first time Mother took me to the art museum, back when I was just a little girl. I was so enthralled by everything there—it was magical. We visited the museum fairly regularly after that. And then, just a few years ago, we attended the most wonderful exhibition—they had Impressionist and post-Impressionist paintings from Gauguin, Monet, Renoir,

Matisse—and van Gogh. Oh, how I love Vincent van Gogh's work."

"Katy is a good artist," Anna told Mac. "I told her she could probably get some inspiration during our visit here."

"And I have," Katy declared with enthusiasm. "I already took my sketchbook and charcoals down to the beach. I did some sketches of driftwood and seabirds."

Mac looked thoroughly impressed, and Anna couldn't help but experience a flush of motherly pride. "Katy has decorated our Portland apartment with numerous paintings."

"And I'll make you a painting, Grandpa," Katy told him. "I heard there's a handsome lighthouse around here. I'd like to create a painting of that."

Mac nodded eagerly. "Yeah. Goo' ligh' house."

"It's really picturesque," Anna told Katy. "If we knew someone with an automobile, we could probably be there in a couple of hours. Otherwise, it takes a good part of the day. We used to take the horses and wagons up the beach. Then we'd camp a few days."

"I ha' car," Mac said.

"You do?" Anna blinked.

"Yeah." His lopsided smile was rather charming. "Ni'tee' ten...run...a...bow."

"What?" Anna tried to decipher.

"You have a 1910 Runabout?" Katy asked eagerly.

He nodded. "Yeah."

"Oh, Grandpa, that's a wonderful car! Do you think we could take it to the lighthouse? Mother has never had a car, but I know how to drive."

"You know how to drive?" Anna frowned at her daughter.

"My friend Samuel taught me to drive in his dad's car." Katy grinned. "He says I'm a natural."

Anna slowly shook her head. "A working mother doesn't always know what her darling daughter is up to."

"Wor'...ing father too." Mac gave her a knowing look.

Anna grimaced to remember. "Yes, I suppose that's true."

"Time for chess," Katy announced as Bernice began clearing the table.

"I don't know." Anna glanced at her father. "I don't want us to wear you out, Mac."

"No, no. I...am...fine."

"All right." Anna stood. "But I did meet with your doctor today." As they walked to his sitting room, she explained how Dr. Hollister had talked about Mac's need for therapy."

"Yeah...I know." Mac peered curiously at her. "You li'e... Doc Dan?"

"Did I *lie* to him?" Anna asked with concern.

"No...*li'e* him. Do you?" Mac looked flustered.

Katy laughed. "Grandpa wants to know if you *like* him, Mother."

"Oh, well." Anna shrugged. "He seems nice enough."

"I think Grandpa must think his doctor would be a good catch for you, Mother," Katy teased. "Right, Grandpa?"

He chuckled, nodding.

"Well, the doctor gave me a helpful book." Anna decided to ignore them. "I looked through it and was impressed with all the good exercises and activities that are supposed to hasten your recovery."

"I'd like to see that book too." Katy sat on the ottoman, setting the chess pieces back in place. "Maybe I can help Grandpa with his exercises."

"That's a wonderful idea." Anna sat down. And it really was. Mac seemed to be very responsive to his charming granddaughter. He probably wouldn't even complain too much if Katy put him through his paces.

"You go fir'," Mac said to Anna.

As she moved a pawn, Anna decided to take it easy on him. Poor Mac didn't need any more discouragement. But after a few moves, she realized there was no need to hold back. Katy was right—he was ruthless. As a result, the match ended fairly quickly. But instead of feeling defeated, she felt encouraged.

"Nicely done, Mac." Anna put the pieces back on the board. "You might stumble over your words, but your chess game is unimpaired."

He nodded, tapping the side of his head. "Brain...wor's fine."

"Well, we are going to get the rest of you working fine too," Katy assured him.

"Wor'..." Mac's brow creased as he glanced at Anna. "Pay...per. Nee' hel'."

"Pardon me?" Anna frowned.

"The paper?" Katy tried. "You mean the newspaper? You need help with it?"

"Yeah." He nodded eagerly. "Nee' hel'."

"Mother can help," Katy offered. "She's a newspaperwoman."

"Yeah." He looked at Anna with hopeful eyes.

"Do you want me to go to the newspaper office for you?" Anna asked with uncertainty.

"Yeah!" he exclaimed. "*Plea'!* To...mo...row."

"What?"

"He wants you to go in *tomorrow*," Katy told her.

"Tomorrow?" Anna looked to see Mac nodding eagerly.

"You have to go in, Mother," Katy insisted. "Grandpa needs you."

"I guess I could do that," Anna told him. "But I wouldn't

want to offend any of your employees. You know I'm an outsider now, and people in the workplace can become—"

"No!" He shook his head. "You are...my daugh...'er. You go for me."

"So are you giving me your authority?"

"Yeah." He shook his finger at her. "You go...repor' ba' me."

Anna tried to make sense of that.

"You report back to Grandpa, Mother. That's what he said. Right, Grandpa?"

He nodded again. "Yeah."

Anna chuckled. "Katy is a good interpreter."

Katy slipped an arm around Mac's shoulders. "It's because we understand each other, don't we, Grandpa? We are simpatico."

Mac nodded, and Anna couldn't help but laugh. "Of course, you are. I think you are two of a kind."

"Well, I hate to say it, but I think we have worn Grandpa out." Katy smiled sympathetically at him. "And you probably won't admit that it's true, but I have a feeling I'm right."

"I must agree." Anna slowly stood. "Tomorrow is a new day, Mac."

"Want me to go get Mickey to help you get ready for bed?" Katy offered.

"Yeah." Mac barely tipped his head.

After Katy went to find Mickey, Anna turned to her father. "Just to be clear, Mac. You want me to go to the newspaper and, well, sort of stand in for you?"

"Yeah!"

"And then to come back and tell you what's going on?"

"Yeah...I...uh..." His brow creased as if he wanted to communicate something but couldn't.

"Is there some sort of a problem there? Some difficulty?"

"Wesley."

"Wesley Kempton?"

"Yeah." Mac's eyes grew sad.

"But I thought Wesley was your right-hand man."

Mac used his left hand to lift his right elbow, shaking the limp appendage to show how useless it had become.

"Oh..." She knew what he was suggesting but still felt confused. Could this be related to Mac's memory loss? "But you treated Wesley like a son, Mac. I thought you planned to teach him everything you knew about the newspaper business. I always assumed he would take over for you someday." She didn't add how often she'd felt jealous of Mac's attention to Wesley when they were both in high school...or how she'd resented Wesley getting the best writing assignments from Mac...or how her father had still embraced the attitude that women were inferior to men in the newspaper business.

But before Mac could offer any more stilted explanations about Wesley, Mickey and Katy returned, and it was time to say good night.

Well, Anna had always considered herself a good investigative reporter. Perhaps she would simply have to get to the bottom of this Wesley Kempton dilemma on her own.

CHAPTER 8

"Grandpa is such a dear," Katy declared as she and Anna sat together on the settee in the guest bedroom, admiring the sunset over the ocean. "I can't imagine how he ever disowned you like you claim he did, Mother."

"You mean you don't believe me?" Anna felt slightly defensive.

"Oh, I suppose I believe you. I did see you both saying you were sorry and all that. But it's difficult to imagine such a sweet old guy ever saying a mean word to anyone."

Anna sighed. "Well, Mac is much changed since the last time I saw him. And according to Bernice, the change came with his stroke. Trust me, Mac used to have a very sharp tongue—if he ever laid into you, you would not forget it."

"Maybe his stroke is a blessing in disguise."

Anna smiled. How many times had she used that same line to get Katy to look at things differently? She slipped an arm around Katy's shoulders, squeezing her closer. "I love how well you're getting along with Mac. And I can tell he's already a great admirer of his granddaughter."

"I meant what I said." Katy opened the book Dr. Hollister

had sent home with Anna. "I plan to read up on this and do all I can to help Grandpa recover."

"And I will do all I can to help out at the newspaper."

"In some ways, it's too bad we only plan to stay for the summer." Katy smoothed her skirt. "Although I really do want to get back to my school and my friends in the fall. But I suspect Grandpa will be sad to see us go."

"Let's not think about that now." Anna grimaced. "And it's probably best not to mention it to Mac either."

"I wish we could move this lovely house and Grandpa to Portland." Katy sighed. "And Mickey and Bernice too."

"That would be quite a move."

"I wish we could move that too." Katy nodded to where the sky was painting the ocean in shades of coral, purple, and gold.

"Does that make you want to unpack your art supplies?"

"I already did." Katy stood. "In fact, if you don't mind, I think I'll go attempt a pastel sketch right now—before the light is gone."

"Good idea."

"Good night, Mother." She leaned down to kiss Anna's cheek. "Thanks for bringing me here for the summer. Sorry I made such a fuss about coming."

"Good night, darling." Anna let out a long sigh of contentment as Katy went to her room. Despite the inconvenience of dipping into her savings and even giving up her editorial job at the *Oregonian*, Anna was glad that they'd come. And if she could do anything to help Mac during the next few months, she was happy to do it.

After the sun was down, she pulled the drapes and turned on the gaslights, taking time to look more closely at this room. She hadn't really taken the time earlier, and it was surprisingly reassuring to see that little had changed in here. She remembered how her grandmother had taken great care in setting up this room, back when Anna was a girl. The improvements were in anticipation of a visit from her grandmother's niece. She'd gotten a new bed and bedding and a settee. Then she'd made lace-trimmed curtains and hung up pretty pictures. The room had seemed quite splendid to Anna's ten-year-old self, and she'd greatly anticipated the arrival of Cousin Rose from the East Coast.

Anna had been quite taken with her independent spinster second-cousin. Impressed that Rose had traveled all the way from Boston by train, Anna immediately recognized that Rose was educated, very set in her ways, and she was a suffragette. During her visit, Rose had been a real inspiration to Anna, constantly reminding her that women could do anything men could do...and possibly better. Of course, Mac had accused his cousin of putting fancy ideas into his impressionable daughter's head. But the truth was, they'd already been there. By the time Rose left, Anna insisted on being allowed to work at the newspaper. Mac protested at first, insisting it was no place for a female, but with her grandmother's backing, Anna was eventually allowed to work after school and weekends at the newspaper. And she loved it!

By the time Anna was fourteen, her friends were accusing her of having printer's ink in her blood. They couldn't understand how she would rather work at the newspaper than attend a silly social event with her peers. But she loved being part of the biweekly publications—and she didn't even care when friends teased her over her ink-stained fingers.

Anna was sixteen when Grandmother died—and that's when Mac laid down the law. "A woman's place is in the home," he'd insisted, claiming it was high time Anna honed her homemaking skills. Anna had tried to comply, even taking cooking lessons from Bernice, but her heart was not in it. She missed the newspaper, the smell of ink and paper. Mostly she missed being Mac's right-hand girl. It wasn't long until Wesley Kempton, just two years older than her, was hired to help Mac at the paper. Before long, she began to suspect Mac wanted to make Wesley a permanent member of their family—by marriage. But Anna wanted nothing to do with it. She preferred Randall Douglas to milk-toast Wesley. But then Darrell came along, and all the local boys had paled in comparison.

In some ways, it felt like Mac had set her up to run away. By fencing her in like that, taking away her responsibilities at the newspaper, insisting she focus on homemaking when he knew she wanted challenges and excitement and adventure... Well, it was no surprise that she fell for the first charming fast-talker who came along. Who could blame her?

Anna went into the bathroom and surveyed the modern space. Commode, lavatory, and a big claw-foot bathtub—with running hot water! She was still amazed that Mac had sprung for such opulence but then remembered Bernice's words about his hopes to sell the house. Perhaps he still planned to do so, but in the meantime, she intended to enjoy it. She wanted a nice, long soak in that beautiful bathtub. She'd longed to do so after her visit in town but knew there wasn't time. Now she had all the time in the world. And her Portland apartment, with its tiny bathroom and community showers, didn't have such amenities.

Bernice had laid out nice white towels that smelled like sunshine, and there was a bottle of scented bath salts just waiting. Before long, Anna was steaming herself in lavender luxury. By the time she slid into the big, comfortable bed, she was so relaxed that she felt like she could sleep for a week. Just in case, she set the alarm clock.

————————————————

With Mickey's help, Mac was the first one to the breakfast table the next morning. To his relief, Bernice didn't comment about how this was only the second time in two weeks that he'd made it to the dining room. Instead, she just handed him the newspaper. But what he read on the front page made his blood boil. Wesley Kempton needed a swift kick in the—

"Good morning, Grandpa." Katy slid into the chair across from him.

"Goo' mor'ing'," he grumbled, tossing the newspaper to the floor.

"Is something wrong?" She laid the napkin in her lap with a curious expression.

"No, no." He attempted a crooked smile. "The...news."

"Bad news?" Katy asked as Anna joined them with a cheerful greeting.

"What bad news?" Anna sat down.

"No ba' news." Mac tried to appear undisturbed.

"You look like you're ready for work," Katy told Anna. "You're wearing your I-mean-business suit."

"You're very observant." Anna made a sly smile as she poured her coffee.

"Mother is used to working around a bunch of bossy men," Katy told Mac. "If she has an important meeting, she wears that suit."

Mac studied his daughter's charcoal-gray jacket. It had a very severe, almost masculine cut that was accentuated with a crisp white shirt and a narrow black tie. And yet, with that curly auburn hair and pretty face, no one would mistake Anna for a man. Still, he thought he understood. "Goo' for you," he told Anna. Hopefully her appearance would help her to win Wesley's respect. Now if only Mac could remember why it was he felt this concern over Wesley. Because Anna was right. Mac had taken Wesley in, almost like a son...so why was he so disturbed about him now?

"I was wondering about something last night, Mac." Anna reached for a piece of toast. "Have you tried writing with your left hand?"

"Doc say...to try," he confessed.

"And have you?" Anna pressed.

"No."

"Then we will work on that," Katy declared. "Grandpa can practice writing while I work on a sketch."

"Excellent." Anna nodded as she spread butter. "I thought if you could write things out for me, Mac, that might help me to understand what you'd like done at the paper. It could be a way for us to communicate better."

"But we're going to keep working on his speech," Katy said. "I read a lot of that book the doctor gave you, Mother. It's given me some ideas."

Anna grinned at Mac. "I think you'll be in very good hands with Katy."

Mac nodded. "Goo'."

"If you haven't already figured it out, Katy is a very persistent young woman. Sometimes I even call her stubborn."

"Thin' of tha'." Mac made a feeble attempt at irony. To his relief, both of them laughed. He considered Anna's suggestion that he attempt to write with his left hand. Suddenly it seemed like a good idea. It was possible that his left hand would be able to communicate more quickly and clearly than his tongue. That would be a relief. "Anna," he said eagerly. "Bri'...tie...wry...ter to me."

Anna looked stumped. "Pardon me?"

"Tie...wry...ter," he tried again.

"I think he wants a *typewriter*," Katy translated.

"Yeah!" Mac grinned at Katy, marveling at how well she understood his bumbling speech.

"That's a fine idea," Anna told him. "After seeing you play chess last night, I'll bet you can type just fine. How about I have Virginia send one home to you?"

Mac nodded, hoping she was right about his one-handed typing skills. Being able to communicate via typewriter would be a tiny taste of freedom. Perhaps it would help him to remember things too. And he might even be able to help Anna with the paper. Because, although he couldn't exactly explain why, Wesley needed to be dealt with. And not only because he'd put a political slant in today's paper, a slant that Mac did not approve. There was something else too. Mac was certain of it. If only he could remember. He knew it wouldn't be easy or pleasant to put Wesley in his place, but hopefully Anna would be up for the challenge.

"What's this?" Bernice stepped over the newspaper that was still splayed across the floor behind Mac's chair.

"Sor...ree." Mac pointed to himself with a sheepish expression.

"Is that today's paper?" Anna knelt down to gather it up, scanning it as she straightened again. "I guess I should get caught up on the latest news." She turned to Mac with a puzzled look. "I can't believe it—Calvin Snyder is the mayor of Sunset Cove? I remember him as kind of a shady character. Of course, that was years ago."

"Snyder barely won," Bernice grumbled as she set down a platter of eggs and bacon. "Some people still think he bought his votes...or stole them. But we've got a new election coming this fall. Hopefully we'll throw the crook out on his ear."

"This article makes it sound as if he's well-liked by townspeople," Anna pointed out.

Mac let out a low growl.

"It implies he's working on economic development and—"

"The only development Calvin is interested in is lining his own pockets," Bernice declared. Then, as if worried she'd overstepped her boundaries, she glanced to Mac. But he simply nodded, actually hoping she would continue.

"Calvin bought Charlie's Chowder House," Bernice told Anna.

"Oh, I forgot all about the Chowder House." Anna looked at Katy. "I'll have to take you there for—"

"Don't bother," Bernice told her. "Calvin is running it into the ground."

"Why would he do that?"

Bernice wiped her hands on her apron, glancing at Mac again, but again he just nodded. He wanted her to clue Anna into the goings-on in town.

"Rumor has it that Calvin is making the most of prohibition," Bernice whispered. "Don't say you heard it from me, but that's what some folks think. Some of us suspect he's using the Chowder House to conduct his dirty business."

"Are you serious?" Anna looked at Mac with worried eyes.

Mac simply nodded, but his brain seemed to be scrambling all about. Like trying to connect the dots that kept hopping around on the page.

"Do you think there's rum-running going on nearby?"

Katy asked with far too much interest. Mac wanted to know how a sweet, innocent girl like her would know anything about rum-running.

"I saw a moving picture about it," she told Mac. "Very exciting."

"Wha'?" He felt alarmed, wondering what other sorts of worldliness his granddaughter had been exposed to in the big city. He'd heard bad things about some of those moving picture shows, and there'd been a recent debate in town whether or not a moving picture theater would be welcome here.

"I saw it at Sunnyside Theatre," Katy explained. "My friends and I go there sometimes. Mother doesn't particularly approve, although she hasn't exactly forbidden it. I'm not sure if her worry is that the theater used to be a brothel—but honestly, it's perfectly respectable now. Although sometimes my friends and I pretend it's haunted. You see, it used to be a mortuary and—"

"*Kathleen Rebecca.*" Anna looked up from the newspaper article, dismally shaking her head at her daughter before turning to Mac. "This article is, uh, interesting...and it seems that Wesley wrote it."

"Yeah." Mac scowled.

"Very enlightening, I think."

"Yeah." Mac felt hopeful. Anna was an intelligent woman. It wouldn't take her long to find out what Wesley was up to. He felt a tiny wave of hope as Anna quickly finished her breakfast and excused herself, saying she wanted to get to the newspaper office while it was still early. Hopefully she would handle this right. But, as he heard the front door close, he wondered...what if he'd just put his only daughter in danger? And why did he think there was danger? What was it that he couldn't quite remember?

Anna knew how to "speak softly and carry a big stick," as Teddy Roosevelt used to say. But maybe Mac should've warned her to watch her back—but against what exactly? He wished he knew.

CHAPTER 9

Anna had no idea what to expect at the newspaper office, but she was eager to get there and get started. It felt right to return. Perhaps it was something she should've done years ago. As she walked the few blocks, she began to build a plan. Since the paper wasn't due to come out for another few days, the staff shouldn't be overly busy. They should all have time to attend an employee meeting. And she would keep the meeting short and sweet. Hopefully sometime this morning. At the meeting she would make it clear that, for the time being, she was in charge—but that nothing else would change. Employees were always reassured to know that new management wouldn't disrupt their status quo. She remembered when Harold Scott passed away a few years ago and how Edgar Piper took his place with a relatively smooth transition. She would follow that example.

"My word!" Virginia's eyes opened wide as Anna entered the building. "Is it really you? All grown-up?"

Anna smiled. "Hello, Virginia. How have you been?"

"I'm all right. Just as fat and sassy as ever." She set a stack of newspapers in the rack by the front door. "How about yourself?" She cocked her head to one side. "You're looking as pretty as ever—although that manly suit doesn't do much for you."

Anna just laughed. Leave it to Virginia to speak her mind. "I'm fine, thank you."

"What are you doing here? Has Mac seen you yet?"

"Mac sent me here." Anna quickly explained about bringing Katy to meet her grandfather. "We plan to stay for the summer."

"You have a little girl?" Virginia just shook her head. "Seems like just yesterday you *were* a little girl."

"Katy is not exactly a little girl." Anna told her a bit more about her daughter and about having been widowed. "I've been working for the *Oregonian*. And now I plan to help Mac out here for a while."

"How is Mac?" Virginia asked with genuine concern.

Anna gave her a quick update, trying to make it sound optimistic. "But it will be a while before he can return to work."

"Do you really think he'll ever be able?" Virginia asked quietly.

Anna shrugged. "Hard to say. But in the meantime, I'm in charge."

Virginia's brows lifted. "Is that what Mac said?"

Anna considered this. "Well, those weren't his exact words, but he's still struggling with his speech. That reminds me. He asked to have a typewriter sent to the house. Could you arrange for that? We're hoping he can type faster than he can talk. That will help communication immensely."

"That's a good idea. I'll have Willy take one right over."

"And I'd like to have a staff meeting." Anna looked at the big clock above Virginia's desk. "How about eleven o'clock? Can you please let everyone know?"

"Will do."

Anna surveyed the main office, looking through the wall of windows that separated the editorial area from the reception area. All the editorial desks were occupied, and a young woman was seated in the open office area next to Mac's private office. "Did Mac hire a secretary?"

"Not exactly. That's Miss Kelly. She's new."

"I thought that desk area was reserved for the assistant editor in chief."

"Used to be."

"I guess things have changed. Anyway, if you need me, I'll be in Mac's office, and I'd like to—"

"Hold on there, honey." Virginia placed a hand on Anna's shoulder.

"What?"

She glanced through the window toward the editorial section, where a couple of the men were curiously watching them now. "You should know that Wesley has set himself up in Mac's office."

"What?"

"Well, he felt that since he was running things, it was a reasonable move." Virginia frowned like perhaps she didn't agree.

"But Mac didn't give him permission to move in there, did he?"

"Not that I've heard."

"Well then." Anna smiled stiffly. "I suppose I'll just have to ask him to return to his own desk—"

"That's where Wesley put his new secretary. Miss Kelly."

"Did Mac authorize this?"

"Not that I've heard."

"Looks like I've got my work cut out for me." Anna set

her satchel on Virginia's desk. "Mind if I leave this with you?"

"Not at all."

"And would you mind taking minutes at our meeting, Virginia? I have a feeling we'll need them."

"No problem."

Anna thanked her and, bracing herself for some sort of confrontation, strode back through the building, passing by the wide aisle between the editors' desks, warmly greeting the writers along her way. A couple she knew from years ago, and a couple looked vaguely familiar. All of them wore very curious expressions. She stopped by the large desk just outside of her father's private office, the desk that she had one day hoped to occupy...back before Wesley took over. An attractive blonde woman looked up at Anna with a slightly bored expression. "Can I help you?"

"You must be Miss Kelly." Anna kept her tone pleasant.

"That's right." The woman gave what Anna considered a "business" smile.

"Is Mr. Kempton in?"

The woman's face grew serious. "Do you have an appointment?"

"No, but—"

"Mr. Kempton doesn't wish to be disturbed this morning. But if you'd care to make an appointment..." She opened a datebook, running her finger down it. "I think he might be able to see you later this afternoon. Or tomorrow perhaps." She looked up at Anna with one brow lifted. "And this is regarding?"

"This is regarding newspaper business," Anna said crisply. "Excuse me." She moved past the desk. "I'll just speak directly to—"

"You can't go in there." Miss Kelly leaped up to stop her.

"I'll let myself in."

"Mr. Kempton has the mayor on the phone—"

"That's all right." Anna reached for the doorknob and quietly opened the door to see Wesley with his back to her. Reclining in Mac's big leather chair, he had his boots propped up on the windowsill and a telephone receiver pressed against his ear. His hair was still mousy brown, but there was a shiny bald patch in the center of his head. And he was smoking one of Mac's cigars! She recognized the sweet, fruity aroma.

"Listen, Calvin, I know exactly what you mean." His tone sounded boisterous, completely unaware that he was not alone. "And I couldn't agree with you more on this, but we have to—" Miss Kelly loudly cleared her throat, and Wesley stopped in mid-sentence, swiveling the chair around with an angry expression, which immediately turned into astonishment. "Uh, if you'll excuse me, Calvin, something urgent just came up. I'll call you back as soon as possible." Wesley hung up the phone and stiffly smiled, snuffing out the cigar in Mac's big brass ashtray.

"I tried to stop her, Mr. Kempton, but she just burst in here." Miss Kelly's scowl was indignant. "Acting as if she owns the place and—"

"That sounds about right," Anna crisply told her.

"I'll handle this, Miss Kelly. Thank you." Wesley got to his feet, extending a hand to his unexpected visitor. "What a surprise, Anna."

"Sorry to burst in on you like this."

"No need for apologies. It's a pleasure." His smile was too slick. "You're looking well."

"Thank you. Mac asked me to come here today."

"I'm so sorry about his health troubles. How is he doing? Not any worse, I hope."

"As a matter of fact, he's improving," she said curtly.

"Oh?" His brows arched. "That's not what I've heard around town."

"Well, you can't always trust rumors."

"Have a chair." He motioned to one of the leather side chairs across from the desk. "Tell me, Anna, how have you been? What have you been doing all these years? Let me guess, you probably have about four children by now." He smiled, preparing to sit back in Mac's chair. But, seeing she was still standing, he waited.

"This isn't a social call, Wesley." She smiled stiffly. "But I'm sure we'll have time to catch up...*later*. Right now, I've got work on my mind."

"Work?" He tipped his head to one side.

"Yes. Mac wants me to take over managing the newspaper."

"*You?*" Wesley's expression was a mixture of confusion and suspicion.

"Yes." She glanced around the surprisingly uncluttered office. Nothing like how Mac had kept this space. And the walls looked stark and bare, with square and rectangular shadows of the items that had been removed. She spied the large stack of framed photographs against the wall. Next to them was an apple crate filled with various pieces of Mac's collection of historical memorabilia and another box overflowing with miscellaneous paperwork and file folders. Wesley had obviously made himself comfortable in here. "Mac wants me to handle things for him while he's recovering."

"Anna, you do understand that your father has suffered a very debilitating stroke, don't you?"

"Of course."

"And you're aware that he may not recover and that it's unlikely he'll ever return to work?"

"That's not true."

He folded his arms in front of him. "I don't want to upset you, Anna, but I've been told by a medical expert that Mac might not make it to the end of the year. Most elderly patients don't last long after a stroke like that."

"That is not what his doctor told me." Anna felt her temper rising but was determined to remain in control. "Besides, we cannot predict the future regarding Mac's recovery. All I can do is what Mac has asked of me. I am here to take over the management of this newspaper until Mac can come back and handle it himself."

"Not so fast." He held up a forefinger. "There are some things you don't know."

"I'm sure there's much I don't know, Wesley. But I do know this is my father's newspaper. And if Mac wants me to run it, you have no right to stand in my way."

"Are you aware that Mac took out a rather large bank loan a few years ago?"

She just shrugged, trying to feign nonchalance.

"He needed funds to modernize our outdated equipment and make some much-needed repairs. This was all quite expensive. It required a considerable loan from the bank."

"And your point is?"

"If this newspaper isn't running—and running right— we'll be unable to make payments on the loan...and in that event your father will lose the newspaper."

"Well, then be assured, I plan to run the newspaper *right.*"

"Do you honestly believe the bank is going to entrust their investment to your hands, Anna? Even if they're very pretty hands." His smile was disturbing.

She shoved her hands into her skirt's pockets. "I think the bank can trust me."

"I've already met with the bank president. I convinced him that nothing at the newspaper would change, that we would continue to operate as always, even if Mac should pass away."

"That was good of you." She locked eyes with him. "Thank you for managing everything these last two weeks, but I will take over now."

"You don't seem to realize that, with you running things, the bank could become quite concerned. They might even revoke the loan, force us into bankruptcy, and shut down the whole operation. Do you really want to take that risk?"

"I don't see it as a risk." She maintained her straight business face despite her uncertainty beneath it. Would the bank really do that? *Could* they do that?

"Be realistic, Anna. Do you honestly think you can waltz in here and take over operations of the whole newspaper?"

"That is exactly what I plan to do." She frowned. "Short of the waltzing part."

He went ahead and sat down in Mac's chair, leaning back and pressing his fingers together, smiling smugly as if he had everything under control—or planned to before long. "Anna, Anna, Anna."

"For the sake of the newspaper, I would prefer you call me Miss McDowell."

"Miss McDowell? What about your married name?"

"I returned to my maiden name after my husband's death."

"You're a widow?" His brows arched.

"That is neither here nor there. The topic of discussion is the leadership of this newspaper. Mac has appointed me and—"

"I completely understand your sentiments, Anna—I mean *Miss McDowell*. We all love Mac. Everyone wants to do whatever they can to help him. But I have everything under control here. The best thing you can do is to go home and spend time with your father. After all, you don't know how long he has and—"

"I wish you'd quit implying that Mac is about to kick the bucket," she snapped. "He's the one who wanted me to come here today. He wants me to manage the—"

"I think I understand now." He sat up straighter. "Of course, you'd like to help out some around here. And that'd be just fine. In fact, we could use an extra writer. Reginald handles the society column, but he and the others writers have had to step up since Mac's illness. I'm sure Reginald would be glad to hand that column over to you. Some women in town have insinuated it's a job a woman could do, and you used to be a fairly good—"

"I have no interest in writing your society column," she declared. "Although I would like to hire a woman to fill that—"

"Are you really this obtuse that you don't—"

"I am not obtuse, Wesley." She reached for the doorknob. "And I'll give you the rest of the day to get your things out of here."

Wesley hit his fist onto the desk so hard that Anna actually jumped. "Why won't you listen to me?"

"I did listen to you." She kept her voice calm but firm. "Unfortunately, you have not listened to me."

"I think I know what you're up to." He stood, getting his face close to hers with narrowed eyes. "You don't want to run this newspaper, you want to ruin it. This is probably something you've plotted for years, your way to get even with Mac. You'd like to take down this paper for revenge, wouldn't you? Just because your father didn't approve of your husband. Isn't that what this is all about?"

"You couldn't be more wrong."

"Because I will go to the bank and tell them what's going on. They can put a stop to it. Is that what you want, *Miss McDowell?*"

She stepped away from him and, with her back to the door, squared her shoulders and took a deep breath. "Apparently you have assumed that I know nothing about running a newspaper. You have erroneously assumed that I've been tending the home-fires and mending the socks and having babies. But a good investigative reporter doesn't rely on assumptions or innuendo. A good reporter relies on facts—he does his research and uncovers the true story, not some trumped-up fiction that suits his fancy."

Relieved that he seemed to be rendered speechless, she placed her hands on her hips, a position of authority she'd learned from her previous bosses. "If you'd done any research, Wesley, you would know that I've been working for the *Oregonian* for the last *fifteen years.* Or perhaps you're not familiar with the largest newspaper in the state, second largest in the Northwest. Their circulation is only hundreds of times larger than the *Sunset Times.*"

She glared at him, waiting for him to respond. He didn't, though she did notice his cheeks flushed with anger. "I took leave from my editorial job at the *Oregonian* in order to come home and spend the summer with my father. Certainly, I hadn't planned to take over management of this paper, but since Mac has asked me, I am willing. Even more willing after seeing what I've seen today. So, as far as my ability to run a small-town paper like this, well, I'd be happy to go and discuss it with the bank. Right now, if you like."

Wesley just stared at her, still saying nothing. Was it possible she had silenced him?

"Now," she continued firmly, "I'll give you until one o'clock to get your things out of this office and restore it to what it was before you trespassed."

"But I can't—"

"If you need help, perhaps Miss Kelly can assist. And, while you're at it, you can inform your secretary that her employment is terminated." Anna wanted to point out that Mac, as far as she knew, had never hired a secretary for himself, but decided it was pointless.

"You can't just—"

"I don't have time to argue with you." She checked her pocket watch. "I have scheduled a staff meeting for eleven o'clock. If you still consider yourself to be an employee, I will expect you to attend. If not, you can settle up with Virginia, and I will talk to Mac about writing you a letter of recommendation."

"But you—"

"I told you I don't have time for this." She waved her hand. "I expect this office ready for my occupancy by one. If not, I will not hesitate to call in legal authorities to clear you out." Without giving him a chance to say another word, she left. Seeing Miss Kelly eying her with suspicion, Anna simply tipped her head.

As Anna marched up to Virginia's desk, her heart was still racing. She had no idea if she'd handled the situation right or not, but she almost didn't care. Wesley had not only overstepped his position, he'd been disrespectful and arrogant. Truly, he had left her with no choice. Still, she wished she could discuss the whole thing with Mac right now. Unfortunately, she knew that Mac, with his tongue-tied, jumbled words, would be unable to advise her. But at least she could report back. Hopefully he would approve.

"How did it go?" Virginia quietly asked.

"I'm not sure." Anna grimaced. "I may have just fired Wesley. Or maybe not. I guess we'll find out at today's staff meeting. Did you let everyone know?"

"I did. And I'm sure it'll be a very interesting meeting." Virginia's smile was catty. "I know I am waiting on pins and needles."

Anna glanced around the office, trying to decide on her next best course of action. She hadn't planned to mix with employees until *after* the staff meeting. Even then, she would maintain a careful and professional distance. But with Mac's office occupied, there was no private space to hole up in until the meeting.

"Is Harvey Rollins still on the police force?" she asked Virginia.

"Harvey's been the chief for the past several years." Virginia's brow creased. "Are you expecting trouble with Mr. Kempton?"

"I'm not sure, but I think I'll pay Chief Rollins a little visit—just in case." Anna picked up her satchel and headed out. Part of her still wanted to run home and tell Mac all that had just happened and seek his advice, but another part of her wanted to continue to manage this situation on her own—to prove to him that she was able.

CHAPTER 10

To Anna's relief, Chief Rollins was in his office and happy to see her. He warmly greeted her and inquired about his good friend Mac. She filled him in and even described a bit of the pleasant time of getting-acquainted that Mac had been enjoying with his granddaughter.

"I'm so glad to hear that." He nodded. "Mac has seemed lonely these past few years. He must be thrilled to finally have family around."

She nodded. "Now I wish we hadn't waited so long. But you know how stubborn Mac can be...and I suppose the apple doesn't fall far from the tree in our family."

He chuckled, then grew more serious. "So, Anna, I don't get the impression this is purely a social visit. Is there something I can do for you?"

She quickly told the chief about Mac wanting her to manage the newspaper and the prickly situation with Wesley Kempton, even explaining her qualifications for running the business.

"I knew it." He pointed a finger in the air. "I'd noticed that byline in the *Oregonian* a while back and even asked Mac about it, but he claimed it wasn't you."

"My boss had suggested I use a man's name for my pseudonym but agreed to my initials—as long as I maintained the pretense I was a male writer. Women are not very welcome in the newspaper business." She sighed. "As Mr. Kempton has just made clear. He offered such extreme opposition, even threatening to go to the bank for their support. But I held my ground. I told him to be cleared out of Mac's office by one o'clock and suggested I would get legal backup if necessary." She smiled sheepishly. "I hope that wasn't out of line."

"Not if you have Mac's authority. As long as Mac is living and breathing, that newspaper belongs to him. If he's asked you to manage it, then it's your legal right to do so." His brow creased. "Although it might be helpful to consult an attorney if Wesley doesn't back down."

"I thought about talking to Randall Douglas. He's an old friend."

"Well, keep that in mind. For now, I suggest that you see how your staff meeting goes. If you have any trouble, tell Virginia to give me a call, and I'll send a couple of officers over. And if Wesley's not cleared out of Mac's office by one o'clock, you give him one last warning. Tell him that you will be calling me. If he disregards that, we'll come in and escort him out."

She thanked him and, seeing that it was nearly eleven, told him good-bye and promised to stay in touch. Then, feeling somewhat more confident, she returned to the newspaper office, where Virginia met her at the door. "The staff is in the break room," she whispered. "I'm not sure if Wesley is in there. Last I saw, he was still in Mac's office. Miss Kelly too."

"Packing up?"

"Hard to say." She shrugged as she locked the glass front door and flipped the Closed sign over.

"Well, let's not keep the staff waiting." With Virginia by her side, Anna entered the smoke-filled break room, politely smiling at the small group gathered there. Most sat in chairs around the two long tables—some nursing mugs of coffee—and a few lingered nervously on the fringes. All looked understandably curious and slightly uneasy. But Wesley and his pretty secretary were noticeably absent. Anna surveyed the group as she went to the spot where Mac used to stand when conducting his rarely held staff meetings. Not surprisingly, aside from Virginia and her, the staff members were all males, and most appeared older than her. She recognized about half of them...writing editors, typesetters, pressmen, ad salesman, circulation boss, and what she assumed was the office boy. But all eyes were on her.

"Good morning," she told them. "Thank you for coming. Some of you probably remember me, but I am Anna McDowell, Mac McDowell's daughter. My father sends his greetings, and I assure you that he is doing his best to make a full recovery. In the meantime, he has asked me to manage this newspaper for him." She paused to allow for their reaction. Clearly, they were taken aback. She was about to begin again when the break room door opened and Wesley and Miss Kelly entered the room.

Deciding to ignore the newcomers, she turned her attention back to the others, continuing her speech. "I can tell by your expressions that you are all wondering what qualifies me to assume this leadership position, but I want to assure you that, besides being Mac McDowell's daughter and growing up in the newspaper business, I am experienced and capable." She gave them a brief history of her fifteen years at the *Oregonian*, including the confession that she ghostwrote articles for years before her promotion to editor. She could see by their eyes that they were both surprised and impressed...but she could tell they were not convinced. Perhaps they would never be.

"Believe me, I know that most people believe the newspaper business is a man's world, but let me remind you that women won the vote in our state nearly four years ago. And, according to a recent survey by the *Oregonian*, women constitute more than one third of newspaper readership. Many think that's a conservative estimate. Also, as I'm sure you know, women consumers dominate much of the marketplace, and newspapers cannot survive and thrive without retail advertisements. So the time has come for women to be accepted in the journalism world— not only in large, progressive cities like Portland, Boston, San Francisco, and New York, but small towns like Sunset Cove as well."

She paused to catch her breath and gather her thoughts, but before she could start again, Wesley spoke up. "Excuse me, everyone, but I'd like to say something." She raised a hand, ready to stop him, but he proceeded. "I will be the first one to say that I was rather stunned to learn that Mac had asked his daughter to take over the newspaper, but after having given it some careful thought and having considered her experience as an editor at the *Oregonian*, I am willing to concede that Miss McDowell is well equipped for the task of managing our newspaper."

Anna blinked in surprise. "Well, thank you, Mr. Kempton."

"My apologies for questioning you earlier," he said. "My only defense is that I care deeply about this newspaper. I have only had its best interests at heart."

"As have I." She nodded. "And I believe that everyone

here feels the same way. At least I hope you do. As you probably know, the *Sunset Times* was established by my grandfather when Mac was a youth—back in the 1860s. The McDowell family has been committed to providing current quality news to this community for decades, and I, for one, hope that it continues for many more decades. It's no secret that small-town papers are folding around the state. I realize this is mostly due to large papers like the *Oregonian* and greatly improved circulation methods. But I must admit to feeling a very real sense of sadness over this modern-day phenomenon. Like my grandfather and father before me, I believe that small towns need a strong, local voice. I hope and pray that the *Sunset Times* will continue to provide that voice for generations to come."

Wesley began to clap, and slowly but surely, several others joined in, until finally they were all applauding. Anna wasn't sure if they were clapping because of Wesley or because of her, but perhaps it didn't matter.

"I will be most appreciative of your support," she continued, "during this interim when Mac is unable to return to work. As I already mentioned, this is a temporary solution. My home is still in Portland, and my plan is to return there by fall—and hopefully to get another editorial position at the *Oregonian*." Of course, she knew this was easier said than done after leaving the way she'd left. But it was possible she could get hired in a different department.

After exchanging brief and polite introductions with the staff, Anna suggested that everyone start their lunch hour a few minutes early, and the room quickly cleared. Except for Wesley and Anna.

"Thank you for your vote of confidence." Still feeling cautious, she headed for the door. "That was quite unexpected."

"Well, like I told you, I thought about your concerns and realized the error of my ways."

"Meaning you want to remain on staff here?" She studied him closely, wondering if this was some kind of game.

"Of course." His smile seemed a bit sheepish.

"And you're certain you can work for a woman? You won't balk at a female giving the commands?"

"I'll do my best."

"And what about Miss Kelly? Did you give her the news?"

"I did, but she didn't believe me. That's why she insisted on attending the meeting. But it appears she got the message."

"Good. And you'll move out of Mac's office by one?"

"I'm almost done."

Anna wasn't sure whether to be happy or suspicious.

"And unless you have any objections, I plan to occupy my old desk as well as my position as assistant editor in chief."

Anna tried to conceal her dismay. Having Wesley second in command was unsettling, especially considering their earlier disagreement. Just the same, she nodded. "If that's what Mac wants, who am I to object?"

"Great." He stuck out his hand. "Still friends?"

"Still friends?" She frowned. "I'm not sure we were ever really friends."

"Oh, Anna." He put a hand over his mouth. "I mean *Miss McDowell.* You must've known how much I admired you all those years ago. I always thought of you as a friend."

"Well, how about if we set friendship aside in the effort to maintain civility and congeniality." She reluctantly shook his hand. "And then we'll see how it goes."

"I suppose that's a wise plan."

"Now, if you'll excuse me, I'd like to go home for lunch." She moved toward the door.

"To give Mac a full report?" His tone sounded like an attempt at lightness laced with concern.

"Of course." She reached for the doorknob. "I promised to keep him informed of everything."

"Well, I hope you don't paint me in too bad a light." His smile looked uneasy.

"All I can do is be honest." She forced a polite smile. "See you at one."

As Anna walked home, she felt a mixture of relief and concern. On one hand, she was grateful that Wesley had shown up and made his speech at the staff meeting—it probably helped her more than she cared to admit. On the other hand, it would've been so much easier if he'd just packed up and left—for good. Now she'd have to keep a close eye on him. Because, despite his amazing turnabout, she was suspicious.

CHAPTER 11

Anna joined Mac in his sitting room for lunch. Bernice had already informed her that Katy had been putting him through his paces all morning, and Anna could see that he was tired. But he seemed glad to see her. She told him about her morning, playing down her interaction with Wesley. Although she did tell him that she was evacuating the interloper from Mac's office.

"My aw...fuss?" he stammered. "Wesley...in my aw...fuss?"

"He'll be out by one," she assured him as she dipped into her soup. "He promised."

"Goo-ood." He nodded.

"And Wesley was surprisingly supportive of me at the staff meeting," she told him. "I think it helped."

Mac scowled as if not so sure.

"I wasn't sure how well your staff would respond to a woman manager." She buttered her roll. "But I told them my qualifications and about my experience at the *Oregonian*. I reminded them of some important facts regarding modern-day women, including that we got the vote in 1912." She chuckled. "But I suspect that some of those fellows are fairly old fashioned."

"Yeah." His eyes looked sad as he tapped his own chest.

"Yes, Mac, I know you've been old fashioned too. But I think Katy and I can help nudge you into the twentieth century." She grinned. "It's about time."

He let out a frustrated sigh, as if he wanted to communicate something but knew it was impossible.

"Did the typewriter come yet?" she asked.

His eyes lit up. "In my den."

Anna smiled. "Your speech seems to be improving, Mac. Have you been practicing?"

"Yeah. Katy make me." His lip curved into a half-smile.

"I hope she's not overdoing it. Katy is an energetic and determined young lady, but sometimes she gets carried away."

"Is goo-ood for me."

"Well, it does seem like you're doing better. I'm impressed. Where is Katy?"

"Pay...tee." He held up his fork, waving it up and down. "Beash."

"Painting on the beach?" Anna tried.

"Yeah. Pick...sure...for me."

"Wonderful. A seascape painting would be nice. And that will give you a little break from her too." She set her spoon in the empty soup bowl. "Mac, I'd like to know more about your staff. I realize it's difficult for you to talk. Besides, I can tell you're tired. But sometime, when you feel like it, do you think you could type up a little bit about each employee?"

"Yeah!" He nodded eagerly.

"I'd like to know who will be easy to work with and, well, the ones who won't be so easy. I know they're all good, dependable employees, but I'm sure they're questioning a woman at the helm. Some maybe more than others."

"Yeah." His brow creased. "Jim." He pointed his thumb toward the ceiling.

"Do you mean that Jim is a good guy?"

"Yeah."

"So I can depend on him?"

He nodded. "Reginald." He held up his thumb again.

"Great, Mac. This is helpful."

"Wesley..." He frowned, turning his thumb down.

"Oh, that's sort of what I thought." Now she confessed that she'd hoped that her earlier confrontation would've resulted in his quitting. "Should I fire him?"

Mac's mouth twisted on one side as he scratched his fuzzy, white hair. "Not sure."

"But I should be wary him?"

"Yeah!"

"I already decided I'd keep a close eye on him."

"Goo-ood."

Anna glanced at the mantel clock. "Well, it's already past one. I better get back there to make sure Wesley cleared out of your office."

Mac held up his hand. "Pay...per."

"Paper?" she asked. "You mean the newspaper?"

He shook his head. "No. *Aw...fuss* pay...per," he spoke slowly. "My file. Bree ho'."

Desperately wishing Katy were here, Anna attempted to repeat his jumbled words in her head. "Office papers...files? Bring your files home?"

"Yeah!" He slapped his knee. "Nee' them."

"I saw a box of papers and files on the floor. I assume they were the ones from your desk. Do you want me to have Virginia send those home to you?"

"Yeah." He nodded. "Will...ee bree."

"Willy? Is that the office boy?"

"Yeah." He held his thumb up again.

"So Willy is dependable." She laid her napkin on the tray. "That's good to know, Mac." She leaned down to kiss his cheek, just like she always did as a girl, and hoped it wasn't offensive. But seeing his eyes light up provided her answer. "I'll tell Willy to bring your box of papers home. You can sort through them at your leisure."

He nodded with what seemed relief, and she reminded him to take a rest this afternoon. "Don't let Katy wear you out." She winked. "See you at dinnertime."

"Goo'-bye."

Anna felt reassured as she returned to the office. So far so good. Mac seemed pleased with what she'd accomplished so far. And she now knew she could trust Jim and Reginald and Willy. And, of course, Virginia. Anna wasn't overly concerned over the no-nonsense typesetters and printers—they would soon see that she only wanted to keep things going.

That left half a dozen others...and Wesley. Suddenly she didn't feel quite so confident. If Wesley had the persuasive power to sway employees her way, he also had the power to turn them against her as well. And it was plain to see that Mac didn't trust him. Yet he hadn't encouraged her to fire him. Perhaps he had reasons for wanting Wesley around. After all, wouldn't he have gotten rid of Wesley long before this otherwise? Once again, Anna wished her father could communicate more clearly.

To her relief, Wesley had cleared his things out of Mac's office, and Miss Kelly didn't appear to be around. The desk she recently occupied was now piled with boxes and things that Anna assumed belonged to Wesley, but he was nowhere to be seen.

Anna carried Mac's box of papers and files and set them on the reception desk. "Can you ask Willy to send this home to Mac?" she asked Virginia. "He wants to go through these papers."

"Will do." Virginia handed Anna a small stack of mail. "And Wesley said to tell you he was taking a quick lunch break."

"Oh." Anna sighed. "I was hoping perhaps he'd quit."

Virginia laughed. "Good luck with that."

"Are you busy right now?" Anna asked.

"Not terribly. Just the usual things."

Anna motioned toward Mac's office. "I'd like to ask you a few things."

Virginia's brows arched with curiosity. "I'll have Willy keep an eye up here for me, and I'll be right with you."

Anna went into Mac's office, attempting to organize it the way Mac used to have it. But it was like putting a puzzle together to get the photographs and pictures into the same places. Finally, deciding that the office walls could use a good coat of paint anyway, she set them back on the floor.

"Here I am," Virginia announced. "What can I do for you?"

Anna closed the door. "I want you to fill me in on everything you know about the newspaper staff." She pulled out a notepad, and they both sat down. "Mac already briefed me a bit. I understand that Jim and Reginald are trustworthy. And Willy too. Would you concur?"

"Absolutely."

"Tell me a little about Jim and Reginald. I know they're both writers, but little else."

"Jim Stafford is the lead news editor. He's relatively new

to Sunset Cove. I believe he hails from Salem. He's friends with Randall Douglas. Mac really seems to like Jim, and from what I've seen, Jim is a good man and a good writer." Her eyes twinkled. "He's not married."

Anna glanced to the ceiling. Why were people always trying to match her up? "And I do remember Reginald, and I know he writes the society column, but I've never been very well acquainted with him."

"Reginald is a sweet man. He's got a lovely little wife named Rachel. No children. He covers all the meetings, school activities, weddings, obituaries, and the society column. He's been with the paper for around twenty years. Very trustworthy."

"Very good. And Mac feels Willy is dependable too."

"Dear Willy. He's been working after school and weekends here since he was twelve. His father is sick and unable to work, so Willy's income helps them a lot. He's been our delivery boy, office helper, custodian. Mac's been like a dad to him. After Willy finished school a couple weeks ago, Mac had plans to promote him—but then Mac got sick. So, for now, Willy is just doing the same old odd-jobs, but full time. I guess you can sort that out."

"I'll talk to Mac about it." Anna made a note.

"Now the other editors. You probably remember Ed from when you were a girl. He covers business news, current events, and national and international news. We never used to have much international news, but with the war in Europe, that has changed. If Ed isn't at his desk, he can be found lurking by the telegraph machine." Virginia's brow creased.

"So is there something about Ed that I should know?"

"I think he's trustworthy enough. It's just that he's rather, well, *prickly*. He doesn't like to be crossed by anyone. He can act like he's an expert on just about everything. And he was strongly anti-suffrage. And he most certainly does not approve of women in the workplace. He will strongly oppose you, Anna, simply because you're not a man. He's not even very nice to his own wife."

"Oh, well, I'm used to male superiority. Now what about Frank?"

"Frank has been here about fifteen years or so. He covers sports, hunting, fishing, weather, agriculture, and so on. He's got a wife and three boys. A nice enough fellow, although, in some ways, he's very much like Ed. He feels a woman's place is in the home—*period*. For that reason alone, he will give you a hard time. Take it from me."

"And I know where Wesley stands...." She frowned. "Well, sort of. In a way, he's a bit of an enigma. Mac doesn't seem to fully trust him. I don't either."

"Wesley's a hard one to figure. He's what I call *slippery*. Sometimes I think he's loyal and sincere...other times I think he's about to pull the rug out from under someone." She shook her head. "I couldn't have been more surprised when he offered his support to you at the meeting this morning."

"I was too. But I suspect it's because I was about to hand him his walking papers."

"Oh..." She nodded. "I see. He just wants to secure his employment. At least for now." She chuckled. "You missed the scene with Miss Kelly and him. She was not happy about being let go."

"I can imagine. By the way, is Wesley married? I got the impression he wasn't. Unless he's just one of those married men who acts like he's still single."

"Wesley is single. He's had a few relationships with women over the years, but they always seem to fizzle. I

suspect they figure him out and run the other direction."
She chuckled.

"I wonder that Mac has kept him on all these years."

"Wesley knows how to play Mac." Virginia pursed
her lips. "I hate to say it, but it's true. Wesley has always
gone along with Mac. He agrees to everything Mac says. I
suspect it's always been because he hoped to run the paper
when Mac retired. And you saw how quickly he moved in
here." She waved her hand toward an emptied wall. "But
what Wesley doesn't seem to realize is that Mac has a lot
more respect for the editors who stand up to him. In fact,
I'd been halfway expecting Mac to promote Jim to his
assistant editor in chief." She shook her head. "Although
Wesley would probably have a fit if that happened."

"Interesting."

"As for the other employees," Virginia continued, "I
think they're all fairly dependable and trustworthy...in
their way. Oscar is a good advertising salesman, with solid
relationships in the community. And Hank manages to
keep circulation up and running. And the typesetters and
pressmen just want to do their jobs without any fuss or
interference from anyone. You give them that, and they'll
accept you."

"So it seems that Ed and Frank present some challenges,
and I better keep my eye on Wesley."

"That's what I'd suggest, but Mac could probably fill you
in better."

"Not right now, he can't. Unless he—" She stopped at
the sound of knocking on the door. Virginia hopped up to
answer it, and to their surprise it was Chief Rollins.

"Sorry to bust in on you like this," the chief told Anna,
"but thought I'd follow up with you."

"Come in, Chief Rollins." Anna waved him in as Virginia excused herself to the reception area.

"I know you must have your work cut out for you here," the chief removed his hat as he sat across from Anna. "But I thought I might let you in on a few things. Some things Mac and I had been talking about recently. And since Mac's laid up and you're running the paper, I think there are things you should know."

"Of course." She nodded. "I appreciate any insight you can share."

"I probably shouldn't mention this to you, but I read Wesley Kempton's article in the newspaper this morning. Got me a little riled up."

"Mac too," she told him.

"I'll bet it did." He set his hat on the corner of the desk and leaned forward. "I know as well as anyone that newspapers have got their politics. And I'm aware that not everyone in this office agrees on everything. I think that keeps the news interesting. But when I read Wesley's article in support of Calvin Snyder—well, I knew Mac never would've let it run. Not on the front page anyway. Maybe in the editorial section, since it was obviously more about opinion than truth. And certainly not Mac's opinion. As well as a lot of folks in town."

"I've heard Calvin Snyder's not very popular with some people," she admitted. "And that he bought Charlie's Chowder House and isn't doing a very good job of managing it."

"Yes, and as far as I'm concerned, that's just the tip of the iceberg."

"Do you think he's involved in anything illegal?" she pressed. "I've heard there's rum-running along the Oregon

Coast. Any chance it's going on around here? Or that Calvin is involved?"

The chief looked surprised. "I can tell you're a good newswoman."

"I can sniff out a story."

"Well, I'm not at liberty to say too much about Calvin's involvement in any illegal activities, and I strongly advise you to do the same. But I will say this—Calvin Snyder has his fingers in an awful lot of pies these days. Political and otherwise. And I know Mac was keeping an eye on things." His brow creased. "In fact, I've worried that might've contributed to his health problems. Doctor Hollister mentioned how anxiety could've been a factor."

"He suggested something like that to me as well." Anna hoped that the lunch conversation today wasn't too stressful.

"Anyway, I know Mac had been collecting and compiling some facts in regard to our mayor. Perhaps you can look into it. But I wanted to let you know that, according to a source of mine, Calvin's bankroll has grown considerably in the past few months. Not only that, but he just bought a roadhouse a few miles out of town. Paid cash for it too. So if you put two and two together, it seems to add up...to something."

"And this is an election year...." She leaned back in her chair, considering. Familiar with Portland politicians, Anna knew how some liked to build up their campaign funds to ensure a victory.

He nodded. "Sounds to me like you're on the right track."

"Can I tell you something, Chief?"

"Do you mean, can you trust me?"

She smiled. "I know I can trust you. You've been friends with my father for as long as I can remember. But I don't want to cross any lines here. I want to tell you something—not so much to tip you off but to get your advice."

"Go ahead."

"I heard Wesley talking to the mayor on the phone this morning. And he sounded pretty cozy with him. But when he realized I was in the office, he shut it down—fast." She shrugged. "Seemed suspicious."

"After reading that article this morning, I have no doubt that Wesley is in cahoots with the mayor. That's one reason I wanted to come by this afternoon. By the way, did you resolve things with him? I see you got your dad's office back, and I didn't notice him in the office. Did you fire him?"

"No. He's on a late lunch break." She hurriedly explained about Wesley's quick turnabout and how Mac had not encouraged her to get rid of him. "I know he doesn't trust Wesley, but Mac almost seemed like he didn't want him gone."

The chief rubbed his chin then smiled. "Maybe old Mac has a plan. Keep Wesley around so you can keep an eye on him." He chuckled. "Yeah, I like that idea. There's an old saying, Anna: Keep your allies close and your enemies closer. Hey, maybe that's what Mac's been doing all this time."

"I don't know about that. But if Wesley really is up to something, I'd like to find out what it is." She grinned. "I'm pretty good at investigative reporting. I like getting to the bottom of things. And, as a woman, I'm sometimes able to ease into places and situations without people figuring out why I'm there."

"You're not suggesting women's wiles?" He grinned.

"No, of course not. But if a man assumes I'm not too smart because I'm a woman and that helps me to make some discoveries, well, I'm not above it."

"Good for you. Just keep me informed—and don't get involved in anything dangerous." He stood, taking his hat. "Be sure to let me know if you discover anything new or if there's anything I can do to help." He frowned. "But like I said earlier, I don't want you to mention this to anyone else, Anna. It's not that most folks in town aren't trustworthy. But some are given to gossip. And some are loyal to the mayor. Mac and I were keeping this to ourselves."

"I understand." Anna wondered how much she should tell Mac. She didn't want to give him cause to worry.

"Give my regards to Mac." Chief Rollins reached for the doorknob.

"Wait a minute." She held up her hand. "Don't go out that way. If Wesley's at his desk, he'll see that you've been talking to me. Might make him suspicious." She pointed to the bookshelf wall. "Do you know about *that*?"

"You bet I do." His eyes lit up. "Haven't used it in years. But that's not a bad idea, not at all."

Anna went over to the window, looking to the sidewalk and street to see if anyone was coming or going into the nearby alley. "Coast seems clear," she told the chief. "I'll lock up after you go out."

A moment later, Chief Rollins pulled out the thick copy of *Moby Dick*. He released the lever behind it, slid back a section of the bookshelf, and slipped through the opening into the narrow hallway. A few steps would deliver him to the secret door that let out into the back alley. Anna couldn't help but smile as she went into the dark, musty hallway and fastened the deadbolt on the door. She remembered the first time Mac had shown her this covert escape, swearing her to secrecy about it. She'd only used the passageway a few times—and only for fun—but she'd never forgotten about it. She knew her grandfather had built it early on, but she never knew why exactly. Mac had suggested it was to escape his collectors, but she suspected he'd been joking. Still, it was exciting to be able to put it to use today. She hoped that Mac wouldn't mind.

CHAPTER 12

By the end of the week, Anna was well aware that her work at the newspaper wasn't going to be a walk through the park. Despite Wesley's bravado of managing the paper in Mac's absence, much had been overlooked. To be fair, some of this neglect appeared to have occurred during her father's shift, but it left her to wonder what Wesley had been doing these past two weeks to remedy things. It almost seemed that he wanted the newspaper to fail.

"I don't understand why Wesley didn't pay this already." Anna waved the overdue bill for newsprint paper in front of Virginia. "Did he think we wouldn't need it?"

"Maybe you should ask Wesley." Virginia reached for the bill, adding it to her growing stack. She'd been helping Anna sort through everything these past few days.

"I already did ask." Anna reached for another bill. "Naturally, he had lots of excuses."

"A five-foot-two, blonde excuse?" Virginia peered over the top of her glasses. "Anna, you should hire a secretary—I mean a real secretary."

"Am I taking unfair advantage of you?" Anna frowned. "You've been so helpful and—"

"Oh, I don't mind, honey. You know I care about this paper. It's just that—"

"Virginia, why don't you be my secretary? We could find someone else to mind the reception area."

Virginia pursed her lips. "Oh, I'm too old to make a change like that. Besides, I like being out in front, rubbing elbows with the riffraff." She chuckled. "You should find yourself a young woman—someone who's been to business school, with good typing skills. I've been telling Mac this very thing the past few years."

"Yes, you're probably right." Anna looked at the ledger that she'd just been going over. "I wonder if we can afford it."

"We could easily afford it if you let Wesley go."

Anna had already told Virginia that, for some reason, Mac wanted to keep Wesley around. She hadn't told her about Chief Rollins's suspicions, but she wouldn't be surprised if Virginia had already drawn her own conclusions.

"Tell you what, honey." Virginia took the ledger and stack of bills. "I'll go over all of this for you up at the front desk."

"Oh, that'd be fabulous. Sure you don't mind?"

"I might not be much of a typist, but I'm darn good at arithmetic." She tapped the side of her head. "I've managed my household budget for more than twenty years. Never got an overdue notice yet."

"Thank you!"

"In the meantime, there's still time to drop a Help Wanted ad into Saturday's edition. Want me to talk to Oscar?"

"Why not? If we discover we can't afford a secretary, we just won't set up any interviews." Anna picked up the mock-up of Saturday's paper. "I better finish going over this. The typesetters need it back before noon."

Virginia stood. "Well, honey, you've done real good for your first week here. And you didn't even have a full week. Next week you'll probably do even better."

As Virginia left, Anna thought about Mac...how demanding this job must've felt to him, day after day, week after week, year after year. Did that have anything to do with his recent health troubles? Virginia was right, he should've hired a secretary. But she knew that he'd relied on Wesley for assistance. Maybe too much.

Anna hadn't mentioned her visit with Chief Rollins to Mac. She had begun to understand that talking about the newspaper office was stressful to him. She could see the frustration in his eyes—as if he felt guilty for being ill and unable to do anything about it. For that reason, she'd kept her conversations with him lighthearted and positive. She could tell that his time spent with Katy was helping with his speech. And he'd been spending time at his typewriter too. But if Anna wanted Mac to have the best chance at getting well, this was a load she needed to carry without him. At least for the time being.

By the time Anna was halfway through the mock up, she was thoroughly angry. It was Wesley's job to final proof for the editors, and yet this mock-up was full of mistakes. Although she'd been making corrections as she found them, the process was taking far longer than it should. What on earth had Wesley been doing the last couple of days? She carried the mock-up out to his desk, ready to rake him over the coals, only to discover he'd already left for lunch. Though it was past twelve, and the others had left too.

She was tempted to throw the whole mess on his desk and go to lunch herself, but she knew the typesetters expected the proof by now. So she returned to her office and finished the process. By the time she left her office, employees were returning from lunch. She just glared at Wesley as he sat down at his desk. Without saying a word, she stomped off to hand the paper over to the typesetters. She apologized to Ronald for the condition of the mock-up. "Wesley was supposed to do the final proof," she told him. "But apparently he...uh, it seems he forgot."

Ronald scowled with disapproval at the messy mock-up. "Well, we need to get this set straightaway."

"I know." She nodded. "Sorry for the delay." Now she marched back to Wesley's desk and demanded to know what had happened. She knew that she should probably do this in the privacy of her office, but just now, she didn't care.

"Oh? I thought *you* wanted to proof them." Wesley acted surprised, but Anna wasn't buying it. "You claimed you were managing *everything*, Miss McDowell. I could only assume that when you said 'everything,' you meant 'everything.' Perhaps you should make yourself clearer in the future."

"Perhaps you do not understand the responsibilities of an *assistant* editor in chief," she shot back at him. "I'm well aware this is a small-town paper, but I don't think it's been run that much differently than a large city paper. And I would think you would know what your job is meant to be, Mr. Kempton. You are to assist the editor in chief. But since that doesn't appear to be the case with you, I am forced to reassign you to a straight editorial position." She pointed to the one vacant space in the office, clear on the other end of the editorial department, looking almost like a detention desk. "Please, vacate this area and relocate yourself to—"

"*What?*"

"I think you heard me correctly." She locked eyes with him. "Am I clear now?"

"Have you lost your senses?" he hissed back at her. "Mac will never agree to—"

"Mac has placed me in charge," she said firmly. "And if you wish to continue your employment here, I suggest you do as I ask, Mr. Kempton."

"Well, I—"

"It's your choice."

"You can't get away with this. I've been second in line for more than ten years. You can't just come in here and—"

"Excuse me." And without another word, she turned and went into her office. Her hands were shaking as she sat down at the desk. Had she just made a stupid mistake? She thought about what Mac might do under similar circumstances.... Back in the old days, he used to bluster and explode on employees who didn't meet his expectations. But they always seemed to take it in stride. Perhaps she really was her father's daughter—auburn hair and a fiery Scottish temper to match. Or maybe she was simply hungry. And yet she couldn't bear to walk through the office right now. Besides the likelihood of crossing paths with Wesley again, she knew they'd all be looking at her. And so, she called the reception desk.

"Virginia." Anna glanced over her shoulder. "I'm going to—"

"I heard it all," Virginia interrupted. "Good job, honey. He had it coming."

"Yes, well, it's late, and I'd like to get some lunch. I thought I'd slip out the, uh, out the back."

"You mean the *secret* back door?" Virginia spoke in a hushed tone.

"Yes." Anna felt relieved to hear that Virginia knew about

the clandestine exit. That was just one more confirmation of Mac's trust in the older woman.

"Just be sure to lock your office door—that way no one will pop in there and figure out that you're gone. In the meantime, I'll let it be known you do not want to be disturbed."

"Thank you."

"And you'll be pleased to know that, right now, Wesley just fetched a box from the storage room. Looks to me like he's getting ready to empty his desk."

"Good to know." She thanked Virginia. Then, after locking the office door, she put on her hat, got her bag and gloves, and made a sly getaway. She was barely out on the sidewalk when she heard a male voice calling her name. At first she jumped, then she realized it was Daniel Hollister.

"Dr. Hollister." She took in a relieved breath. "How are you?"

"I'm doing well." He nodded pleasantly. "But remember, you promised to call me Daniel." He walked alongside her. "Isn't this a fine day?"

"Yes." She glanced around, surprised to see the sun had burnt through the morning fog. "It's gotten quite nice."

"Do you mind if I walk with you?"

"Not at all. I was just out to get a late lunch."

"As am I." He grinned. "Would you care to join me?"

"I usually go home for lunch." She frowned.

"You seem uneasy." He peered curiously at her. "Anything wrong?"

"Just the stresses of work." She glanced at him, realizing that the newspaper wasn't the only thing troubling her. "Do you mind if I ask...is there a Mrs. Hollister?"

His smile was sad. "There was...and she was a lovely

woman...but that was long ago. I've been widowed for quite some time."

"Oh." She nodded. "I'm sorry for your loss."

"Thank you. So there is nothing improper about your joining me for lunch."

"That sounds nice. I would appreciate your company."

"How about the hotel restaurant? They have delicious fish chowder on Fridays."

She considered this, wondering if Lucille might still be lodging at the hotel. But at the same time, she wasn't sure she cared since it seemed her warning must've registered, given that Lucille had not attempted to see Mac. "Fish chowder sounds wonderful."

They made polite small talk as they strolled down Main Street, eventually being seated by the front window in the hotel restaurant. "I saw your father this morning," Daniel told her after their order was taken. "I was impressed by his improvement—and in such a short amount of time."

"That's much to do with Katy."

"Ah, yes. I also had the pleasure of meeting your delightful daughter. She told me about putting her grandfather through therapy sessions." He grinned. "Leave it to a pretty, young girl to accomplish what I couldn't."

"Katy is persistent."

"And talented too. I saw the painting she was working on for Mac."

"I'm so glad she's found activities to occupy herself. She was so reluctant to spend her summer here. Yet I think she's having a much better time than her mother."

Daniel looked concerned. "I heard you're working at the newspaper. Is that not going well?"

"It's been a challenge, that's for sure." She slowly shook her head. "But hopefully I'm up for it." Now, although she hadn't meant to, she told him about demoting Wesley Kempton this afternoon. "That's my reason for anxiety today."

"Well, I can't say I know him very well, but I've never had a particularly favorable impression of Mr. Kempton. He's always seemed a bit self-important to me."

"I honestly don't know how Mac put up with him all these years."

"I suspect Mr. Kempton has shown a completely different side around your father. I'm sure he's harbored hopes for promotion in the event of Mac's upcoming retirement. Probably even more so after Mac's illness."

"Yes, I've had similar thoughts." She paused as big bowls of fish chowder were set down. "This looks delicious."

They quietly sampled their soup, then Anna asked Daniel about Mac. "I've been torn about talking to Mac about the stressful goings-on at the office. Especially after what happened with Wesley today. I suspect it might be hard on him. Do you think that sort of anxiety could be detrimental in his recovery?"

"I absolutely do. You're wise to keep your encounters with him positive. Mac may say he wants to know all the happenings at the newspaper, but I'm fairly certain it won't help him get better. And it might possibly set him back."

"Yes, that's what I thought."

"But I do understand your need to talk to someone." He smiled. "I'm a pretty good listener. And, as a physician, I'm accustomed to confidentiality."

"Thank you." Although she felt she could trust him, she knew that, after promising her discretion to Chief Rollins, she wouldn't be able to disclose everything. So, changing the subject, she explained her hopes to hire a secretary. "I honestly don't know why Mac didn't do this years ago. I can't imagine the load he must've been carrying. It's no wonder it took a toll on his health. I'd like to discuss this idea with him, but I'm afraid he would be stressed by it. I feel stymied."

"Mac asked you to manage the paper, Anna. It sounds to me that he trusts you implicitly. So if you think hiring a secretary is a good move, why not simply do it?"

"Yes, I'm sure you're right." She smiled. "It's funny... sometimes I forget that I'm a grown, independent woman in this town. There are moments when I feel just like the young girl I was before I left—not much older than Katy and not nearly as confident. Sometimes I even imagine Mac looking over my shoulder, about to tell me what I'm doing wrong."

He chuckled. "Well, I've heard that Mac could be a hard taskmaster at times. But I suspect he was always harder on himself than he was on others."

"You could be right." Anna had never really considered this before, but it did make sense. Sometimes it had seemed to her that Mac carried the world upon his shoulders. As a girl, she'd associated that with running the newspaper. Now she wasn't so sure.

As they finished their lunches, Anna felt surprisingly relaxed and refreshed. So much better than when she'd left the office. The doctor really was good medicine. She was just about to thank him when she saw something that made her stomach knot up. "Oh dear!" She laid her napkin beside her place setting, ready to make a quick getaway.

"Something wrong?" He glanced around the restaurant.

"Lucille," she muttered. "She's still here."

"Lucille?"

"My mother. Mac's ex-wife." She shifted in her chair, an attempt to avoid being spotted by Lucille.

"Oh?" His brows arched. "Not the woman in the frilly pink dress?"

"That's her." Anna cringed. "She's quite the clotheshorse."

His smile looked fixed. "Looks like she's coming this way."

"Just my luck."

"Anna," Lucille bubbled cheerfully as she came to their table. "Fancy seeing you today. I was just thinking of you, darling. And here you are with your handsome young gentleman friend. How perfectly delightful."

Anna stiffly introduced Lucille to Daniel. "He's been caring for Mac. We were just talking about his progress."

Without being asked, Lucille pulled out a chair and sat down next to Daniel, then leaned closer to him. "Tell me, dear doctor, how is my old Mac doing? I want to know everything."

Daniel's brow creased. "Mac is doing as well as can be expected for someone who's been through such difficulties. I still recommend much rest and quiet for him. No undue excitement. Anna and I were just discussing this."

Lucille frowned. "So he isn't receiving visitors yet?"

"No, not until he's much stronger," Daniel told her. "For now, I recommend that only Anna and Katy and his housekeep—"

"*Katy?*" Lucille looked suspicious. "Who is Katy? Please, don't tell me that Mac has gotten himself a new wife. No one in town has informed me of anything like this."

"Katy is Mac's granddaughter," Daniel answered before Anna had a chance to send him a message with her eyes. Now she wanted to kick him in the shin.

"Granddaughter?" Lucille's blue eyes lit up. "Are you saying that I am a grandmamma?" She turned to Anna. "You never mentioned a word of this to me."

Anna mutely nodded.

"How old is the dear child?"

"She's not exactly a child," Anna confessed. "She's a young lady of sixteen."

"Sixteen! Oh my goodness." Lucille giggled. "Surely, I'm not old enough to have a full-grown granddaughter. Why, just look at me."

Anna exchanged glances with Daniel. "I'm sorry, if you two will excuse me, I must get back. I've already been gone too long." She reached for her purse to extract a bill, but Daniel stopped her, reminding her that he'd invited her. "Thank you," she told him. "I wish you both a most pleasant afternoon."

She felt slightly guilty leaving poor Daniel in the clasps of her pushy and intrusive mother, but he'd revealed his mettle by reminding Lucille to keep her distance from Mac. That was reassuring. However, he'd also let the cat out of the bag regarding Katy. For that alone, he probably deserved a few more minutes with Lucille's inquisitive chatter. If nothing else, it should give him a pretty good idea of what Anna and Mac had been up against with a woman like that.

Chapter 13

It was after two o'clock when Anna slipped back through the secret passageway. The first thing she did was call Virginia, asking her to send Jim Stafford to Anna's office.

The lead news editor looked slightly uneasy as he sat down in one of the leather chairs. "Planning to make more heads roll today?" he casually asked.

She smirked, rolling a pencil between her fingers. "Not that I know of."

"I'll warn you, Wesley is not in the best of spirits." Jim leaned back, gazing evenly at her. "But according to what I heard from the typesetting room, he deserves it."

Anna felt relieved to know that the typesetters had understood the situation—and weren't blaming her. "I asked you in here because I'd like you to take over as assistant editor in chief, Mr. Stafford."

"First of all, call me Jim." He folded his arms in front of him. "Second of all, why should I accept that position?"

She blinked. "Well, because it's a promotion."

"With a raise?"

"Yes, of course." She considered this. "I can't say what exactly. We're currently going over the books and the budget. But I can assure you that whatever Wesley was getting will be matched for you."

"I suppose that's something. Trouble is...I *like* being a reporter. I'm a writer, not a manager. I like writing news stories."

"And you're excellent at it."

"Thank you."

"So why would you balk at this promotion?" She was confused. "You don't want to be an assistant editor in chief?"

"An *assistant editor in chief* is just a fancy title for a *yes-man*."

"A yes-man?"

"That's what Wesley was for Mac. And we all knew it. Mac would say, 'Jump,' and Wesley would say, 'How high?'"

Anna couldn't help but smile. "I sort of wondered about that."

"Wesley brought Mac his coffee with cream and sugar, he took letters for him, he even ran errands in town—whatever Mac asked of him, he did it. A yes-man."

"Well, I'm not asking you to do those sorts of things, Mr. Stafford."

"Jim." He narrowed his eyes.

"Sorry. Jim." She nodded. "Anyway, I am planning to hire a secretary as soon as possible. There'll be an ad in the classifieds tomorrow. She will handle some of the things you just mentioned—but she'll work for both you and me. You'll still be the lead news editor, but you'll also be second in command of the office, and your opinions in running this place efficiently will be greatly appreciated."

"Really?" He sat up straighter. "You honestly think you can pull this off?"

"Yes. Mac put me in charge, and I'm determined to bring

this office into the twentieth century. I realize we will never be the *Oregonian*, but there's no reason we can't be the best newspaper on this section of the Oregon Coast. I'd like to improve everything from content to circulation."

"I do like the sound of that." He brightened. "So as long as you don't expect me to be your 'yes-man,' count me in."

"Great. You can start on Monday. In the meantime, I'm going to have some rearranging done around here. I want you to have a semiprivate office, separate from the editorial section, and we'll have the secretary situated so that she's easily accessible to both of us. How does that sound?"

"Sounds like progress." He grinned. "And Mac won't mind?"

"He put me in charge, Mr.—*Jim*."

"All right, then." He stood, sticking out his hand. "It's a deal."

As she shook on it, she hoped that she hadn't overstepped her bounds. What would Mac say? Or maybe she'd take the doctor's advice and not tell him. What could it hurt? Eventually, when everything here was working like a well-oiled machine, she could tell him.

"Mind if I say something?" Jim paused with his hand on the doorknob.

"Not at all. What is it?"

"Watch your back with Wesley."

"What?"

"I'm not suggesting that he's dangerous exactly, but he could be vindictive regarding this demotion. And I suspect he's got some questionable connections. The truth is, I don't trust him."

Anna studied him for a moment. "Thank you for the warning, but I must admit, it's not news to me."

"Really?" He tipped his head slightly. "Then here's a question for you...why not just fire him?"

She smiled, remembering what the chief told her. "There's an old saying...keep your allies close and your enemies closer."

"Machiavelli?"

She shrugged. "To be honest, I'm not sure who said it originally. But I see the wisdom in it."

Jim looked slightly impressed as he opened the door. "Well, this should be interesting...at the very least."

At the end of the day, Anna asked Virginia to join her. She gave her the updates regarding Jim's promotion and asked for suggestions on the best way to accommodate a semiprivate office for Jim. "And I'd like to get some separation for the other editors too. This open room design is rather old fashioned. I think writers work better with a bit of privacy. It instills confidence." They went over the possibilities of creating semiprivate office spaces with screens between the desks. Anna even sketched out some design ideas on paper. "This is similar to what we had at the *Oregonian*." She held up the paper. "But we obviously have to keep costs down."

"I've been going over the books," Virginia told her. "It seems we're not in as bad of shape as we assumed. I have a feeling Wesley was trying to make it appear worse...by not paying the bills. But from what I can see, we're solid."

"And Mac recently upgraded a lot of the equipment," Anna pointed out. "It looks like the paper is well positioned for the future. We just need to keep moving forward with it—and keep track of the bottom line."

Virginia took Anna's sketch. "How about if I ask my brother-in-law about this? He's a retired carpenter, but, according to my sister, he's got too much time on his hands.

Maybe he can come in during the weekend and put up some partition walls."

"Fabulous."

"And I'll see if Willy can be around to lend a hand. Who knows what might happen."

"Say, before you go..." Anna sighed. "Any thoughts about Wesley? According to Jim he's disgruntled and not hiding it."

"I heard him talking to Ed and Frank in the break room right before I came in here. I couldn't catch everything, but the gist of it was that you were going to ruin the newspaper, that no good would come of having a woman in charge."

"Do you think Ed and Frank are siding with him?"

"Hard to say, but I didn't hear them offer any opposition."

"Well, maybe it's for the best. If they're going to give me trouble, we might as well get it out into the open. Thanks for letting me know." She patted Virginia's back. "And thanks for all your help today—and this week."

"Hopefully next week will be smoother." She glanced at the clock on a shelf. "Quitting time."

"You have a good weekend," Anna told her. "I'm going to stick around awhile to finish up a few things."

"And avoid crossing paths with Wesley?"

Anna shrugged. "Maybe." She smiled. "But not really. I want to go say a word to the typesetters as well as the pressmen—let them know I appreciate them."

"Good for you." Virginia nodded with approval. "You'll never regret showing those hardworking men your respect."

"I know." Suddenly Anna had an idea. "And maybe I'll run over to the bakery for donuts first."

Virginia laughed. "Now you're talking."

So it was that, after the editorial office cleared out, Anna took a box of donuts to the pressroom. She kept her words simple, just telling the ink-stained employees how much she'd admired them as a child. "But I admire you even more as an adult. Thank you for your hard work." She set the donuts on a work bench. "This paper would be nothing without you men." She could see they were surprised, but before they could respond she left.

As Anna walked toward home, she breathed deeply of the fresh ocean air. Having grown up on the Oregon Coast, she was well aware that clear, sunny days—with no wind— were not necessarily the norm in summertime. Of course, that was what compelled tourists to make the trek over the Coastal Range, hoping to escape high temperatures and stale air in the inland regions. And based on the traffic in town, it was already in full swing.

How many summers she had longed to come back here... to breathe in this lovely air and simply relax? And now— amazingly—she was here. She paused on Shore Avenue, next to the beach-access stairs and just steps from her father's house, and gazed out over the ocean. So incredibly beautiful...and yet she'd been so busy, she'd had little time to soak in any of the splendor. Thankfully, she had the whole weekend ahead of her. And she needed it!

"Anna!" Rand waved from a gleaming automobile, parking it across the street. She greeted him as he hopped out and strode toward her. Dressed impeccably in a pale-blue citified lawyer suit, he looked surprisingly handsome. "So good to see you!" he exclaimed. "I was hoping to cross paths with you today."

"How are you, Rand?" She adjusted the brim of her hat to look into his face, suddenly wishing she had worn something more feminine than her serious business suit.

"I'm doing well, thank you. Especially now that I

managed to catch up with you." He beamed down at her. "I hear you're working hard at the newspaper these days."

"Word travels fast in these parts."

"Don't forget my mother runs the mercantile." He chuckled. "Anyway, I suspect you've been rather busy this week, but have you heard that it's Founders Day weekend?"

"As a matter of fact, I have heard. We have some pieces in tomorrow's paper about the celebration. Sounds as if it's grown into quite a big shindig since the last time I was here for the festivities. There's a parade, a picnic, a carnival, and a—"

"Founders Day dance." He grinned. "So, tell me, are you free tomorrow night? Made any plans for the big dance? You know that I mean *big* in a small-town way."

"To be honest, I've been so swamped at the newspaper, I haven't given it much thought."

"Mother!" Katy exclaimed happily as she came up from the beach. "You're home." As Anna greeted her, Katy rushed toward them with her art case, easel, and canvas. "Hello, Mr. Douglas." Katy's eyes lit up to see the sleek black car parked across the street. "Is that yours?"

"It is. Brand-new Model T Town Car. Had it shipped out from the East Coast. She just arrived a couple weeks ago." He grinned. "She's a honey, that's for sure."

"Oh, yes! She's a beauty!" Her easel slipped from beneath her arm, and Rand stooped down to get it.

"Looks like you've been painting." He peered at the seascape painting still in her hand.

"It's for Grandpa." She held up the canvas, narrowing her eyes. "It's nearly done, but I still need to add some white foam on top of the waves. I thought I'd finish today, but I met some kids down on the beach." She peered at Anna. "Do you know the Krauss family?"

"I'm not sure."

"Of course you do," Rand told her. "Your old friend Clara Baxter married Albert Krauss. Remember, she was only sixteen when they got married?"

"Clara?" Anna nodded. "Of course—she married the good-looking fellow from Newport. They had a baby as I recall...but I haven't seen her in years."

"Well, I was just talking to AJ Krauss—that's short for Albert Junior. He's seventeen and his younger sister, Ellen, is fifteen. Clara Krauss is their mother. They were digging clams on the beach, and they let me help, and we got to talking, and they knew all about Mac. When I told them he was my grandpa, they told me their mother had been friends with you."

"Yes, of course. I wonder how Clara is doing."

"I guess she's fine. The Krausses own Sunset Fish Company," Katy explained, "and AJ said that I could go out on one of their boats if I wanted—and I do!" She was so excited that she dropped her art case, and paint tubes spilled onto the street.

"Let me get those for you." Rand stooped down to gather the paints. "How about if I help you get these supplies into the house," he offered Katy. "Seems you've got your hands awfully full."

"Thank you." She led the way, chattering about AJ and Ellen and how much fun they'd been and how she hoped to spend time with them during the weekend.

In the house, Rand set Katy's art supplies on the foyer table and then turned to Anna. "So, what about my invitation? Care to accompany me to the Founders Day dance tomorrow night?"

"Oh, Mother," Katy exclaimed. "AJ and Ellen were just talking about that. I'd love to go too."

"How about if I escort both of you lovely ladies?" Rand removed his pale gray bowler hat, sweeping it in front of him in a gentlemanly bow. "It would be my honor."

"Yes, yes." Katy clapped, her eyes wide. "Can we go, Mother? *Please*?"

"I think that's a yes," Anna told Rand.

"Oh, hello," Bernice came into the foyer, wiping her hands on her good white apron. "Are we having another guest for dinner?"

"Yes." Katy nodded eagerly. "Mr. Douglas, can you join us—please?"

"Well, I—"

"I'll just go set an extra place." Bernice bustled away without waiting for his answer.

"We'll understand if you have other plans," Anna said to Rand.

"As a matter of fact, I'd love to join you."

Anna didn't know what to say and so she simply smiled.

"Come say hello to Grandpa." Katy grabbed Rand by the hand. "He still has trouble talking, but it's good for him to practice. Just be patient and give him time to speak. You can entertain him while Mother and I clean up for dinner."

Anna just shook her head at her determined daughter's enthusiasm and then, excusing herself, hurried up the stairs. Eager to shed her serious workday suit—as well as the weight of responsibilities that went with it—she quickly freshened up and donned a light, airy summer dress of shell pink. It was one that Katy had insisted she get the previous summer, but Anna had only worn it once. With its tiny pearl buttons and a gracefully layered skirt, it felt feminine and slightly carefree. As she pinned up her auburn curls, she felt grateful for Katy's cheerful hospitality. It would actually be refreshing to have Rand join them for dinner. A nice change of pace for all of them.

Although Katy was good at chattering about next to nothing, poor Mac still struggled to complete a sentence of just a few words. For the past several evenings, Anna tried to do her part, but after her long, hard days at the newspaper office, she sometimes felt too weary to contribute much to the conversation. Perhaps Rand would fill in the gaps tonight—and hopefully Mac wouldn't mind.

Anna poked her head into Katy's room to discover she was still in her dressing gown. "I'm going down," Anna told her. "Looks like you'll be awhile."

"I had to scrub off paint and sand and—"

"Don't worry, it's not even six. Come down when you're ready." She smiled. "It was nice of you to invite Rand."

"He seems to really like you, Mother."

Anna waved a dismissive hand. "We're old friends, that's all."

Anna could hear Rand talking as she reached the bottom of the stairs. She halted by the door to Mac's private sitting room, listening unobserved as Rand described a legal case he was representing. He paused as Mac asked a stilted question, waiting for him to get the words out before answering. It was so nice hearing Mac engaging with someone else that Anna almost hated to interrupt them. Then she heard another voice and realized that Dr. Hollister was also in the room. What was he doing there? Had Mac been ill? Hopefully Daniel wasn't here to tell Mac about Lucille being in town. In that case, Mac might very well need a physician.

CHAPTER 14

Still feeling a bit confused as to the purpose of Daniel's presence, Anna entered her father's sitting room to see the three men visiting congenially.

"Hello, everyone," she greeted them cheerfully. "I don't mean to interrupt, but—"

"Anna!" Mac's face lit up, and the other men turned toward her. "Very...pretty."

She thanked him as Rand and Daniel both stood, politely greeting her. Then she went over to Mac and kissed his cheek. "You're looking well. But I hope you're not overdoing it." She glanced curiously at Daniel. "I assume this isn't a professional visit."

"Not at all. Mac kindly invited me for dinner after his examination this morning. I planned to mention it to you earlier today, but then we, uh, we were interrupted, and you had to return to the newspaper office." He smiled knowingly.

Relieved he'd had the sensibility not to mention Lucille as the source of their interruption, Anna returned his smile. "Well, this is very nice. And so unexpected. Like a real dinner party."

"Nice." Mac nodded, speaking slowly but more clearly. "Friends...and family."

"Here," Daniel waved to the chair he'd been seated in. "Please join us."

"Thank you. But if you gentlemen will excuse me, I'd like to go see if Bernice needs a hand with anything." She made her exit then hurried to the kitchen. Hopefully Bernice wasn't feeling too overwhelmed by this evening's festivities.

"I didn't know we were having a dinner party tonight," Anna told Bernice.

"Isn't it wonderful?" Bernice dipped a ladleful of drippings over a large roast. "Just like the old days."

"I just hope it's not too much for Mac."

"Well, at least we've got the good doctor here to help." Bernice winked as she closed the heavy oven door. "But I have a feeling it'll be just what Mac needs."

"Is there anything I can do to help?"

Bernice used a dishtowel to wipe her forehead. "Well, you could tell everyone that dinner will be served a little later than I expected."

"I'm sure no one will mind."

"And you could check the settings in the dining room. It's been so long since I've served a formal dinner, I'm not sure I got it right. And I meant to get the silver candlesticks from the sideboard. And Mickey set a bucket of fresh roses out on the back porch—they should go into a vase."

"I'm on it." Anna was glad to be busy. For some reason the idea of having both Daniel and Rand as dinner guests was a bit unsettling. She didn't like to admit, not even to herself, but it was simply because they were both rather attractive and available men...both of whom had shown a fair amount of interest in her. And although their attention was flattering, it made her uneasy. Like a fish out of water. She'd never had time—or taken the time—for involvement with romance. And she wasn't even sure how she felt about this sort of thing now—or even how to behave. It was all rather unnerving—yet nice.

"This room looks so beautiful," Katy gushed as Anna set the crystal vase of pink roses in the center of the table. "May I light the candles, Mother?"

"Sure. I don't think it's too soon."

"These plates are so delicate, so pretty with the tiny pink rosebuds."

"Yes, I was surprised that Bernice put them out. It was my grandmother's best bone china. She used to tell me how it was shipped here from Austria about the same time that this house was built."

"How long ago was that?"

"Well, this house was finished when Mac was around ten. So about fifty years ago. My grandmother took great care with this china, only bringing it out for special dinner parties...holidays, birthdays." Anna sadly remembered the last time she'd dined on this china...the Christmas before Grandmother passed away.

"Well, Bernice must've thought this was a special occasion." Katy reached across the table to light the candles. In her periwinkle voile dress, she truly looked as pretty as a picture. And so grown-up that Anna felt a clutch inside of her chest. Was this really her little girl?

Anna smiled at her. "Katy, darling, I must say, you look quite fetching tonight."

"Thank you. After all, it's Founders Day weekend." Katy blew out the match. "I felt it was time to be festive."

"Well, it feels like we're about to kick off a real celebration with our little dinner party." Anna led Katy out into the living room, glancing around to see that the carpet looked recently cleaned and the wood furniture gleamed. Plus there was a pretty bowl of fresh flowers on the big, round coffee table.

"Everything looks so nice and inviting in here."

"Bernice has been busy." Anna explained about Dr. Hollister's being an additional dinner guest.

"Goodness, Mother." Katy's brows arched. "Are both those men vying for you now? Seems you have suitors coming out of the woodwork."

Anna laughed. "Hardly. And it was Mac's idea to invite the doctor."

"Which one do you prefer?" Katy asked in a hushed tone. "The doctor or the attorney?"

"Oh, you and your romantic notions." Anna nodded to the mantel clock. "Bernice said dinner will be a bit later than planned. I should probably go play hostess with our guests. In the meantime, could you see if Bernice needs help with anything? I'm afraid she's gotten out of the habit of dinner parties."

"And then I'll ring the dinner bell when it's ready," Katy offered.

Anna didn't feel too surprised by Katy's romantic assumptions just now. It simply fit her age and youthful fixation on beaux and love. But it did bother Anna that her daughter wasn't too far from the truth, since Anna had been harboring similar thoughts. Even so, she reminded herself as she prepared to rejoin the gentlemen, Rand was simply an old friend and Daniel was Mac's physician. Nothing to get overly excited about. After all, she was thirty-four years old! Ridiculous to go around acting like a schoolgirl.

"Dinner will be served a bit later than expected," she informed the men. She started to fetch a straight-backed chair for herself, but Rand insisted she take his easy chair. She thanked him as she sat down and, folding her hands in her lap, turned her attention on Mac. "Did you remember that this is Founders Day weekend?"

He nodded. "I know."

"I'll bet you remember the original Founders Day celebration," Rand directed this to Mac.

"Yeah...I do."

"Mac's parents helped to found Sunset Cove," Anna told Daniel. "They came over on the Oregon Trail with a wagon train when Mac was just a tyke. Wasn't it around 1860?" she asked Mac.

"Yeah. In spring...I was four." He held his left hand out to show how small he might've been.

"And yet you still have a lot of memories about that time." Anna remembered the exciting tales he used to share with her when she was a little girl. "I've often thought you should write about your memories of that trip. I know I'd like to read it. I'm sure Katy would too. Perhaps you could write them on your typewriter."

He rubbed his chin with a thoughtful expression. "I could do that."

"Eighteen sixty?" Rand mused. "Not long before the Civil War."

"Mac's family hailed from Pennsylvania," Anna told him. "My grandmother lost two brothers, who fought for the North."

"So your family traveled here in a covered wagon?" Daniel asked Mac.

"Tha's right. Came from..." As Mac pointed to the old family portrait on the wall, he struggled to pronounce where the photo was taken.

"Mac was born in Philadelphia," Anna spoke for him.

"That photograph was taken shortly before they left. That's Mac's mother and father." How many times had Mac told her about the people in this picture? "Our family were newspaper publishers from way back, and my grandfather came out West to start a newspaper."

"I assume the little boy with the mop of curly hair is Mac, but who is the solemn-faced girl in the photograph?" Daniel asked.

"That's Mac's sister, Rebecca." Anna glanced at Mac. "She was a few years older than him."

"Does your sister live in town?" Daniel asked Mac.

Mac sadly shook his head. "No..."

"Rebecca died on the Oregon Trail," Anna explained somberly. She remembered how her grandmother would memorialize Rebecca on her birthday, retelling Anna the sad story of leaving her daughter behind in an unmarked grave. "Cholera. Mac's mother got sick as well. She lost an unborn child and nearly died."

"That's too bad." Daniel shook his head. "Unfortunately, there were many casualties on the Oregon Trail. Deprivations, harsh conditions, and lack of sanitation led to much disease...and death."

"What about you, Rand?" Anna hoped to change the subject. "What brought your family to Sunset Cove? As I recall, your folks started up the mercantile when I was still a little girl. I remember how excited I was about a new store—and so thrilled that they had a candy counter."

Rand laughed. "That was probably my doing. My parents came to Oregon by ship from New York, a few years before I was born," he explained. "My mother still goes on about how rough it was going around the Horn—"

"And to think how ships so easily pass through the

Panama Canal nowadays," Anna said. "Imagine how that would have shortened your parents' trip."

"The Panama Canal has greatly improved shipping time for the store's merchandise," Rand told them. "Mother was just marveling at how quickly an order from Atlanta arrived this week."

"But you say your parents came to Oregon *before* you were born," Anna said. "So they must not have settled here in Sunset Cove."

"That's right. They built a general store in Portland. But the competition was growing, plus it was my mother's dream to live near the ocean. So they moved here in the mid-1880s. I was about seven then."

"So your parents were almost like founders," Anna told him.

"What about your family?" Rand asked Daniel. "When did they come out West?"

"My family is still on the East Coast," Daniel explained. "They live in Boston. My father still practices medicine there."

"What brought you way out here, then—and all by yourself?" Anna asked.

"Well, as I mentioned to you before, I lost my wife some time ago," he told Anna. "We were married in June of 1898. I had just finished Harvard Medical School and was doing my internship in a clinic located in a rather rough part of town. My wife died in childbirth—ironically, in one of Boston's finest hospitals." He shook his head. "It made me feel rather lost and helpless at the time. A physician who loses his wife in one of the country's most modern medical facilities."

They were just expressing their sympathy and regrets when Bernice burst into the room, holding her hands in the air. "Anna Rebecca," she said urgently. "I need your help. Something has—"

"What is it?" Anna leaped out of her chair. "Has Katy been hurt—burnt on the stove?"

"I'll come too," Daniel was by her side.

"No one is hurt," Bernice directed this information to Mac. "Katy is just fine."

Even so, Daniel exited the room with Anna. Out in the hallway, Bernice lowered her voice. "It's *Lucille.*"

"What do you mean?" Anna felt confused.

"I mean she's *here.* In the living room—with Katy."

"Oh dear." Anna looked at Daniel.

"Let's go see what we can do to avert this." He straightened his jacket.

"Go on back to the kitchen," Anna instructed Bernice. "We'll handle Lucille."

"Good luck with that." Bernice looked grim, but she hurried away.

"I appreciate your help with this," Anna told Daniel as they headed for the living room.

"Mother," Katy exclaimed with raised brows. "There you are. Look who is here."

Anna tried to organize her thoughts and words as she took in her mother's appearance. As usual, Lucille was dressed to the nines. Tonight it was layers of magenta silk dripping with ecru lace—and perhaps a bit too youthful for a woman of her age. "Lucille," Anna used a polite yet firm tone. "What are you doing here?"

"I brought my granddaughter a little gift."

Katy held out a frilly magenta parasol with a slightly amused expression. It had obviously been part of Lucille's own ensemble, probably used as a ploy to get herself into Katy's good graces and inside of the house. How typical.

"Well, that was very generous of you." Anna looped her arm through Lucille's, hoping to escort her to the front door. "Thank you for your thoughtfulness. And now, if you don't mind, we're about to sit down to—"

"I see you've got your attractive doctor friend with you, Anna." Lucille frowned but remained in place. "I hope Mac isn't feeling unwell."

"Mac is fine." Anna gave a slight tug on her mother's arm, but Lucille remained anchored to the floor, peeking over Anna's shoulder toward the dining room.

"Oh my, it looks like you're having a nice dinner party." Lucille glared at Anna. "But you told me that Mac is not receiving guests due to his poor health."

"It's only a small affair." Anna tugged harder on Lucille's arm. "But we really should—"

"What is go...ing on?" Mac boomed, using a tone reminiscent of the old Mac.

Anna turned to see Mac, with Rand at his side, entering the living room. It was too late to shield her father from this.

"Mac McDowell," Lucille gushed, and, breaking loose from Anna's grip, she rushed toward him. "Oh my word, Mac, you are more handsome than ever." She hugged him, then stepped back, still holding on to his arms. "Goodness, you are so distinguished." She turned to Daniel. "And here you made it sound as if the poor man was on his deathbed earlier today."

"Lu...cille." Mac stared at her with a stunned expression.

"This isn't good for Mac's health," Anna insisted. "He shouldn't be—"

"Well then, let's all just sit down and relax." Lucille took charge and was soon guiding Mac toward the couch. "Although I do think your young doctor is wrong about your health." She glanced toward Daniel. "Mac appears to be in fine shape." She helped Mac onto the couch, nestling right next to him and keeping her hand wrapped around his arm.

"Wha—what?" Mac blinked at her.

"Oh, it's so good to see you, Mac. I know you won't believe it, but I have missed you. Genuinely missed you." She reached over to tenderly touch his cheek. "I came up to Sunset Cove hoping to make amends, but then I heard about your illness, and no one would let me see you. They claimed you were too ill." She waved to the group that was still standing around, watching with wide-eyed interest. "But then I come over here to discover you are hosting a dinner party. Goodness gracious. Surely, they exaggerated your condition, Mac. Because truly, you look perfectly fit to me. A fine specimen of an elderly gentleman."

"I...I..." Mac looked flustered and confused.

Anna knew it was time to intervene.

"Lucille, I'm sure you don't want to cause Mac any undue—" Anna was interrupted by the clanging of the dinner bell.

"Bernice says that dinner is served," Mickey proclaimed. He tossed Anna a worried glance then hurried away.

"I'll just go set an extra place for our new guest," Katy announced lightly.

"Oh, thank you, dear girl." Lucille beamed at Katy. "What a delightful surprise to find out I have such a well-mannered granddaughter." She frowned at Anna. "It seems that someone has raised her right."

Feeling a mix of anger and anguish, Anna knew there was no graceful way out of this messy dilemma. Not without Mac's help. She went to the couch, sitting on Mac's other side. "What do you think?" she quietly asked. "Is this too much for you? This is your home, Mac, you have the final say."

"I...I am fine." The left side of his mouth curled into what seemed a somewhat amused half-smile. "Don't worry, Anna. It is fine."

Anna tossed a questioning glance at Daniel, but he simply shrugged. And so she stood, giving up with a deep sigh. "Well, at least we have our doctor on hand," she attempted to sound light, "in case anyone needs him before the night is over."

"Come in to dinner, everyone," Katy called out cheerfully. "There's roast beef and potatoes and asparagus—and it all looks delicious."

Anna tried not to feel irritated at her overly hospitable daughter. Katy probably thought this was simply fun and games—like a scene from one of those silly moving pictures she liked to go see with her friends.

"And I almost forgot. I brought a gift for you, Mac." Lucille turned to Katy. "I left a parcel in the foyer, dear. Can you fetch it for me?"

As Katy hurried off to get the mysterious parcel, Lucille helped Mac to his feet. "I think you're going to like my little surprise." She chuckled as they all migrated to the dining room and, before anyone could stop her, Lucille took the seat on the opposite end of the table from Mac's chair, as if she planned to play the hostess tonight. Then, after everyone was seated, Lucille opened the bag that she'd collected from Katy. "I brought your favorite port, Mac." She held up a dark red bottle.

"But there's prohibition," Anna told her.

"Oh, prohibition schmo-hibition." Lucille set the bottle on the table. "Bernice, dear, please, bring us some wine glasses. Those delicate crystal ones that Kathleen kept for special occasions."

Anna looked at Mac, surprised to see that he was still smiling. It was almost as if he was enjoying this whole debacle. Anna turned to Daniel, seated to her left, and once again, he simply shrugged. "A sip or two won't hurt him," he whispered to Anna. "Might actually help his circulation."

Anna looked at Rand now, wondering if any of the adults at the table felt as concerned as she, but he was actually helping Lucille to open the bottle. And before Anna could launch further protest, Lucille began to pour, presenting the first glass to Mac. After everyone—including Katy—was served, Lucille lifted her glass.

"To Mac," Lucille proclaimed. "To his health and happiness—and to *auld lang syne.*"

The others lifted their glasses, making Anna feel she had no choice but to follow. After all, the toast was to Mac—and, despite her concerns, he didn't seem troubled.

"What does *auld lang syne* mean?" Katy asked as they set down their glasses.

"It's Scottish," Anna told her, removing Katy's unfinished wine with a stern expression. "Like Mac." She forced a smile. "As I recall, it means something like *days gone by.*" She glanced at Mac. "Is that correct?"

"*Old...long...ago,*" Mac proclaimed.

Anna nodded solemnly. Of course, it was fitting—whether it was days gone by, old long ago, or auld lang syne...Lucille's toast was uncannily appropriate. And not due to Founders Day, although that worked, but mostly for their uninvited dinner guest. Because like it or not, Lucille was a big part of Mac's past...and of Anna's too. She just hoped that Lucille didn't intend to become a part of their future.

CHAPTER 15

Sunset Cove seemed to have pulled out all the stops for Founders Day weekend. Early on Saturday morning, as Anna and Katy strolled through town, bright banners hung from lampposts, American flags blew in the breeze, and colorful bunting was draped in business windows. "I've never seen the town looking so festive." Anna paused by a plate-glass window to adjust the pins in her wide-brimmed hat, securing it against the sea breeze that was wafting through town. Katy, after declaring none of Anna's summer dresses cheerful enough, had loaned her a frock in a delicate forget-me-not floral print and a white lace collar to wear for today's festivities. Anna had worried it was too youthful, but Katy insisted it wasn't.

"Oh, look, Mother." Katy pointed across the street. "There are Ellen and AJ."

It took Anna a moment to remember. "Oh yes, you mean the Krauss children."

"Oh, Mother. Please don't call them *children.*" Katy waved, called them over, and performed polite introductions. Ellen smiled shyly, and AJ removed his straw hat to reveal thick, wavy blond hair.

"I was friends with your mother," Anna told the young people. She nodded to Ellen. "I can hardly believe how much you resemble Clara."

"Our mother is in the mercantile right now," AJ told Anna. "You should go tell her hello."

"Yes, you should," Ellen agreed. "Mother was just saying how eager she is to see you again."

"Yes, Mother," Katy urged. "Do go and see her right now. And if AJ and Ellen don't mind, I'll walk around with them for a bit."

"Not at all." AJ nodded with what seemed a bit too much interest.

"Yes," Ellen added. "And then we can all watch the parade together."

Anna simply nodded. "Just don't forget your promise to drive Mac over to the park at lunchtime, for the picnic."

"You know how to drive an automobile?" Ellen asked Katy.

"Of course." Katy laughed lightly.

"Katy is a *modern* girl," AJ teased.

Anna felt the need to bite her tongue—instead she excused herself, crossed the street, and entered Douglas Mercantile, but after looking around the somewhat busy store, she didn't see Clara anywhere.

"Anna McDowell," Marjorie Douglas declared. "How are you this fine morning?"

"I'm doing well, thank you."

"Randall told me about your dinner party," Marjorie said quietly. "It sounded very interesting."

Anna smiled stiffly, wondering how much Rand had revealed to his mother. "Yes, it was quite an evening."

"So, tell me, are Mac and Lucille on good speaking terms now?" she whispered.

"That's hard to say. But I believe it was a relatively pleasant evening—I hope for everyone." Anna didn't care to mention Lucille's determination to win Mac over last night or how Mac had managed to keep the upper hand, maintaining a polite distance. Certainly, it had helped having Rand and Daniel there to buffer things. And Katy, the ever-cheerful magpie, had kept conversation moving along.

"Can I help you with anything?" Marjorie asked.

"No, thank you. I stopped in because I thought my old friend Clara—"

"*Anna?*" A woman placed a hand on Anna's arm.

"Yes?" Anna peered at the pale woman, trying to place her.

"It's me—Clara."

"Oh my." Anna forced a pleasant smile. "Of course it is." She hugged Clara then stepped back to study her more closely. She seemed so old! Although her blue eyes were the same, everything else seemed old and faded—from her frowzy felt hat to her dusty, worn shoes. What had happened to her?

"I heard you were in town, Anna. How is your father doing?"

Anna gave a quick update on Mac then told Clara about meeting Ellen and AJ just now. "Such lovely children. They told me you were in here."

"And they told me how they met your daughter on the beach. They were both quite taken with her." Clara's eyes seemed to grow wider. "Oh my, Anna, you haven't changed much. You don't look any different from when we were girls."

"I've told her that very thing." Marjorie folded tea towels

from behind the counter, smiling as if she'd listened to every word.

"Oh, well, thank you both." Anna smiled. "You're too kind." She noticed Clara's partially filled basket. "I don't want to interrupt your shopping."

"I'm all done." Clara set her basket on the counter with a frown. "Albert doesn't like me to dillydally in town. I need to get back quickly."

"Will you come to town for the festivities later?" Anna asked as Marjorie began to ring up the purchases.

"Dear me, no. I've got far too much work. You remember the Sunset Fish Company, don't you? Well, Albert runs the family business now. And this is our busy time of year."

"Then I won't keep you." Anna suppressed the urge to question why Clara couldn't have time off to enjoy the holiday. "But I do hope we can catch up again. It's been so long."

"Yes, of course. That would be nice." Clara laid her money on the counter.

Anna quickly explained about how she was covering for Mac at the newspaper. "Stop in any time you can. We'll have a nice, long chat."

Clara's smile seemed uneasy as she pocketed her change. "Yes, I'll try to do that." She tipped her head to Marjorie, told Anna good-bye, and then hurried out.

"Don't count on it." Marjorie's brows arched.

"Count on what?" Anna asked her.

"On Clara coming by the newspaper office to *chat*." She made a doubtful expression.

"Why not?"

"That husband of hers." Marjorie's tone grew hushed. "He's working poor Clara into an early grave."

"What?"

"The poor woman slaves for him, long hours...late into the night." Marjorie stopped talking as another customer approached the counter. "No time to *dillydally*." She glanced upward then greeted the next customer and started to ring up groceries.

Anna was about to leave the store when Rand emerged from the backroom. "I thought I heard your voice." He walked her to the door, then paused outside on the sidewalk. "That was quite an interesting dinner party last night." He chuckled. "I hope it didn't wear Mac out too much."

"He was cheerful at breakfast," she told him. "Said he hadn't slept so well in a long time."

Randall's brows arched. "Do you think Mac has any genuine interest in Lucille?"

She considered this. "To be honest, I think he's amused by her interest in him. And he hinted this morning that he's curious as to her motives." She frowned. "For that matter, I am too. Why is she trying so hard to endear herself to him?"

"I wondered the same thing myself." He glanced around, as if to see if anyone else was listening. "I don't want to sound crass, but I always say, 'When in doubt, *follow the money.*'"

"Follow the money? But Mac's not wealthy. From what I've heard, both his house and the newspaper were mortgaged to the bank for recent improvements."

"Maybe Lucille doesn't know about all that."

"Maybe. But I thought she'd married into money. She appears to be quite well off."

"Things aren't always what they seem."

"Yes, I'm sure you're right." Now Anna told him about talking with Clara. "Things didn't seem quite right with her either. And your mother suggested as much. What do you think?"

"I think..." He lowered his voice. "Albert Krauss is not very trustworthy."

"Oh?"

"But don't say you heard it from me." He smiled. "I don't want to be slapped with a slander lawsuit."

"Your mother said that Albert Krauss is working Clara too hard." Anna glanced down the street to see that Katy was still strolling with AJ and Ellen. "But the Krauss children don't appear to be overworked or abused."

"I believe that's greatly due to Clara. I've heard that she sacrifices herself to spare her children. Oh, I'm sure they help out some, but Clara carries most of the load."

"Poor Clara." Anna remembered how many times she'd made sacrifices for her own child. But nothing like Clara seemed to be making.

Rand waved to an older man coming down the street. "And there's my morning appointment." He tipped his hat to Anna. "I'm looking forward to tonight's dance." He grinned. "Until then."

Anna checked her pocket watch. The parade wouldn't begin for an hour, and now Katy was nowhere in sight. Not wanting to loiter on the street but not eager to go home, she decided to take a peek into the newspaper office. Although Virginia had seemed fairly sure that her brother-in-law would want to help in remodeling the office spaces, Anna had been a bit skeptical. After all, it was short notice as well as a celebratory weekend. But to her surprise, the door was unlocked. The bell jangled as she went inside, but it was nearly drowned out by the sound of hammers and saws.

"Hello?" Virginia popped from around the corner. "Oh, it's you." She wiped her hands off on a pair of dusty dungarees. "George has been here since six this morning. Been hard at work too. He brought his son, Robbie. And Willy and I are helping out as well. We plan to get it all done by mid-afternoon, since Robbie and Willy want to attend the dance."

"That's wonderful." Anna tried to see past her, but someone had covered the glass doors into the editorial section with brown paper.

"No peeking." Virginia placed her hands on her hips. "Not until it's done."

"Do you think it'll look good when they're done?"

"I'm certain it will." Virginia nudged Anna toward the door. "Go out there and enjoy the festivities before that pretty summer frock gets all covered in sawdust."

"Yes, well, thank you." Anna adjusted her hat then went outside. Trying not to feel guilty, both for not helping with this and for keeping it from Mac, she strolled down the street. Already a few people were starting to gather, finding good spots along the sidewalk where they could watch the parade.

"Anna." Daniel caught up with her just as she was in front of his office. "Are you in town for the parade?"

She explained how Katy had enticed her out for a morning stroll. "But then she abandoned me for her young friends."

He chuckled. "Oh, the fickleness of youth." He nodded to the bakery across the street. "I was just going to get a pastry to enjoy while watching the parade. Care to join me?"

"Thank you. That would be nice."

"Great. I have the perfect spot to watch from." He pointed to a terrace outside of his doctor's office. She could see that a small table and a couple of chairs were set out upon it. "You can see the whole thing from up there."

"Lovely."

"How would you like to go on up there and get a pot of coffee brewing while I pick up some pastries?"

"I'd be happy to," she offered.

He unlocked the door then gave some quick directions, and they parted ways. But when she got up to his office, she was surprised to be met by Daniel's nurse. Though instead of wearing her nurse's uniform, Norma Barrows had on a pretty yellow dress.

"What are you doing up here?" Norma asked with what seemed like suspicion. "Don't you know we're closed today?"

"Yes, I assumed you were closed," Anna explained. "But Daniel sent me up here to make coffee and—"

"If Dr. Hollister needs coffee, I am perfectly capable of making it," Norma said sharply.

"I'm sure you're quite capable." Anna frowned. "But Daniel told me the doctor's office is closed today. So why are you up here?"

"I, uh, I wanted to catch up on some filing." Norma went over to a tall wooden cabinet, pulled it open and, as if to prove her point, she began to flip through the folders.

"I see." Anna glanced over to the door that Daniel had explained led to a small kitchen. "Well, I'll just leave you to it then." And before Norma could protest or question, Anna hurried into the kitchen, closing the door behind her. She was just filling the percolator with water when Norma came in.

"What do you think you are doing?" she demanded.

"Like I said, I'm making coffee."

"But *why?*" Norma scowled.

"Because Daniel asked me to." Anna set the pot on the stove and then, with her back to Norma, began to measure coffee grounds into the metal basket. "He's gone to the bakery for pastries. We plan to watch the parade from the terrace."

Norma made a huffing sound, and the kitchen door banged closed, followed by the slamming of what Anna assumed was the doctor's office door. But as Anna arranged cups, saucers, and pastry plates on a wooden tray, she felt certain that she hadn't heard the last from Nurse Norma. Clearly, she was not happy about Anna's presence in this office this morning. And it was no great leap to guess why. After all, Norma was single, and Daniel was single. Norma was obviously hoping for more than just a professional relationship with him. But did Daniel know about this?

After giving the terrace table and chairs a quick wipe-down, Anna was just getting the tray when Daniel showed up with a white paper sack. They soon had everything set outside, and Anna could hear the sound of marching drums a few blocks away.

"Sounds like they're warming up." He checked his watch. "About ten minutes now."

"This is such fun." Anna filled his coffee cup. "Thank you for inviting me."

"Shortly after moving to Sunset Cove, I watched my first parade up here," he confided. "Probably because I felt like I didn't really belong in Sunset Cove and wanted to keep to myself. But then I realized how much I liked it up here. And so this is where you'll find me whenever there's a parade in town."

"Can't blame you—it's a fine vantage point. And to be honest, even though I grew up in this town, I still feel like an outsider myself...sometimes."

"Did you feel a bit like that last night?" he asked gently. "I mean, when Lucille showed up?"

"Was it that obvious?"

"You seemed to become a different person." He picked up his coffee cup. "In fact, you seemed to change when Lucille surprised us at the hotel restaurant too. Like a switch was flipped, and you suddenly weren't yourself."

"I know." She sighed. "That seems to happen whenever I'm around her. It's hard to explain, but it's almost like I'm six years old again. So frustrating."

"Let me guess...you were six when your mother left."

She somberly nodded.

"I remember a psychological piece I read a few years ago. I think it may have been by Titchener. Anyway, the theory is that a person can become somewhat trapped emotionally—at a certain age—when something traumatic occurs in their life."

Anna considered this. "Do you think that's why Lucille makes me feel like I'm six?"

He smiled. "It seems possible."

She nodded then turned to him. "What about you? Is it possible you became trapped when your wife passed on?" She suddenly wished she hadn't asked him that question. Why was it that the news reporter in her always popped out like that?

He set down his cup with a furrowed brow. "I guess I used to feel a bit stuck in my grief."

"But you don't anymore? You've managed to find a way out of it?"

"That was one reason I decided to come to the West. I felt that starting a new life might help. Plus I knew good doctors were scarce out here. And I must admit that the change has helped me. And making new friends helps too." He brightened. "I've really enjoyed getting to know you and your family, Anna."

She felt warmed by his words. Perhaps he really did have some romantic interest in her. But this reminded her of Norma. Did Daniel have any idea of what his nurse's intentions toward him might be? Should he be warned? But before she could form any intelligible words, the sound of band music grew louder.

"Here they come!" Daniel said eagerly. Suddenly they were both peering down Main Street, watching as the marching band with drums and horns and waving flags opened the parade.

"I wish Mac were well enough to see this." Anna gazed happily at the various floats, horse-drawn carriages, automobiles, bicycles, and marchers parading by.

"Look at that car." Daniel pointed to a shiny blue vehicle coming slowly down the road. "Brand-new Studebaker. I've seen it around town but don't know who owns it." Like the other cars, its top was down, and it was decorated with colorful bunting and flags. But Anna was surprised at the words on the banner along the side.

SUNSET COVE NEWS CELEBRATES FIFTY YEARS
1866 – 1916

"I didn't know the newspaper was that old," Daniel exclaimed.

"My goodness—that's Mac in the passenger seat!" Anna stood in excitement. "And it looks like Wally Morris is driving!"

"Wally Morris?"

"He's an old family friend." Anna waved both arms, calling down to the car. Both men grinned up at her, happily waving back.

"Wally worked for my grandfather at the newspaper a long time ago," she told Daniel. "I can hardly believe he's still around. Goodness, he must be nearly eighty by now."

"He looks rather spry for his age. And that must be Wally's car since Mac has a little Runabout."

"And to think Mac told me he was too tired to attend the parade." She chuckled. "Said he was saving his strength for the picnic."

"Mac doesn't look overly tired to me." Daniel winked at her. "I think your dad is on the road to recovery."

"Really?" She turned hopefully to him. "Do you honestly think he'll regain his arm and his speech and everything again?"

Daniel's smile faded. "Well, no...I doubt that. But he can still regain his spirit. And that's probably what matters most."

Although Anna knew that he was right, she felt disappointed to think Mac might not progress any more than he already had. Still, she was determined not to give up. Hopefully Katy wouldn't either.

CHAPTER 16

Anna knew she had mixed motives when she invited Daniel to join them for the Founders Day picnic at the park. It was true that she enjoyed his company, but she also liked the idea of having a physician nearby for Mac's sake. It concerned her that he'd participated in the parade and still planned to attend the picnic at the seaside park. But at least she'd gotten him to lie down for a while in between.

"I've got the food all packed up," Bernice told Anna and Katy. "Mickey put it in the car. Now we'll walk this basket of place settings down to the park and get the table ready."

"Why don't you just ride with us?" Anna asked. "Or are you worried about Katy's driving skills?"

Bernice chuckled as she pinned her straw hat into place. "You must not have seen Mac's automobile yet."

"Yes, Mother," Katy said. "You may prefer to walk too. Or else you can hold the food basket in your lap and ride in the rumble seat. Grandpa's Runabout is rather small. Only two can ride in front."

So it was that Anna walked to the seaside park with Bernice and Mickey. "I hope you made enough food for an extra guest," she directed to Bernice.

"Oh?" Bernice's brows arched. "Please don't tell me that Lucille is joining us."

Anna cringed. "No, no. At least I hope not." She explained about Daniel.

"Oh, we've got plenty for Dr. Hollister." Bernice nodded. "That's fine."

"I don't think anyone mentioned the picnic last night at dinner." Anna pursed her lips. "Hopefully Lucille doesn't know about it."

"Don't count on it."

Anna glanced at Bernice. "You've known Lucille for a long time, haven't you?"

Bernice nodded grimly. "Since the day Mac brought her back from San Francisco. I'd been working for your grandmother for several years by then, and I'm sure I was as shocked as she was."

"What was your first impression of Lucille?" Anna pressed.

"First impression?" Bernice shrugged. "Pretty much the same as now."

Anna knew what she was saying. "So you were quite surprised that Mac chose Lucille for his bride."

"Not entirely. There's no denying Lucille was a striking woman. No doubt she had turned Mac's head. But it happened too fast. They didn't know each other. Too different." She elbowed Mickey. "Wouldn't you agree?"

"I guess." He looked away as he shifted the basket to his other hand.

"What do you remember of Lucille as a mother?" Anna quietly asked Bernice.

"She never took to it." Bernice sighed. "Maybe she just wasn't the maternal type, or maybe she was too young. But she never really got the hang of it."

Or, Anna wondered, perhaps Lucille was just plain selfish.

"Well, thank goodness for your grandmother," Bernice declared. "Mrs. McDowell was the maternal type."

"I know." Anna almost wished she hadn't asked and was ready to change the subject now. "So did you two see the parade this morning?"

"I did." Mickey nodded eagerly. "Bernice didn't want to go."

Anna told Bernice about Mac riding in Wally Morris's car. "They both looked so dapper, and the car was all decorated. I couldn't have been more surprised. And I didn't even realize it was the newspaper's fiftieth birthday."

"I believe the official date is in mid-October," Bernice told her. "I know Mac wanted to have a big celebration. Hopefully he'll be up for it by then."

The seaside park was getting crowded, but Anna spotted Daniel already seated by himself at a table. "Looks like the good doctor got us a table." She waved to him, and soon Bernice was spreading out a big red-and-white gingham tablecloth.

"Katy is driving Mac over," Anna told Daniel as she laid out the plates and silverware. "They have the food."

"Let's go get lemonade for everyone," Daniel suggested, "before the line gets too long."

Anna agreed and, as they strolled across the park grounds, the brass band began to tune their instruments in the gazebo. While standing in line, visiting with various friends, old and new, Anna found herself feeling more and more at ease.

"My hometown is growing on me," she told Daniel as they carried several glasses of lemonade back to the table.

"A relief after my rather difficult week at the newspaper. It almost gives me hope."

"I'm glad to hear it."

"In fact, I'm starting to like this town so much, it will be difficult to leave."

"You're planning on leaving?" he asked.

"The plan was to stay for the summer. I promised Katy we'd return to Portland before her school starts in September. Of course, I kept our apartment there." She grimaced to remember how she'd given up her job then siphoned from her savings to pay three months of rent during their absence.

"I see Mac and Katy." Daniel put down the drinks. "I'll go give them a hand with the picnic basket." He was barely gone when the Krauss kids came to the picnic table.

"Katy said we could join you." AJ set a small picnic basket on the end of the table. "Hope you don't mind."

"Do you have room?" Ellen asked.

"We'll make room," Anna told her.

Before long, they were all seated at the table, waiting for Reverend Williamson to say the standard blessing to start the picnic. But instead, it was Mayor Snyder stepping up to the gazebo with the megaphone in hand. Although the band stopped playing and the crowd grew quiet, Anna could tell by some of the expressions that Calvin Snyder was not well liked by everyone.

"Welcome, welcome," he boomed through the megaphone. "I'm so glad you could join us for the annual Founders Day picnic. And what a fine day for our celebration. So much is going on in our fair town these days, and I'm proud to be a part of it. During my past years in office, I've seen such growth and progress and prosperity here. And looking to the future, I have great plans for our little city by the sea. My, how things have changed since the first pioneers arrived here in Sunset Cove. And we all look forward to more changes. During my time as mayor, I've helped to usher in all sorts of improvements..." He continued to ramble, acting as if he were personally responsible for all the good things in Sunset Cove—or perhaps he was making a campaign speech. Whatever the case, Anna could tell that it was starting to aggravate a lot of the townsfolk.

"Why don't you let a *real* pioneer speak?" a man hollered.

"Yeah," another yelled. "Let's hear from someone who was here from the beginning."

"Wally," Mac declared.

"Good idea, Mac." Anna nodded. "We want to hear from Wally Morris," she called out.

Others started to take up the chant and then a couple of men escorted Wally up front, and everyone began to clap with enthusiasm.

"Thank you." Wally spoke into the megaphone that one of the men had removed from the mayor. "I'm honored to be here today. I remember when my folks came to this place back in 1852, when I was just a boy and Oregon wasn't even a state." He looked around the crowd. "Nothing much was here when we first arrived. Just beautiful blue ocean and miles of beach and great big trees. Lots and lots of great, big trees." He went on to tell about how other settlers continued to come over the Oregon Trail, mentioning names and families—including the McDowells—telling about how they worked together to build homes and barns and eventually started the town and the original businesses.

"As you all know, the town officially began in 1856, sixty years ago." He paused to look over the crowd. "Most of our original founders are gone now. But in a way they remain— they are represented here by their descendants—all you good folks. Not only you who hail from families who came in 1856, but also those of you who've chosen to make our fair city your home. I believe this celebration isn't so much about this town and its buildings as much as it's about the people living and working here. So shake hands with your friends and neighbors and rejoice to be part of such a great community."

Everyone cheered loudly. Then Reverend Williamson came up and offered a short blessing. After "Amen" was said, the band began to play, and everyone started to talk and eat.

"That was a nice speech that Wally gave," Anna told Mac.

He nodded. "Good words."

"Better than old Snyder," Bernice muttered.

"You don't like Mayor Snyder?" AJ asked her in a slightly sharp tone.

Bernice simply shrugged, reaching for a deviled egg.

"My dad happens to think Mayor Snyder is the best mayor we've ever had," AJ declared.

"Everyone is entitled to their opinions," Anna told him.

"Mayor Snyder has gotten us through this recession by encouraging local businessmen," AJ told everyone. "My dad says that if Mayor Snyder hadn't been elected, we might have lost our family's fishing business. We all owe the mayor a lot."

"Humph." Mac reached for a roll.

"I don't believe my father is such a great fan of the mayor," Anna quietly told AJ, hoping that he'd take the hint and get off his soapbox.

"Along with a number of other people," Daniel added. "Of course, this only means that the upcoming election could be interesting. That is, if someone will step up and run against Calvin Snyder."

"Here, here," Bernice agreed.

"No one wants to step up because no one wants to lose." AJ sounded a bit pompous.

"*AJ*," Ellen chided her brother in a warning tone.

"It's true," he insisted. "Everyone is saying that Mayor Snyder will run unopposed this fall because no one can beat him. There's not a better man in town."

"Oh, surely someone will want to run against him." Anna looked at Mac. "Have you heard any rumors of interest through the newspaper?"

He just shrugged, reaching for a chicken drumstick.

"Maybe Wally Morris will run for mayor," Katy offered. "He seems like a good guy. I think I'd vote for him."

"You can't vote," AJ said smugly. "You're not old enough."

"Well, I'm old enough," Anna told AJ. "I would gladly vote for Wally."

"And that is why women never should've gotten the vote." AJ grinned as if he'd made a funny joke, but Anna did not find it amusing.

"And why is that?" Anna asked him.

"If women hadn't gotten the vote, we wouldn't have prohibition," AJ told her. "And prohibition has hurt Oregon's economy. Everyone says so."

"Not everyone," Anna shot back at him. "I'm sure the bootleggers and rumrunners are quite grateful for prohibition. From what I hear, they're getting rich."

AJ just laughed. "That's probably true. But other businesses have suffered."

"Well, I think Wally Morris should run for mayor," Katy declared. "And if he did, I might not be able to cast my vote, but I would gladly campaign for him."

"And I would help her," Ellen declared.

AJ scowled at his sister but didn't speak.

"Good girls!" Mac laughed loudly, slapping the table with his hand.

"In fact." Katy stood. "I think I will go speak to Mr. Morris right this minute. I will attempt to talk him into opposing Mayor Snyder."

"Yeah!" Mac lifted his glass of lemonade as if to toast his granddaughter. "Good luck!"

As Katy departed, Rand came over to their table, greeting them. "You folks look a lot more interesting than my mother and her old-lady friends."

Anna invited him to join them. "We're having quite the lively political discussion." She quickly explained their conversation as Rand sat down.

He chuckled. "Well, if anyone can persuade Wally Morris to run, I think it could be our Katy."

"She seemed quite determined," Daniel told him.

"That's actually not a bad idea. Everyone likes Wally." Rand patted Mac on the back. "I hear you old boys were in the parade and—"

"Everyone likes Mayor Snyder too," AJ interrupted. "Well, most everyone."

Tired of politics, Anna pointed across the park. "Say, do they still have the dessert table at these gatherings? I remember Mrs. Meier's famous chocolate cake from my childhood."

"You bet they do." Rand grabbed her by the hand and pulled her to her feet. "And the early birds always get the best sweets."

"The rest of you better hurry up," Anna called over her shoulder as Rand tugged her along. "Before it's all picked over."

"Your mother is here," Rand told her as he led her

through the crowded park. "I just wanted to give you a little warning."

Anna let out a quiet groan. "Where did you see her?"

He nodded toward the gazebo, where the band was still playing and a small cluster of listeners were gathered. "Over there."

Anna recognized the woman in the flamboyant scarlet dress and matching parasol. Lucille must not have heard that older women—particularly widows—shouldn't wear red. "Why's she still here?" Anna muttered to herself, turning away and hoping that Lucille hadn't spotted her.

"The obvious guess is she's set her cap for your father," Rand whispered.

"Yes...you already mentioned that she might be after Mac's money—even though he doesn't have much to speak of." Anna held up a finger. "Perhaps that's a little fact that Lucille should be made aware of...." She looked over the loaded dessert table with interest.

"Meaning you'll inform her?"

"Yes." Anna nodded. "When the time is right, I think I'll do just that." She picked up a piece of rich-looking chocolate cake. "But first, I'm going to enjoy this."

But as the picnic continued, Anna never found the perfect opportunity to speak candidly to her mother. Despite the fact that Lucille invited herself to join their group, once again focusing most of her attention on Mac, Anna decided she'd have to inform her mother of Mac's financial situation later.

"I'm afraid Mac is worn out," Anna whispered to Daniel. Or maybe it was simply Anna who'd had enough. Lucille was currently telling everyone about "surviving" the San Francisco earthquake ten years ago, making it seem like an exciting, dramatic adventure where she'd played the heroine.

"I think you're right," Daniel told Anna.

But Katy was chattering away with Ellen and AJ and several other young people, all seeming to have a good time. "I hate to interrupt Katy to drive him home right now, but I don't know how—"

"I'll drive you home," Daniel offered.

"Thank you." She went over to Mac, cutting Lucille off in mid-sentence. "I'm sorry to disrupt your interesting story, but Dr. Hollister feels that it's time for Mac to have a rest." She turned to Mac. "I'm sure you don't want to argue with your doctor."

The left side of Mac's mouth curled upward. "No...the doc...is right."

So they excused themselves and, with Daniel on one side and Anna on the other, escorted Mac to his vehicle and helped him get inside. As Anna sat in the trundle seat of the little Runabout, holding on to her hat against the ocean breeze, she decided that so far this had been a delightful day. Nearly a perfect day...except for Lucille, the proverbial fly in the ointment. Anna despised feeling so antagonistic toward anyone—and it gnawed on her to think her ill will was aimed at her own flesh and blood—but she just didn't know how to get over it.

CHAPTER 17

Daniel helped Anna get Mac into the house and settled into his bed for an afternoon nap and then led her into the front room. "That was a good call," he told her. "I do think Mac was more tired than anyone realized."

"I'm sure. He's been doing so much lately."

"But it's good that he feels like participating in life again. Although he still needs to pace himself and get plenty of rest." Daniel glanced at the mantel clock. "I hope he's not planning to go to the dance tonight."

"Oh, I'm sure he's not." She frowned. "Although I did hear Lucille mention to Mac that she'd like to go. A not-so-subtle hint. Fortunately, he ignored it."

"Yes, I overheard that too. I hope that you'll encourage Mac to take it easy tonight. I already warned him that overdoing wasn't prudent." Daniel brightened. "Speaking of the dance, do you plan to attend?"

"Rand asked if he could escort Katy and me tonight," she told him.

Daniel nodded. "Yes, and he's recently gotten that handsome Town Car." He made a low whistle. "I'm trying not to be envious of that pretty car. I purchased an old delivery truck from the butcher when I first moved here. I only use it for emergency house calls or in bad weather."

"Well, Rand's vehicle had both front and back seats. Perhaps you'd like to join us?" Anna knew she might be crossing the line here, but she wasn't concerned.

Daniel's grin looked slightly mischievous. "You don't think Rand would mind?"

"I don't see why. You and Rand can ride up front, and I'll sit in back with Katy." She actually liked the sound of this.

"Then I'd be happy to join you."

She told him what time to meet at the house, and Daniel offered to park Mac's Runabout in the carriage house.

If Rand was perturbed by Daniel joining them, he didn't show it. In fact, as the two men rode up front, they seemed to be quite congenial. Perhaps even striking up a good friendship, albeit a bit stiff and formal.

"Where is the dance?" Katy asked Anna. "I thought it might be at the park. It's so pretty there, with the gazebo overlooking the ocean."

"I assume it's at the grange hall," Anna told her. "That's where it always used to be."

"They still hold it at the grange hall," Rand confirmed. "That's because you can never tell about the seaside weather, Katy. It's been wonderful these past few days, but it can change in a moment. Rain and mud are not conducive to ladies' fine silks and delicate shoes."

"And you ladies will probably outshine the rest of them tonight," Daniel declared. "I hope that you don't put any noses out of joint."

Anna laughed. "I'm not too worried about that, but

thank you. I must admit that my ensemble is due to my daughter's refined taste. She insisted on dressing me in a gown that she designed herself."

"Katy is a designer?" Rand asked.

"Her artistic talents aren't limited to paint and canvas," Anna boasted. "She is magical with fabric too."

"My mother has never paid much attention to style," Katy told them. "She's always been more interested in business than in apparel. So I've learned to fend for myself when it comes to fashion. Otherwise, I'd go around looking like some dowdy Victorian from the nineteenth century."

The men chuckled, but Anna didn't mind since Katy was probably right. Anna had little regard for fashion, and her wardrobe had grown more and more sensible—and somewhat masculine—while trying to climb the ladder at the *Oregonian*. With little time to concern herself with frills, she had given Katy loose reins and a somewhat unsupervised wardrobe allowance. Naturally, Katy had run with it. But the truth was, Anna admired her daughter's style, and she appreciated her recent fashion assistance. At least for the most part.

Anna had voiced concerns over the gown that Katy had foisted upon her earlier this evening. It was a concoction of aquamarine-colored fabrics that Katy had designed for a spring dance at her school. The first layer of the gown was such a filmy silk that it had seemed almost indecent at first. But then Katy topped the slip-like dress with a layer of intricate lace, and the results were both exquisite and modest. Plus Anna had to admit that Katy's delicate, turquoise satin slippers looked lovely with the gown. Her daughter truly did have a gift when it came to couture. Anna just hoped that she and Katy wouldn't appear overdressed for this small-town dance.

Rand offered Anna his arm as they went into the grange hall, and Daniel politely escorted Katy. The hall seemed to be bursting at the seams with people, music, and warm air. After alternately dancing with Rand and Daniel, Anna begged for a break. While sipping her punch, she watched with interest as Norma Barrows sashayed over to the table where Anna was sitting with Rand and Daniel.

"Dr. Hollister." Norma's tone sounded flirtatious. "Fancy seeing you here." She politely greeted Rand, muttered a stiff hello to Anna, then turned back to Daniel. "I thought you didn't care for these social functions."

Daniel shrugged. "Thought I might give it a try."

"I noticed you out there," she continued. "Looks to me you know your way around the dance floor."

"Maybe you should take him for a spin," Rand suggested.

"I thought you'd never ask." Norma laughed as she reached for Daniel's hand. "Come on, Doc. I think they're playing our tune."

Daniel tossed a slightly desperate look to Rand and Anna. Rand chuckled, and Anna just smiled. Perhaps it was time Daniel figured out that his nurse had more than just work on her mind.

"I'm going for seconds on punch," Rand told Anna. "Can I get you some?"

"Yes, please." She handed him her punch cup.

As Rand returned to the refreshments table, Anna scanned the crowd for Katy. As before, Katy was mixing with the younger crowd and, to Anna's relief, was dancing with other boys besides AJ. Anna didn't like to think ill of anyone, but her mother's intuition was suggesting that the young man was not to be completely trusted. And his focused attention on Katy made Anna uneasy.

"You must be Anna McDowell." A middle-aged man

pulled out a chair and, without being invited, sat down across from her. With his wavy blond hair, he wasn't bad looking, aside from his slightly flushed face.

"Excuse me?" She studied him.

"Sorry." He grinned. "I'm Albert Krauss."

"Oh?" She nodded slowly. "You're Ellen and AJ's father. And Clara's husband." She glanced around the packed hall. "But I didn't see Clara here."

He waved his hand. "Aw, Clara hates dances." He leaned forward as if to confide something. "She gets all worked up and anxious in a crowded room." He laughed like this was funny. "Me, on the other hand, I enjoy a good time."

Anna pulled back slightly at the aroma of liquor on his breath. She recognized this smell from her short marriage to Darrell. "Excuse me, Mr. Krauss, have you—"

"No need for such formalities." His smile made her uneasy. "Just call me Albert."

"Uh, yes, well, as I was about to say, *Albert*, have you been drinking?"

He just laughed. "Well, you are a clever one, aren't you?" He patted his vest pocket. "Care for a little snort?"

"No, no thank you." She forced a smile. "I was merely curious as to how you obtain your spirits during our current state of prohibition."

He slapped his knee and laughed loudly. "Well, little lady, it's much easier than you'd think. As long as you know how to steer clear of the cops."

She glanced around the bustling crowd. "I see. But how can you be sure they're steering clear of you?"

Albert's eyes darted left and right as he slowly stood. "Well, it's a pleasure to meet you, ma'am. Hope to see more of you around town."

"Please give my regards to Clara."

He nodded with a slightly grim expression and then went off to join up with some other laughing men. One of whom was her recently demoted employee, Wesley Kempton. Judging by his flushed face and overly loud voice, he'd likely been drinking too. The newspaper reporter inside of her was taking furious notes.

"Here you go." Rand set a cup of punch before her.

"Thank you." She smiled as if nothing whatsoever was troubling her. "I just had an informative encounter with Albert Krauss."

"Informative?" Rand nodded with interest.

"Yes. I smelled liquor on his breath and inquired about it." She picked up her punch cup, sniffing it just in case.

Rand's eyes darkened with concern. "You didn't?"

She broadened her smile. "Indeed, I did."

"Anna." His tone grew hushed. "That could be dangerous."

"I'm not worried. After all, I'm a newswoman. Snooping is what we do." She casually sipped her punch.

"I understand that, Anna. But this is a small town. A bit of discretion goes a long way around here."

She considered this. "I'll try to keep that in mind."

After they finished their drinks, Rand invited her back out to the dance floor, but while pretending to enjoy the dance, she kept a discrete eye on Albert and Wesley and the other men...wondering about their politics and business connections. She didn't even feel too surprised to see Mayor Snyder exchanging pleasantries with them. It all just seemed to add up—to no good. Anyway, she felt it would be a fairly easy puzzle to solve. Hopefully she would get to the bottom of it by the end of summer, if not sooner.

At the end of that dance, Daniel and Norma came over, and Daniel insisted that they exchange dance partners. Since Rand didn't object, Anna didn't either.

"I'm sure you must realize that your nurse has more than professional interests in you, Daniel." Anna used a teasing tone.

"As long as she does her job, I can't complain."

"Then it doesn't make you uncomfortable?"

He just smiled. "It's not unusual for a doctor to have a devoted nurse. In fact, it's rather the norm."

"Well, as long as you know." She glanced over to where the mayor seemed to be holding court with Albert, Wesley, and the others. "Have you noticed that there's some imbibing going on here tonight?"

His brow creased. "Unfortunately, that's rather the norm too."

"With the mayor?"

"Afraid so."

"I can't say I feel very good about Albert Krauss," she confided quietly. "I mean, since his son has taken such an interest in Katy."

Daniel nodded a bit grimly. "I've felt concerned too. I didn't want to say anything. But I think AJ is a young man that needs to be watched."

"I'm afraid to say much to Katy," Anna confessed. "It might simply push her toward him." Anna remembered how she'd acted when Mac had opposed her relationship with Darrell.

"I don't know much about these things...but it seems you'd be wise to keep the conversation flowing with her. You two seem to have a good relationship. Best to maintain it, I think."

Anna smiled. "Good advice, doctor."

As the dance ended, Anna noticed Albert Krauss coming their way and, before they could exit the dance floor, Albert stepped up. "I'd like the next dance with Miss McDowell," he told Daniel.

Daniel lifted his brow. "I believe that is up to Miss McDowell."

"If you'll excuse me, I think I'd like to take a break." She waved her hand. "It's getting rather warm and stuff—"

"What? Is my wife's old friend too good to dance with the likes of me?" Albert demanded.

"Not at all." She attempted to feign enthusiasm. "It's just that I'm—"

"Come on." Albert grabbed her hand. "I'd like to tell my little wife that I—"

"Excuse me." Daniel put a hand on Albert's shoulder. "Miss McDowell wishes to take a—" His words were cut off by the swinging of Albert's fist, slamming right into Daniel's jaw and reeling him backward. Suddenly Albert's friends gathered around, pushing Daniel to his feet and jeering on a fight.

"Stop it!" Anna yelled at them, holding up her hands. "Stop it right now!"

"Listen to the lady!" Wally Morris stepped beside her. "Show some respect."

"That's right." Mayor Snyder moved in, pushing Albert and some of the others aside. "You boys break it up. Go outside and cool off, if you need to." He smiled at Anna and Daniel. "I hope you're all right."

"Yes, thanks." Daniel wiggled his chin back and forth as if to test it.

"What happened?" Rand and Norma came over to join them.

Anna quickly explained. "And unless you mind, I'd like to go home," she told Rand. "Before things get even more out of hand."

"Any time you say." Rand nodded.

Norma rolled her eyes. "Are you kidding me? Why, this happens all the time at these little social affairs. The boys always get into a brawl. No one takes it seriously."

Daniel rubbed his jaw. "I'm taking it seriously."

"Did he hurt you?" Norma softened.

"Nothing serious, but I'm with Anna. I don't want to stick around for more."

"I'll go get Katy," Anna told Rand. Of course, Katy wasn't pleased with the decision to leave early, but when Anna told her about Daniel getting socked, she gave in. It wasn't until they were in the car and headed for home that Anna began to tell Katy the rest of the story.

"AJ's father smacked Dr. Hollister?" Katy's eyes widened.

"That's right," Daniel said from up front. "He's got a solid right hook too."

"What did you do to make him so mad?" Katy leaned forward.

"I didn't care to dance with Albert." Anna fiddled with her evening bag. "Dr. Hollister merely defended my choice not to."

"I'm glad Rand wasn't so touchy about dance partners," Daniel teased. "I might've been beaten to a pulp by now."

"What a heel," Katy declared.

"I feel sorry for his wife," Anna admitted. "Poor Clara. What she must put up with."

"Well, I think we left at the right time," Rand told them. "I've been to a few of these dances, and sometimes they can get a little rough...if you stick around long enough."

"One good thing, though," Anna said.

"What's that, Mother?"

"Well, I was somewhat relieved that Lucille wasn't there."

Katy laughed. "Oh, Mother! You're going to have to get

over that. The old girl is starting to grow on me. I'd like to get to know her better."

Anna grimaced but held her tongue.

"Speaking of the old girl." Rand slowed to park in front of Mac's house. "Isn't that her getting into the taxi right now?"

Anna wasn't sure what was more surprising—that Sunset Cove had a taxi service or that her mother had been here. But instead of reacting, she simply thanked Rand for taking them and thanked Daniel for accompanying them. Then she and Katy hurried into the house. Katy went up to her room, but Anna went to the front room to find Bernice huffing around as she gathered up the tea service.

"Looks as if Lucille has been here." Anna could still smell her mother's overly sweet perfume.

"I'll say she was here." Bernice stacked the china pieces so noisily that Anna worried they would break. "She arrived like clockwork, shortly after you girls left for the dance. She stayed all evening long. I finally put my foot down and insisted that Mickey was ready to help Mac to bed. Otherwise, I'm sure she'd still be here." She picked up the tray. "Land sakes, she's a silly woman!"

"Oh dear." Anna shook her head. "How did Mac seem? Was he glad to have her?"

"Hard to say. As usual, Lucille did most of the talking. Dressed in her buttons and bows and hair piled high and acting like she was queen of the castle—or wanted to be— she ordered me around like she owned the place." Bernice scowled. "And Mac just let her."

"Poor Bernice. And here I thought you and Mickey would have a nice, quiet evening in our absence."

"I'll tell you this much, Anna." Bernice lowered her voice. "If that woman becomes a permanent resident here, I'll be giving my notice. Mickey too. That's all there is to it. She comes, and we go."

"Oh my." Anna picked up the teapot and creamer. "I don't think you need to worry about that. I can't imagine Lucille will ever live here again."

"Don't be so sure about that." Bernice marched off to the kitchen.

"I think Mac is simply amused by her." Anna followed her, setting the teapot and creamer in the sink. "Sort of like when he reads the comic strips on Sunday mornings...he doesn't take any of that silliness seriously, but he chuckles a bit."

"So you're comparing your mother to a comic strip?" Bernice frowned.

"Sort of." Anna gave her a quick hug. "Why don't you let me clean these things up?"

Bernice did not object. As Anna washed up the tea things, she hoped she was right in her assumption that Lucille simply was a bit of light, fluffy entertainment for Mac. After all, he knew better than anyone who Lucille truly was. She might've been able to fool Mac once, but she certainly couldn't do it again.

Could she?

CHAPTER 18

Anna braced herself as she entered the newspaper office on Monday morning. A conversation with Virginia at church the previous day had reassured Anna that the newspaper remodel had been successfully completed, but now the question remained. How would the editors respond to their new semiprivate office spaces? Anna knew that change did not sit well with everyone. Especially when the changes were implemented by a female who was younger than all of them.

"Good morning." Virginia's eyes lit up as Anna came in.

Anna greeted her then inquired as to the general climate in the office.

"Not bad. Reginald said it was a great improvement. Ed and Frank didn't say much, but I'm pretty sure they like it." She lowered her voice. "Wesley, as you can imagine, was not a bit pleased. But his nose is still out of joint from last Friday. I doubt that he would've approved of anything today."

"I was sort of hoping he wouldn't show up," Anna whispered as Virginia handed her a small stack of mail.

"You and me both." Virginia pointed to her datebook.

"I've already had two calls from women interested in the secretarial position we advertised on Saturday. Want me to schedule them for interviews?"

"Yes, I'd like to get that position filled as soon as possible. See if they can come by later this afternoon." Anna opened the door to the editorial area, peeking around to see that the divider walls she'd requested looked even better than she'd expected. The dark-stained wood partitions were about four feet high and trimmed in sturdy wood strips that gave them a rather dignified and substantial appearance.

"Good morning." Anna held her head high as she walked down the aisle between the desk areas. "I hope you all had a good weekend." She waited as the gentlemen stood, peering at her over their partition walls. "As you can see, we've made some changes here. This design was inspired by the editorial offices at the *Oregonian*. I hope these semiprivate spaces will make our workplace more comfortable for everyone."

"I think it's a great improvement," Reginald told her. "In fact, I'd recommended something like this to Mac several years ago."

"Really?" She considered this. "Well, I'm eager for Mac to come see it...when he is well enough."

"He seemed well enough at the parade." Wesley's tone sounded sardonic. "And he was well enough to attend the picnic. Seems to me he must be well enough to come back to work too."

"According to his doctor, he's not," she crisply informed him. She turned her attention away from Wesley and back to the others. "I'm sure you've all heard by now that Jim has been promoted to assistant editor in chief." She smiled to see Jim standing on the fringes of the editorial department. "And I'll be hiring a secretary to assist Jim and myself.

Other than that, there are no other changes to speak of, and I'm not planning on making any more. So for now, it's simply time to carry on. Business as usual."

"Well, if it's business as usual, will we still have our editorial meeting at ten?" Wesley's tone was dripping with superiority now. "Or have you changed *that* too?"

"Of course." Caught slightly off guard, she suddenly remembered Mac's Monday-morning meetings. "Like I said, nothing else has changed around here. So carry on." She continued toward her office, pausing to speak to Jim. "So what do you think of the changes?" she asked her new assistant editor in chief. "Is your office area adequate?"

"Very nice." He pointed to the desk situated between his office and Mac's. "And the secretarial space is conveniently placed too. Well done."

"Good. Hopefully we'll find the right person soon," she told him. "And one more thing, Jim. I'd like you to assist me in this morning's meeting. In fact, I wouldn't mind if you took the lead."

He looked somewhat surprised.

"I think the others would appreciate seeing you in that position. It might reassure them that not much has really changed."

He nodded. "Makes sense."

"I'll open the meeting and contribute as needed, but I'd like you to run the show." She opened the door to Mac's office. "By the way, I told Mac about your promotion, and he was in complete agreement."

"That's good to know." He lowered his voice. "How is he really, Anna? Do you think he'll ever return to work?"

She frowned, motioning him into Mac's office and then closing the door. "I honestly don't know if he'll ever be able to work again. But he is getting better. And we're hoping for the best. But he still struggles with his speech."

"It was great seeing him and Wally in Saturday's parade." He smiled. "Gave me hope."

"His mind is as sharp as ever." She smiled and leaned onto the desk. "And he's been typing away on something— something he wants to keep private for now. Only having one hand to type with slows him down some. That and he still tires rather easily and needs his rest. But he's genuinely trying. And he's been in good spirits."

"It must be encouraging to have his family around." Jim's brow furrowed slightly. "I know it's none of my business, but I'm curious as to how he's handling having his, uh, ex-wife in town."

"I'm sure that most of the town is wondering the same thing." She folded her arms over her chest. "To be honest, I don't really know what Mac thinks about it. He's been maintaining a pretty good poker face. But Lucille seems determined to insert herself back into his world, acting almost as if nothing ever happened between them."

"I've always wondered what did happen between them."

Anna smiled. "You're a true newsman, Jim. Always asking questions."

His grin looked slightly sheepish.

"Well, the truth is that the disintegration of their marriage has always been a bit of a mystery to everyone— including me. The most common story is that Lucille grew weary of small-town life, but I've always felt there was more to it. However, I lived in the same house with them, and I honestly do not know what happened. One day my mother was there, and the next day she was gone." Anna still remembered her shock...and the pain that followed.

"Yes, Mac has always been rather tight-lipped about his personal life."

"I've always assumed it was because he was as surprised by it as I felt."

Jim's smile seemed genuinely sympathetic. "Well, Mac is lucky to have you, Anna. And, for the record, I think you're doing a great job with the paper. Keep it up."

"Thank you." She sighed. "That means a lot to me."

As Jim returned to his office space, Anna sifted through the small stack of letters. Although she was grateful for Jim's support and concern, she hoped she wasn't putting too much upon him. Not that he didn't seem perfectly capable, but more because she didn't want to put herself out of a job. Not yet anyway. Maybe at summer's end.

Anna's plan for the editorial meeting was to remain relatively quiet and take careful notes. But after Jim finished going over potential stories and assignments, she couldn't help but speak up. "Before we conclude, I'd like to make one more assignment," she announced. "There's a big story brewing in Sunset Cove that requires some investigative work." The room got quiet. "I'm well aware that there's bootlegging going on around here, but I'm certain there's some rum-running as well. I'd like someone to take it on, to dig around and come up with an exposé—"

"Aw, that's a non-story." Wesley waved a dismissive hand.

"A non-story?" She locked eyes with him. "How can you possibly say that?" Naturally, Wesley wouldn't like this idea—it would probably cast a bad light on some of his good drinking buddies.

"Because everyone knows there's bootlegging and rum-running going on—all up and down the coastline. *Big news.*" His tone was sarcastic.

"It was big news in Portland," she challenged. "It should be even bigger news in a small community like this."

He feigned laughter. "Really? Who do you think wants to read about it?"

"*I* want to read about it," she told him. "And lots of honest, law-abiding citizens will want to read about it—that is, if the story is handled right."

"So what's the story?" he demanded. "What's the angle?"

"You're an editor," she shot back. "You tell me the angle."

"You're editor in chief." He pounded a fist into his palm. "You're supposed to make the assignments."

"That's exactly what I'm doing." She suppressed her aggravation. "If you don't—"

"I'll do the story," Jim interrupted. "And I already have an angle."

"What if *I* want to do the story?" Wesley argued.

"Tell you what." Anna arched her brows. "Why don't you both do a story? If they're good, we'll run one midweek and one on Saturday. Maybe we'll do a series of informative stories on the subject." She stood and gathered her papers to signal the meeting was over. "Thank you."

Wesley scowled but said nothing. As Anna made her exit, she felt certain that he wanted to kill this story and, left to his own devices, probably would. For all she knew, Wesley could be in cahoots with some of the criminals involved. He was so antagonistic that it wouldn't surprise her at all. But with Jim on it, Wesley couldn't stop the story. And, although she didn't want to tip her hand, Anna planned to do some investigating herself. Maybe she'd write her own story. Maybe the *Sunset Times* would blow these crooked lowlifes wide open. And if Wesley was involved...well, that would simply make it a very juicy story—not to mention ensure his termination.

By Tuesday, Anna had hired a secretary. A serious woman named Jeanette Lloyd had just finished a year of business school and needed a job to help support her recently widowed mother. Jeanette seemed intelligent, sensible, confident, and sincere. Besides that, Anna simply liked the young woman and felt she'd be a good fit in their male-dominated workplace.

To Anna's dismay, neither Jim nor Wesley came up with much of a story regarding the locals who were rebelling against prohibition. Wesley had lots of excuses about folks resenting being questioned, and Jim simply claimed he needed more time. But Anna wasn't overly concerned since the midweek paper was already quite full with stories from the previous weekend's celebration.

"Will you have your story finished in time for Saturday's paper?" she asked Jim as she returned his proofed pages.

"I'm not sure." He frowned. "I'm onto something rather interesting. But I don't really want to rush it." He scratched his head. "I remember Mac was working on something...I wish I could talk to him about it."

"I'm not sure that would be too helpful." She told him more about Mac's communication challenges. "Sometimes he's intelligible. But if he's stressed or excited about something, it's like baby babble. I haven't mentioned this because I don't want anyone to get the impression anything is wrong with his mind. Just play chess with him and you'll know his brain is as sharp as ever."

"So are you saying I shouldn't talk to him?"

"I don't know. Let me ask Mac about it." She drummed her fingernails on the desk, thinking. "Perhaps if my daughter, Katy, or I were there with you, we could help. We're somewhat used to his speech. Katy is especially good at interpretation."

"Maybe you could ask him about some of the information he'd been gathering. I know he had been collecting some things. If I could access them, it would help with my research."

So later that day, during her lunch break, Anna explained to Mac what she and Jim were working on. "Jim would like to talk to you about it." She wiped her mouth with the napkin. "He seems to think you've got some information that could be useful to him."

Mac frowned, shaking his head. "Gone."

"Gone?" she echoed with confusion.

"Not in box."

"You mean the box of papers that Virginia had Willy bring home to you?" she asked.

"Yeah. Not in box." He pointed to her. "In my office? You got?"

"I don't recall anything like that in your office." As she explained how she'd cleaned and sorted through his things, she suddenly remembered how at home Wesley had seemed before she'd demoted him. "Do you think Wesley could've taken it?"

Mac made a low growl. "Yeah."

"Well, I'll see if I can find out."

"Goo' luck." He glumly shook his head.

Anna glanced at her pocket watch. "If I get back there before the others, I could poke around in Wesley's desk. What did the paperwork look like, Mac? Typewritten or in your own hand?"

"My hand. Notes in folder. Unmark' folder." Mac didn't look very hopeful.

"Well, I'll do my best."

"Be careful."

Anna hurried back to the office to find Virginia eating lunch at her desk and perusing a magazine. "Is Wesley back?" Anna quickly asked.

"No one here but me and the printer boys."

"I'm going to snoop in Wesley's things." Anna briefly explained. "Mac thinks he might've taken a file from him. Whistle or something if Wesley comes in." Anna went straight to Wesley's desk, flipping through the file drawers, hoping to unearth an unmarked folder filled with Mac's handwritten notes but without success. She was just opening a smaller side drawer when she heard the sound of Virginia whistling "She'll Be Coming Round the Mountain." Anna closed the drawer and scampered away.

Safely in her office, she wondered if Wesley really had taken the file. And if he had, what did he want with it? He certainly didn't want to write an article. And if he had it, would he keep it here in the office—or someplace safer, like his home? She also wondered how much Mac recalled from his notes. And even if he could remember, could he communicate those things with her or Jim?

By the end of the day, Anna had a plan. She'd invite Jim to come to the house sometime this week so that the three of them could sit down and try to sort this out. She intended to keep Katy out of this conversation. In case there were specific names or incriminating information involved, she knew her daughter was safer left in the dark. Hopefully she could schedule a time when Katy was already occupied. And since she'd been spending a fair amount of time with Wally and Thelma Morris lately, it wouldn't be difficult.

Katy, in her enthusiasm for Wally running against Mayor Snyder's reelection, had offered to be Wally's campaign manager. Wally had questioned her youth initially, but after getting better acquainted and with Mac's encouragement, he was starting to take her seriously. And already she'd designed some very attractive and clever posters in support of Wally. Despite his wife's support—since Thelma despised the current mayor—Wally hadn't officially thrown his hat into the ring. But Katy felt certain he would. And if he did, Mac had already told Anna that the newspaper would offer its political endorsement for him. That alone could make for some very interesting stories.

CHAPTER 19

Although Anna knew she needed to have a frank conversation with her mother, she was reluctant to arrange for it. Her hope was that Lucille would eventually realize that Mac was not wealthy, lose interest, and return to San Francisco. But so far, that had not happened. And according to Bernice, Lucille was making regular visits to Mac during the day, while Anna was at work. So when Jeanette announced that Lucille was in the newspaper office, hoping to speak to Anna, it seemed the time was right. Anna told Jeanette to send her in.

"Good afternoon, Anna, dear." Lucille entered the office with her usual flourish of swishing layers of skirt, frilly parasol, and the wafting scent of some overly flowery perfume that made Anna feel slightly sick. "Isn't it a lovely day today?"

Anna went over to open the window. "Yes, it looks like the fog has lifted."

"I do hope you don't mind me dropping in unannounced." Lucille sat in the chair opposite the desk and slipped off her lace-trimmed gloves. "But you're so hard to catch up with sometimes. I thought perhaps this was the best place to corner you." Lucille pointed to the bookcase that concealed the secret getaway. "Well, unless you decide to make your escape through there." She giggled.

Anna felt chagrined to think Lucille knew about the clandestine escape route. "As it so happens, I've hoped for some time with you." She forced a smile. "So I'm glad you came today." Anna covered the typewriter, which still had her half-written editorial in the carriage—an opinion piece about prohibition laws and why the public should respect them. "I've wanted to speak to you in private."

"Really?" Lucille blinked. "I was under the impression you wanted to avoid me completely."

Anna tried to collect her feelings and focus her thoughts. "I want to speak to you about Mac."

"Dear, dear Mac. I just had coffee with him this morning, and he—"

"Why are you here, Lucille?" Anna leaned forward, peering curiously at her mother. "Why are you spending so much time with Mac? What is it you're after? Why did you return to Sunset Cove?"

Lucille's smile faded. "I merely wished to repair my broken bridges with the father of my only child."

"Well, it seems you've done that. Mac appears to have forgiven you for all the deep wounds you inflicted upon him thirty years ago." Anna frowned. "I honestly don't know how he managed to do this, but he seems to harbor no animosity toward you now. So I think your task is accomplished, which makes me wonder why you're still here."

Lucille's countenance grew stern. "Why are you so eager to be rid of me, Anna?"

This was not how Anna planned for this conversation to go. "I'm not trying to get rid of you." She measured her words. "It's simply that I'm curious as to your rationale in regard to Mac. You've been spending so much time with him, giving him so much of your attention...well, it almost seems as if you want to get back together with him."

"Would that be so terrible?"

Anna leaned back in her chair, suppressing the urge to pound her fist on the desk and declare that it would be terrible.

"Mac appears to enjoy my companionship—"

"Or is he simply being polite...or amused?"

"Anna, dear, I do understand that you still bear considerable ill will toward me, but is it fair to impose your bad feelings onto Mac? He's a grown man. He can make his own choices."

Anna didn't know how to respond.

"Furthermore, I wonder if it's good for you to be so hateful toward your own mother. Such bitterness cannot be healthy. If your father and daughter can accept me, I would think you'd at least try to follow their examples."

Anna felt speechless...and seething with anger.

"I am not the enemy, Anna. Certainly, I've made my mistakes. But I am not completely to blame for everything that went wrong all those years ago." She waved her hand. "And look at you. Despite your childhood disappointments over your parents' troubles, you appear to have grown into a strong, intelligent, successful woman." She smiled a bit slyly. "And based on what I've learned about your young adult years, you have made some of the exact same mistakes as your mother. In fact, I think we have much in common, daughter. Perhaps you should make an attempt to get better acquainted with—"

"I don't have time for this right now, Lucille." Anna stood. "But before you leave, there is one thing I'd like to make perfectly clear. *Mac is not wealthy.* He has mortgaged his home and this office building in order to make improvements to the newspaper. So if you think that there is anything financial to gain by winning him over, you will be in for a big disappointment."

"Oh, Anna, do you really think I'm here for monetary purposes?"

"It seems an honest assumption. After all, it's no secret that you married your second husband for his money." Anna knew this was a low blow but couldn't seem to help herself.

Lucille frowned as she slowly stood. "It's true that I married Walter for security. I was a lone woman without family or money. But Walter truly loved me...and over the years I grew to love him. I was quite brokenhearted when he passed away. As far as my current financial situation, I have no need for Mac's money—or anyone's. I am a woman of independent means. Don't concern yourself about me."

Anna wasn't sure she could believe Lucille but decided not to question her. "Well, that's fine. Now, if you'll excuse me, I have a newspaper to run."

"Perhaps we can continue this conversation later." Lucille moved toward the door. "Sometime when you're not so busy?"

"Perhaps." Anna folded her arms in front of her.

"I know what I'll do." Lucille's eyes lit up. "I shall invite all of you—Mac and Katy and you—to join me for dinner this weekend. How about Saturday?"

"At the hotel restaurant?" Anna felt confident that Mac would decline this invitation. He wouldn't want to be made a spectacle in the hotel restaurant. Certainly not on a Saturday night.

"Oh, I've left the hotel. I planned to keep my news as a

surprise for the time being, but if you promise not to tell Mac, I'll let you in on it." She pulled on her gloves.

"Let me in on what?"

"I purchased a home this week." Lucille's smile seemed a trifle smug.

"A house here in town?" Anna cringed to imagine Lucille as a permanent resident of Sunset Cove.

"Yes! I'm so excited about it, Anna. I bought the old Willis house on Harbor Drive. Certainly, it's not as impressive as Mac's delightful home, but it's fairly roomy and has a lovely sea view. And it's fully furnished. I'm on my way there right now. My belongings are to be delivered from the hotel at four." She glanced at the wall clock. "So I should probably be on my way." She reached for the doorknob. "I'll plan on the three of you joining me at, say, six o'clock on Saturday evening. I know Mac doesn't like to eat too late."

"But I don't know—"

"You three will be my first guests in my new house." She wrapped her satin purse straps around her wrist. "Perfectly delightful."

Before Anna could think of a viable excuse to refuse this invitation, Lucille blew a kiss and left.

The Willis house! How was it possible that Lucille could afford to buy a house like that? Perhaps it wasn't as handsome as Mac's old stone house, but it was quite elegant...and quite close to Mac's home. Well, at least Bernice and Mickey couldn't threaten to leave now. Although Bernice would probably have a fit to hear that Lucille would be residing only a few houses away.

Anna's admiration for Jim grew as he joined Mac and her for

lunch on Friday. Katy was at the Morrises', in celebratory mode since Wally had just agreed to run for mayor. So, to Anna's relief, it was just the three of them, talking privately in Mac's sitting room. But watching Jim's interaction with Mac was encouraging. And it seemed the two were on the same track in regard to exposing who they suspected to be behind the criminal element taking a hold on Sunset Cove.

"We have the list of names." Jim held up the notepad he'd been writing on during their meeting. "Including our mayor and several prominent business owners. And another list of folks that have no qualms about breaking prohibition law. But that doesn't make for much of a story."

"No story." Mac shook his head.

"I agree," Anna told him. "It's premature. Although I am running an opinion piece in tomorrow's paper." She handed Mac a copy. "I hope it will rattle some cages."

"Good." Mac paused to scan the page.

"And I talked to Harvey again," she told him.

"Chief Rollins?" Jim asked with raised eyebrows. "He's in on this? Do we know he can be trusted?"

"Yeah." Mac nodded vigorously. "Old friend."

"But I've been watching some of the police force." Jim sounded concerned.

"Chief Rollins hinted that not all his men are trustworthy," Anna confided to them. "Naturally, he didn't want to say who."

"I'm particularly suspicious of Officer Collins," Jim said.

Anna was surprised. "Clint Collins?"

"Some of Clint's friends are on our list." Jim grimly shook his head. "He bears watching too."

"He seems like such a nice man." Anna remembered how friendly he'd been with her while she was waiting to talk to Harvey.

"You engage with any of these fellows in the right place and the right time, and they can charm the socks off you," Jim explained. "But catch them at the wrong time and they can turn on you like vipers."

"Yes." She nodded. "I remember the men at the Founders Day dance."

"What?" Mac asked.

So she told them about the unfortunate encounter. "And the names of those men are on our list too."

"People who bear watching." Jim checked his watch.

"How I wish we could publish the list." Anna could just see the headlines.

"No!" Mac firmly shook his head.

"Of course we won't do that," Jim assured him.

"Need real evidence," Mac slowly told Jim and then turned to Anna. "No lawsuit."

"I understand." Anna solemnly nodded.

"No lawsuit," Mac repeated himself, shaking a finger in the air. "Wesley...lawsuit."

For a moment, no one spoke, but Jim and Anna exchanged worried glances. "Did Wesley threaten a lawsuit against you?" Anna asked Mac.

"No." Mac pointed to his eyes. "Wesley watching...*want* lawsuit."

"Oh...?" Anna considered this.

"Do you think Wesley hopes the newspaper *will* be sued?" Jim asked.

"So that the bank will foreclose on the paper?" Anna added.

"So that someone else can get control of the newspaper?"

Anna's thoughts buzzed. "Like the mayor? Or Wesley himself?"

Mac nodded somberly. "Must be careful."

"I see." Anna remembered what Mac had said about keeping Wesley around. "Were you worried that firing Wesley could bring a lawsuit?" Anna asked.

He shrugged. "Talk to Rand."

"Yes," she said eagerly. "Perhaps we should have him in on all of this. Maybe even keep him on a retainer. You know he practiced law in Salem, Mac. He's probably the best lawyer in town."

"Yeah." Mac nodded. "Good idea."

"Well, we've covered a lot of ground." Jim put his notepad back in his briefcase. "But I still have some proofing to finish at the paper or the typesetters will have my hide. So unless we have anything else to go over, I should probably get back."

"Yes, let's not keep them waiting," Anna told him. "I'll be along shortly."

After Jim left, Anna told Mac that she still hadn't found his missing file. But Mac seemed unconcerned, assuring her that she and Jim probably had gathered as much information by now as Mac had found.

"What about the fact that Wesley might have the file?" she asked. "That he might be planning on using it for some sort of lawsuit or leverage?"

Mac sighed. "Yeah...my worry."

"Well, if we can stay ahead of him, and if we can find some solid evidence that could lead to some arrests, maybe we can stop Wesley before he ever gets a chance." She frowned. "It makes me so furious, Mac. To think that you took Wesley under your wing."

"Bad home." Mac sadly shook his head.

"I know. But you helped him. You hired him while he was still in high school. You taught him everything he knows. And then he turns on you like that." She stood with indignation. "It makes me so angry."

Mac's eyes were misty. "Wesley changed...he likes power now."

"I know. I've seen that in him. The first day I went into the office, I knew he'd changed."

"Friends with mayor...both want power."

"Yes...I suppose that's not surprising. Corruption in the high places. I covered similar stories in Portland occasionally."

"Be careful," Mac said solemnly. "Don't show suspicion."

"I know, Mac." She smiled. "I learned from you how to use my poker face when things get dicey." She leaned down to kiss him good-bye.

"With Lucille?" His pale blue eyes searched her face.

She grimaced. "Well, I suppose you're right about that. I am not good at keeping my emotions under control with her."

"Dinner tomorrow night?"

She sighed. "Like I told you, I want to beg off, but if you really want me there, I will go. And I will do my best to mind my manners. Katy already gave me a speech."

Mac chuckled. "Good for Katy."

She studied him closely. "Tell me, Mac, how is it that you've managed to accept her back so easily? How did you manage to bury the hatchet?"

His countenance grew serious. "Long story, Anna. Two sides." He pointed to his chest. "Blame here too."

"Oh." She was curious to hear more but knew she needed to return to work. Besides, he looked tired. "Well, hopefully you can share some of your deep, dark secrets with me someday. But right now I have a newspaper to get out."

He nodded with a weary sigh. "Yeah. Good for you."

As Anna walked back to the newspaper office, she strained her memory to recall what her parents' marriage had been like during the early years of her childhood. As usual, not much stood out. She remembered Lucille as being beautiful and slightly detached but never unkind. And what was lacking in Lucille as a mother was made up for in Anna's grandmother and Bernice. Meanwhile, Mac had worked hard at the newspaper, trying to create something great, determined to take it further than his father had been able to do before he died.

Although Mac worked long hours during the week, he'd always seemed jovial and energetic and interested in everyone when he came home each evening. It felt as if the whole house came to life when Daddy arrived. Yes, Anna had called him "Daddy" back then. And on weekends, he'd taken Anna down to the beach to wade in the surf or collect seashells or build sandcastles or simply lie in the dunes and watch clouds in the sky. It had been just about perfect.

She remembered how often it seemed that Mac and Lucille had gone out in the evenings. They would both dress up and attend social functions with friends or go to dinner at the hotel. And they had frequent dinner parties at home—some small and intimate, others big and flamboyant. Anna remembered listening to them on the upstairs landing until someone finally ushered her off to bed.

In Anna's childhood memory, it had been a truly idyllic marriage—something Anna had never experienced for herself—and she'd never understood why Lucille hadn't been satisfied. Or how she could turn her back on her husband and child and just leave. She hadn't understood it then.

And she still didn't.

CHAPTER 20

Anna was grateful for Katy's interest in helping Wally's mayoral campaign for several reasons. First of all, Katy was in her element—sharing enthusiasm and creativity for a good cause. Secondly, Anna truly hoped that Wally would beat Calvin in the election. And last, but not least, it occupied much of Katy's time…making her less available to spend time with the Krauss kids. Specifically, AJ.

It hadn't escaped Anna's notice that AJ's father, Albert Senior, was on the "suspicious" list that Jim had made. In fact, he'd made Anna's list as well. And she felt certain that, in the case of the Krauss family, the apple did not fall far from the tree. If Albert was involved in anything illegal, it stood to reason that AJ was as well.

To this end, Anna had decided to make an investigative visit to the Sunset Fish Company on Saturday morning. To cover her motives, she carried a basket and planned to ask about purchasing a whole salmon for their Sunday dinner.

"Anna," Clara exclaimed as Anna came into the small store that was situated in front of the large building. "What are you doing out this way?"

"Good morning." Anna greeted her with a smile, then

tried not to cringe at the strong smell of fish as she explained the object of her mission. "Mac has been craving salmon."

"I'm sorry." Clara frowned. "We are out of salmon."

"Oh?" Anna looked around the small shop. "Well, I wonder if there's anything else you might have that would make him happy." She began to peruse the glass case, surprised to see the fish inventory seemed rather limited. "Hasn't the fishing been bountiful lately?" she asked.

Clara frowned. "Our main boat is being repaired," she explained. "So Albert has been sending the smaller ones out, and apparently they haven't had much luck."

Anna smiled. "Well, that must mean that you're not so busy here, Clara. Perhaps you'll have time to get out more. I missed you at the Founders Day activities."

"Oh, well, I'm not much interested in social gatherings."

Anna frowned. "That's what Albert told me at the dance, but I must admit I was skeptical. You used to enjoy being with people. Remember the parties and socials we attended as girls? I remember you as one of the best dancers around."

Clara waved a hand. "That was long ago."

"Not that long." Anna peered curiously at her. "We're the same age. Remember?"

Clara turned away, busying herself with wiping down a countertop that looked perfectly clean.

"When do you have time off?" Anna asked. "Perhaps we could meet for tea or—"

"I don't think that's possible." Clara let out a sigh.

"I'd like to really talk with you," Anna persisted. "To talk about old times and to catch up. I've seen far more of your children than I have of you, but—"

"Clara?" Albert's voice sounded sharp as he seemed to emerge right out of the paneled wall.

Anna jumped in surprise. "Where on earth did you come from?"

He waved a hand. "Never mind." He smiled but without warmth. "Well now. What have we here?"

"Anna was looking for salmon," Clara told him.

"Doing the household shopping, are you?" He looked suspiciously at her. "Doesn't Mickey usually fetch fish for the kitchen?"

"I felt like taking a walk," she said quickly. "And I hoped to do some catching up with my old friend Clara." She smiled brightly at Albert. "Surely you don't have any objections to the two of us going for a cup of tea? I've been back in town awhile now, and Clara and I have barely had time to say hello."

"Well, I—"

"You wouldn't want anyone to think that you keep your sweet little wife under lock and key, would you?" She laughed like this was funny. "Besides, a little break would do her good, don't you think so?"

"But it's Saturday—"

"Isn't Ellen around? She's such a fine, sweet girl, I'm sure she'd be happy to give her poor mother a little time off."

"Well, I—"

"Or perhaps AJ would like to help out," Anna continued. "Or even yourself. I hear your big fishing boat is getting repaired. You probably have a bit of spare time on your hands." She turned to Clara. "Come on, old friend, I insist you must come with me. And since it's nearly noon, perhaps we should have some lunch."

"Oh, Anna." Clara twisted the cleaning cloth in her hands. "I can't possibly go with you. Albert would—"

"No, no, Clara." Albert stepped behind the counter,

removing the cloth from her hands. "I think Anna is right. You should go out with her. I insist."

Clara looked dumbfounded.

"Wonderful." Anna smiled at Albert. "What a good husband you are."

"You ladies have a real nice time." Albert had a sly twinkle in his eye. "And Clara, when you get back, you'll have to tell me all about it."

"Well...all right." Clara removed her apron and pulled out a worn handbag from beneath the counter. Then she looked down at her equally worn dress. "I don't look very nice."

"You look just fine." Anna looped her arm in Clara's. "We shall have a lovely time." As she walked Clara out of the fish shop, she could feel the tenseness in her. "Wasn't that nice of Albert to let you go like this?"

"I don't know." Clara sounded worried.

"Tell me, how did he do that magic trick in there? Suddenly appearing like that?"

"Oh, that—it's just a storage closet."

"Well, I'm glad he let you go. You don't get much time off, do you?"

"No." Clara glanced over her shoulder, almost as if she expected Albert to charge out and tell them he'd changed his mind.

"Well, that's not right," Anna declared. "And it concerns me. Slavery is illegal, you know."

"Oh, dear, I'm not a slave."

"No, you're not."

"It's just that, well, there's always work to be done."

"Even when there's not much fish to be sold?"

Clara didn't say anything.

"Is your fish company struggling?" Anna asked, trying

not to sound overly curious. "Are you in any kind of financial trouble with it? Is that why your larger boat isn't running right now?"

"Oh, no. Not at all. I keep the books, so I know we're financially stable."

"Then can't you afford to hire an extra employee?" Anna asked. "To help at the shop and give you some time off?"

"Oh, Albert would never agree to that."

"No, I didn't think so." Anna changed the subject then, inquiring about Clara's children and their plans for the future, hoping to sound simply friendly—not suspicious.

"AJ will graduate high school next year and then he'll be helping Albert full-time in the fishing company. Ellen will probably get married and start a family."

"After she finishes high school?"

"If that's what she wants."

"Do you ever regret marrying before you finished high school? You were sixteen, weren't you?"

"Yes...sixteen." She sighed. "For some reason, I was so eager to be married. I thought it meant being grown-up and in charge of my life."

"But instead, Albert is in charge?"

Clara didn't answer, just shook her head.

"I was young too," Anna admitted. "At least I finished high school. But, looking back, I wish I'd listened to Mac. He wanted me to go on to college. Granted, he wanted it so I'd meet a suitable husband, but I would have gained an education too."

"We were young," Clara declared solemnly.

"That's true." Anna nodded as they came into town. "I just hope that my daughter can learn from my mistakes."

Clara turned to look at her. "At least you've made something of your life, Anna. I can't say I don't envy you some. You're so independent. I cannot even imagine what that must feel like."

"Do you remember how you felt when you were sixteen?" Anna asked. "I mean *before* you met Albert?"

"Of course."

"Were you more independent then than you are now?"

Clara pursed her lips but nodded.

"So maybe you won't be too eager to see Ellen married off, then?"

"It's food for thought." Clara let out a weary-sounding sigh.

"Speaking of food, I'm famished." Anna nodded to the hotel. "Lunch is my treat today, Clara. We will try to turn back the clock and talk together like we used to back when we were our daughters' ages."

Clara seemed uneasy as they entered the hotel restaurant, but after they placed their orders and were served a pot of tea, she seemed to relax. After their food was served, Anna continued her attempt to draw her out, inquiring about some of Clara's family members, discovering that her parents had both passed on and that her siblings had both moved away. Finally, after Anna insisted on ordering them each a slice of pie and a fresh pot of tea, she focused her questions on Albert, gently trying to determine if he'd always been so demanding and domineering.

"I learned early on that he planned to rule the roost," Clara admitted. "I didn't really mind at first. I had my hands full with a baby, and I thought it was Albert's way of showing love for me. But then some things happened...." She lowered her voice. "I lost a baby, and Albert seemed, well, rather unsympathetic. That hurt. I felt like he didn't really care about me. Not like I wanted him to anyway. Then Ellen came along, and Albert grew even more distant. He spent most of his time out on the fishing boat or working in the cannery or just out drinking with his crew. Not with me and the children."

"That must've been lonely."

Clara nodded. "Very. But by then I realized that if Albert were home, I would have to put up with his outbursts. It got so I was glad to be alone."

"Did he lose his temper a lot?" Anna asked quietly.

She simply nodded again.

Anna reached for her hand. "I'm sorry, Clara. That must've been so hard on you. You were always such a fun-loving, vivacious girl. It's hard to think of what your life has been like. I wish I'd been around more then, to help you."

Clara had tears in her eyes. "I'm so glad you're here now, Anna." She glanced around the restaurant. "You have no idea how much this means to me...that you invited me here to catch up." She used her napkin to catch a tear.

Anna felt a wave of guilt. It wasn't that she didn't care about Clara. She absolutely did. But her initial motive for getting Clara away from the fish shop had been to gather information. Now she was determined to do anything she could to help her old friend. "We will have to make this a regular thing," she told her.

"I could hardly believe that Albert let me come today," Clara confessed. "I doubt it will happen often."

"Maybe it will...if we work it right. Albert seems to care about his reputation. When I teased him about keeping you under lock and key, he seemed to change course. He obviously knows I run the newspaper. He might be worried I'll go around telling everyone that he's a lousy husband."

"I'm sure there are plenty of folks who already think that."

"Well, for some reason, it seemed to matter." Anna picked up her teacup. "I'm a stubborn woman, Clara. I won't give up. Not easily."

"Thank you."

"I'm curious about something." Anna reminded herself to be cautious. "Albert has a number of fishing boats, right?"

"Yes. Besides the big boat, which is out of commission, we have four smaller boats."

"And you mentioned your company is doing well financially?" Anna lowered her voice. "Do you think there's any chance that Albert could be using any of his smaller boats for rum-running?"

Clara looked genuinely shocked. "Oh, no, I don't think so."

"I'm sorry to question this, but we know that there are some people doing this along the coastline. And I know that Albert and his friends still imbibe alcohol, despite prohibition."

"Yes, that's true. But Albert claims that prohibition laws are a big mistake. He says they don't deserve to be observed. So does the mayor."

"Really? You've heard him say this?"

Clara frowned. "Well, maybe not in person. I suppose I've just heard Albert and AJ saying that he is of that opinion. Why are you asking?"

"Did you read today's newspaper?"

"No...not yet."

"Well, my editorial column will probably answer that question."

"So you are in favor of prohibition?"

"It's the law of the land, Clara. It might be a new law, but that doesn't mean we can ignore it."

"Some people do."

"I know." Anna remembered how Lucille brought Mac the bottle of port and how no one, besides Anna, seemed to object.

"Albert says it won't be around for long."

"I don't know about that, but I do know that when people choose to disobey the laws, it leads to trouble." Anna considered confiding to Clara about Katy's father... and where that had gotten them. But she wasn't absolutely sure she could trust Clara. Not so much because of who Clara was, but more because of who she was married to. Plus Anna knew, Albert would be waiting to grill his wife as soon as she got back.

Anna paid their bill and insisted on walking Clara partway back to the fish company. Once on the street, she shot her friend a cautious look. "I hope that our conversation can be just between us."

"You mean don't tell Albert about it?"

"I'm not comfortable with him knowing what we talked about."

"Don't worry. I say as little to him as possible most of the time."

"Would he ever bully you?" Anna turned to look at her. "I mean, to get information from you?"

Clara shrugged. "I'm used to his ways. I know how to handle him."

Anna put her arm around Clara's shoulders, giving her a squeeze. "Well, you've got me here now. If you ever need anything, or if Albert ever steps out of line with you, all you need to do is call me. I will gladly help you."

Clara thanked her, pausing on the edge of town to embrace, and then, promising to meet again soon, they parted ways. But as Anna headed for home, she felt genuinely concerned for Clara's welfare. What if taking her out like this today and questioning her like she'd done had put Clara in some kind of danger? Or was Anna just being overly concerned and suspicious?

Yet the more she considered it, it seemed entirely possible that Albert could be involved with bootlegging. The idea had been percolating in Anna's head for some time, but out of respect for Clara and the kids, she'd tried to suppress it. But what if she were right? Albert had the perfect setup to run rum. A fishing company located on the harbor with direct access to the ocean, a small fleet of maneuverable boats, a place to hide booze, and plenty of friends—including the mayor—to help him.

And if Anna were right, if Albert really was involved in illegal activities, it was highly likely that his son could be involved too. And if AJ was involved, that meant it could be very dangerous for Katy to be associated with him. Anna suddenly felt like she'd unwittingly opened Pandora's box— and she had no idea of how to put the lid back on.

CHAPTER 21

As if Anna wasn't plagued with enough worries, tonight was Lucille's little dinner party in her new home. Both Mac and Katy seemed to look forward to it, but Anna would prefer to spend the evening having a tooth extracted.

"Oh, Mother." Katy stood in Anna's doorway with a look of dismay. "I don't know why you're dragging your heels like this. Lucille seems to be really trying. And she and Mac have been getting along so well. Can't you just make the tiniest bit of effort?"

Anna feigned innocence. "I am making an effort, Katy. I'm going tonight, am I not?"

"But look at you." Katy wrinkled her nose.

"What?" Anna glanced down at her tan linen suit and sturdy oxford shoes. "I'm perfectly respectable."

"You look like you're going to work. This is a dinner party."

"Lucille didn't tell me it was a *formal* dinner party. She simply invited us to come eat at her house."

"But you know how she is, Mother. She will expect you to be *dressed*. For that matter, so will Mac. Don't you care what he thinks?"

Anna grimaced. Katy was right. Suddenly Anna could imagine her father's face to see her appear in her boring suit. "All right." She opened her closet. "You win. Go tell Mac that I'll be down in a few minutes."

When they were finally walking down the street to Lucille's house, Anna was glad she'd listened to her daughter. If she'd stubbornly gone to dinner in her work suit, it would've simply drawn more attention to the fact that Anna resented being part of the dinner party. And, really, what would be the use in that? Besides, her lightweight silk dress was actually more comfortable.

"Welcome, welcome, please, come in," Lucille gushed as she opened the door wide, waving them into the foyer. Anna hadn't been in this house since she was a teenager and her friend Dorothy Willis lived here. According to Mac, the Willises had moved to the southern part of the Oregon Coast. As Anna recalled, this house had always been overly full with ornate furnishings and layers of carpets, heavy drapes and too much dust. The Willises had owned the furniture store in town, and Mrs. Willis seemed determined to utilize their home as something of a warehouse. But as Anna peeked into the living room, she could see it had been considerably thinned out. In fact, it now looked rather attractive and inviting.

"It's a beautiful room," Katy gushed to Lucille. "So much better than the first time I saw it with furniture piled all about."

"You've been here before?" Anna asked her daughter.

"Sure. Grandmother had me over when she moved in the other day. I helped her rearrange a few things."

Anna ran a finger over the entry table. "Yes, it's much better."

"Very nice." Mac handed Lucille his hat.

"Come, my darlings, let's sit." Lucille led them into the living room. "Dinner should be ready in about twenty minutes."

"Are you cooking?" Anna looked doubtfully at Lucille.

"No, of course not. I wouldn't subject you good people to that." Lucille laughed as she sat next to Mac on the dark blue velveteen settee. "I hired a woman as a live-in housekeeper and, as it turns out, she's quite a good cook as well." Lucille pointed toward the gleaming wood coffee table where a crystal decanter and four matching goblets were prettily arranged. "Can I offer you a before-dinner *apéritif?*"

"Lucille." Anna used a firm tone. "Although California has no prohibition laws, I'm sure you must be aware that Oregon does have such laws."

"Yes, of course. But I'm also aware that many of your fine citizens ignore them."

"Well, out of respect for your granddaughter—and out of respect of the fact that Mac and I are responsible for the town's newspaper, which has taken a prohibition stance, I would think you'd want to respect our laws."

Lucille blinked. "To be honest, I hadn't thought of it quite like that." She turned to Mac. "What do you think, dear?"

"Anna is right." He nodded.

"Well then." She picked up the tray, carrying it toward the dining room. "We'll just get rid of this."

Anna thanked Lucille when she returned. "I don't know if you read the newspaper today, but I have written an opinion piece that might help you to understand our position better. I mean the newspaper's position."

"I will be sure to read it." Lucille smiled. "And I will be respectful of the law."

"Do you mind if I inquire as to where you purchase your alcoholic beverages?" Anna asked.

Lucille's eyes twinkled with mischief. "Well, dear, I promised not to reveal my source. But I can assure you, it's not difficult to procure."

Anna fought down feelings of aggravation, deciding this was neither the time nor place to question Lucille about her illegal connections. But she was determined to do so later. Instead, she let Katy take the lead by telling everyone about her plans for Wally's mayoral campaign.

"He's agreed to let us hold a fundraiser event, but we haven't decided yet whether it'll be a pie social or a dance."

"Why not do both?" Lucille suggested.

"What a great idea," Katy exclaimed. "And I told Wally we should hold it on Independence Day, but he's worried it will interfere with the holiday."

"Wally is right." Mac nodded.

"What about the Saturday after July Fourth?" Anna suggested.

They discussed campaign ideas for a while and then Katy told them about how she'd gone fishing today. "My first time being out on the ocean—it was so exciting."

"Fishing?" Anna asked. "I thought you were at the Morrises' all day."

"I was at the Morrises' this afternoon," Katy clarified. "But I went fishing with AJ this morning and—"

"You went out in a boat with AJ and didn't even tell me?" Anna scowled.

"Well, Mother, I don't usually report in to you over everything. And if you're worried about me being alone with AJ, don't concern yourself. Ellen and another one of AJ's fishing friends were with us."

"But I don't—"

"Did you catch anything?" Lucille asked eagerly.

"No, but AJ caught a salmon." She glanced at Anna.

"And AJ's dad said you'd gone to the fish shop looking for a salmon earlier, that Mac had wanted one but they were all out, so AJ sent his fish home with me." She turned to Mac. "I didn't know you liked salmon."

To Anna's relief, Mac maintained his poker face as he nodded. "I like salmon. Good for you, Katy." Then as Katy continued to describe their escapades on the ocean, Mac tossed Anna a curious glance, but she simply smiled. Still, the idea of Katy going out in a boat with AJ was disturbing. Somehow Anna needed to make it clear that was not acceptable. But after allowing Katy so much freedom, it wouldn't be easy to rein her back in...not without revealing the real reasons.

As the evening progressed, Anna tried to be polite, attempting to engage in the conversation at appropriate times, but she knew she was preoccupied...distracted. Not only with concerns for her friend Clara's welfare or her eagerness to discover who was selling alcohol to Lucille, but she now had her daughter's safety to worry about too.

Determined to enjoy a day of rest, Anna informed Katy and Mac that she didn't plan to be up early for breakfast in the morning. "I hope you'll both excuse me." They were walking back to Mac's house after dinner, moving at a tortoise's pace for Mac's benefit, and Anna was wishing they'd taken the car like Katy had suggested earlier.

"Poor Mother." Katy linked her arm into Anna's. "You've been working so hard. You need a break."

"Maybe just a little one." Anna turned to Mac as they made their way up to his door. "What do you think of Lucille's house?"

"Nice."

"Do you like having her for your neighbor?" Katy asked him.

"Yeah." He nodded as he hobbled along. "Nice."

"I was impressed with how well the house looked." Anna opened the door and waited for Mac to go in. "Much better than I remember from when the Willises lived there." Mickey met them in the foyer, then helped Mac to his room to get ready for bed.

"Katy." Anna put a hand on Katy's shoulder. "I want to talk to you before we turn in."

"I know." Katy let out a long sigh. "I've been just waiting for it. You don't want me to go fishing out on the ocean without—"

"It's not that I don't want you to go fishing or to have fun." Anna paused to think. "But I don't want you to go out without informing me of your whereabouts."

"But what if you're at work?"

"Then tell Mac or Bernice."

"Is that all?" Katy looked exasperated.

"Not really. You know I don't like to judge people, Katy, and I try to give them the benefit of the doubt. But I have a bad feeling about AJ."

"Oh, Mother. Just because of what he said about women getting the vote?" Katy made a face. "I've been straightening him out on that. Ellen and I have both laid into him on women's rights."

"It's not just that." Anna led Katy into the front room. "I'm going to tell you something in confidence, trusting that you won't repeat this."

"What?" Katy's eyes lit up with interest.

"It's about AJ's father. Albert is not a good man, Katy."

"Oh, I know that. Ellen's told me all about him."

"Really?"

"Yes. He's very bossy with her mother, and he yells at Ellen and AJ sometimes. But that's just the way he is. My friend Amanda's dad is like that. She just makes herself scarce when he blows up. Sounds like Ellen and AJ do the same."

"But it isn't only his temper that concerns me. I had a long conversation with Ellen and AJ's mother, and, well, I just don't trust Albert. I don't want to say too much, because right now it's mostly suspicion. But I strongly feel he's not of good character."

"Are you saying that I shouldn't be friends with AJ and Ellen just because their dad is a louse?" Katy made a pout. "That doesn't seem fair, Mother. It doesn't seem like you."

"But it's more—"

"What if people knew that my father was a convicted criminal? Would you want my friends to cast me aside just because of him? Would that be fair?"

"No, of course not. That's not what I'm trying to say."

"Then what are you trying to say?" Katy put on her defiant look, face set and arms crossed.

"I guess I'm just saying—be careful. And like I already told you, Katy, you do not have permission to go anywhere alone with AJ or with any other boy."

"I know that, Mother. And I haven't."

"Also, if you go out in a boat, or anywhere for that matter, specifically with AJ and Ellen, I want to know about it. Or, if I'm at work, I want Mac or Bernice to know about it." She gave Katy her I-mean-it look. "I know you feel very grown-up, Katy, and I've given you a lot of independence. That's because I trust you. But you are not an adult yet. You are still sixteen, and you have to abide by my rules. Is that understood?"

Katy nodded with a glum expression.

"You know it's because I love you, don't you?"

"Yes, Mother." Katy nodded.

"And it's possible that I know some things about this town that you might not be aware of. Things you don't need to worry about...but that could be dangerous."

"Yes, Mother. I know you're worried about rum-running and bootlegging and the criminal elements involved."

Anna tried not to look surprised.

"But that doesn't concern me." Katy smiled. "In fact, I think it's all rather exciting. And besides, aren't I doing my part to help?"

"What?"

"I mean by being Wally's campaign manager, trying to boot out the crooked mayor."

Anna couldn't help but smile as she hugged Katy. "I'm so lucky to have such a mature and responsible daughter. And for clarity's sake, it's not that I'm worried about *you* doing something wrong. I'm not. It's just that I'm a little worried that someone else might do something that could put you in danger." She kissed Katy's cheek. "And that would devastate me."

"Don't worry, Mother. I'm a lot smarter than you think."

Anna knew this was true. Katy was very smart. But Anna also knew that the "smartness" of youth was exactly what got young people into trouble sometimes—they felt they were infallible and then they fell on their faces. After all, wasn't that what she had done? Still, she knew she'd said enough...for now.

CHAPTER 22

On the Monday before Independence Day, Anna wrapped up the editorial meeting to announce the newspaper's decision to endorse Wally Morris's mayoral campaign. "As you know, the *Sunset Times* supports prohibition," she said at the end of her short speech. "And although we don't force the editor in chief's views on individual editors, we ask that you respect them—and that you respect the laws of the land. Naturally, you are all entitled to your own political opinions, and you're welcome to submit such views on the editorial page." She glanced over to Jim. "And unless you have anything to add to our meeting, I'll let everyone get back to your desks. Since Tuesday is a paid holiday, we all have plenty to accomplish today. Thank you."

As Anna went to her office, she felt that the atmosphere at the paper had improved considerably in the past several weeks. Quite a change since that first day when she'd stepped in for Mac. Other than Wesley, who still continued to be a bit of a challenge, the rest of the staff seemed to accept her. As she closed her office door, she wondered why she even concerned herself with Wesley's offhanded comments, pesky questions, and generally cocky ways. Hadn't she worked with fellows just like that at the *Oregonian*? And she knew the editors with attitude were often the most talented.

Anna had sometimes been envious of them, wishing she could pull off the same sorts of stunts the men got away with. Unfortunately, they expected a lady to exhibit better office etiquette. And it would've been useless to point out the different standards to management, since her complaints would've been received by a male with the authority to terminate her at will. The few women existing in the newspaper world had been trained to *mind their manners*. Well, unless their father owned the paper. Anna smiled as she returned to her midweek editorial. At least there was that.

Now if only Mac could agree to letting Wesley go. But each time she raised the subject, he glumly refused. Anna wondered if it was because a part of Mac still considered Wesley his son. Albeit a slightly disrespectful and rebellious and somewhat disappointing son. Still, there was no denying that Anna had been impressed with Wesley's most recent pieces. He was definitely a gifted journalist when he applied himself. Mac had taught him well. Just proving the point that, as Mac had recently said, she couldn't just fire him for "no good reason." And, really, a part of her didn't even want to fire him. She occasionally saw in Wesley what she felt Mac had seen...and she agreed that they shouldn't give up their hopes for him. But at the same time, not unlike a mischievous toddler, Wesley bore careful watching.

Similar to Founders Day, the town was all decked out for the July Fourth celebration. Only this time the bunting was all red, white, and blue. And now, besides Mayor Snyder's reelection posters, Wally Morris's much more attractive posters were liberally displayed on various, not all, store windows. Naturally, as Anna walked to the hotel restaurant where she'd agreed to meet Rand for a business lunch, she took mental notes on the businesses with Snyder posters. Not that this meant they were involved in any criminal activity, but just in case.

As Anna went into the hotel, she smiled to herself. Since coming to Sunset Cove, she had managed to attract two very eligible bachelors, and she'd been dividing her time between the two of them. Lunch with Rand today. Watching the July Fourth parade with Daniel tomorrow. But there had recently been another interesting development. Jim had asked her to join him at the Independence Day dance and fireworks show. Although he'd claimed his purpose was to attend the dance incognito with Anna on his arm, so that they could clandestinely spy on anyone who might be celebrating in some illegal ways, Anna had her own suspicions. Or maybe she was just acting like a silly schoolgirl, imagining things.

"There you are." Rand met her at the door, looking dapper as usual. "Right this way. I've got a table saved for us."

"Town is certainly busy." She followed him to the table and sat in the chair he held for her.

"The tourists have arrived." He waved his hand over the crowded restaurant.

"Is that what it is?" She picked up the menu.

"That's right, you've missed out on all this over the years."

"There were times I really did miss it," she confessed. "Summers in Portland could get awfully sticky and hot. I remember longing for a cool sea breeze and the need to wear a sweater in the middle of summer."

"And our summer fog?"

"Yes, I even missed the summer fog. And most of all I missed the beautiful sunsets."

"Well, with the increased availability of automobiles over the past decade, our little beach town has turned into quite a vacation destination for more and more people."

"I have noticed a couple of small inns that weren't here before."

"And a couple more just outside of town. To be honest, I was a bit surprised when I first moved back home. And I'll warn you, it gets even busier in August."

"Mac mentioned that it was time to start increasing the numbers on our print runs. That must be why."

"Speaking of Mac, I don't want to forget that this is a business meeting. You asked me to go over some things for you." He reached down to remove a large envelope from his briefcase. "I think you'll be pleased with what I've written up in regard to the bank loans and the provision I've made in the event of Mac's inability to return to work or even in his demise."

"Oh." She frowned. "Well, fortunately, he seems to be getting better every day."

"I know. Just the same, I think it was very prudent. Mac wanted it written up and witnessed. He wants to shut down any possible loopholes that might pop up...just in case."

"And you also researched our liability issues in regard to slander lawsuits...just in case?"

"I most assuredly did. They are in here as well." He handed her the envelope. "But as your counsel, I still encourage you to be cautious." He glanced around the crowded room, then lowered his voice. "Our mayor is a cagey fellow with his own legal counsel close at hand. I assure you, he will let nothing slip past him. Anyone can file a claim—whether it's legitimate or not is decided in court. And, as I'm sure you know, law is very fluid when it comes to libel and slander, and precedence is often set in the courtroom." He smiled. "Not that I wouldn't enjoy trying a case like that, but I still advise you to tread carefully."

"I understand." She nodded as she slid the envelope into her own briefcase. "I appreciate your advice."

"Okay, now that we've covered the business part of this meeting, promise me that I can take you to the Independence Day dance tomorrow night. And I'm even happy to invite Daniel and Katy to join us again, if you'd like."

"As lovely as that sounds, I've already made other plans." She quietly told him of Jim's idea to spy on the local riffraff. "You know how there's likely to be a fair amount of drinking and such going on."

"But the police will be there."

"Yes, but in uniform. Jim and I will have the opportunity to mix with the crowd and observe without drawing attention to ourselves."

"Good point. Perhaps I should do the same."

"Yes," she said eagerly. "We need all the eyes we can get. Chief Rollins is glad for the support. He is doing all he can to gather evidence. But so far, he doesn't have enough to make a raid on anyone, much less an arrest." She quickly explained the chief's suggestion that they write down any suspicious activity and then Anna would slip it to one of his men. "Wade Brooks is playing detective by being out of uniform."

"A plainclothes policeman?" Rand chuckled. "Although locals might recognize him and suspect he's on duty."

"That's why I'll do the passing to him. Make it look like I'm simply being friendly."

"I see." Rand frowned. "And you're sure that's not dangerous?"

"I'll be careful. And the chief and his men will be around. I'm not worried."

"So what about the parade tomorrow? Are you planning on going? Or will you be playing detective for that too?"

"I told Daniel I'd watch it with him from his terrace, but I'm sure he wouldn't mind if you joined us up there."

"Yes, I'm sure he wouldn't." Rand's tone was sarcastic, and he looked disappointed. "No, thank you. I won't crash your parade-watching party. I suppose I'll just have to watch the parade with my mother out in front of the store."

Anna felt bad. "If you go to the dance, I promise to dance with you a time or two. I mean, if you're interested."

"Well now, I don't know." He gave her an impish grin. "What if I bring a date of my own?"

"Then perhaps she'd like to trade dances with Jim." She sipped her tea. "That way we all can have some fun."

He brightened. "All right, it's a deal."

The Independence Day parade wasn't quite as large and exuberant as the Founders Day parade had been, but it was nice to know patriotism was alive and well in Sunset Cove. Anna even got teary to see the young, uniformed soldiers marching behind the high school band. She knew that, despite President Wilson's decision to remain neutral, the likelihood of the United States going to war in Europe was probably just a matter of time. All one had to do was pick up a newspaper—even the *Sunset Times*—to discover the atrocities the Germans were imposing on their neighbors.

Anna waved the small flag she'd brought with her.

"What brave young men," she told Daniel. "God bless and be with them if the US goes to war."

"Do you think that will really happen?" Daniel asked. "Wilson seems determined to keep us out of it."

"I think it's inevitable." She sighed. "Much as I wish we won't have to, I feel doubtful it will resolve itself. Germany seems intent on dominating and destroying much of the European world. I thought they'd keep it to the Continent, but now they're encroaching on the British Isles. I don't see how we can remain neutral."

"Then our boys will really need God's help." Daniel grimly shook his head. "I've done some reading about the lethal gases and other modern killing machines the Germans are utilizing."

"I know. It's terrifying. And to think our young men are being recruited and trained all across the country. Just like these sweet boys marching down Main Street today. It's chilling to think that they're not much older than my Katy."

"As a member of the medical profession, it's chilling to think of the care many of them will need out there on the battlefield...and then afterward."

"Would you ever consider going over there—to help out?"

Daniel frowned. "It's crossed my mind. They'll need experienced physicians."

"Yes...I'm sure they will." She felt sad to think that Daniel might leave Sunset Cove. Partly for Mac and partly for herself. Of course, she and Katy still planned to return to Portland in the fall...so what difference did it really make?

Anna watched as the horse-drawn fire wagon rolled along behind the soldiers, loudly ringing its bells, signaling the end of the parade. "I wonder when Sunset Cove will get a real fire engine." She remembered the noisy modern trucks that Portland had recently acquired. "They're so much faster than the old wagons."

"Maybe you should ask Mayor Snyder." Daniel nudged her. "Speak of the devil." He nodded down to the crowded street.

"Where? What am I looking for?" She'd already seen the mayor waving from a fancy car early on in the parade.

"It seems that Mayor Snyder and one of your reporters are having some sort of disagreement in front of the bakery."

Anna peered down to see the mayor's creased brow and flushed face as he shook an angry finger at Wesley. Meanwhile Wesley looked slightly wide-eyed and taken aback. Not his usual, swaggering self. "Interesting. I wish I could hear what they're saying."

"Looks to me like Wesley's getting chewed out."

"Or perhaps he bit off more than he could chew."

Daniel chuckled. "Whatever the case, Wesley is tucking his tail between his legs."

Anna watched with interest as Wesley hurried down the street. "It actually gives me hope to see Wesley stood up to the mayor. If that's what he did. He usually comes across as one of Calvin Snyder's best buddies."

"Not today."

Anna wondered...had the mayor gotten wind of tomorrow's paper and their endorsement of Wally Morris? Or perhaps Wesley had just informed him, and Calvin was throwing a fit. Well, maybe that was a good thing. It was about time Wesley realized the mayor was a fair-weather friend. Perhaps this would be a much-needed jarring.

As the spectators began moving along, Anna thanked Daniel for sharing his terrace with her. "It really is a great place to watch the parade," she told him. "Although there's

❦

something to be said for standing down there, mingling with the others."

He nodded. "Yes, I've had similar thoughts. Maybe I'll do that for the next parade."

"Will you be attending the dance tonight?" she asked as she got ready to leave. She'd already told him of her plan to do surveillance with Jim.

"Only if you promise me a dance or two."

"Of course." She smiled. "I think that will simply make our little act more convincing." She spied Clara Krauss zigzagging through the crowd with a loaded basket on her arm. Had she actually been allowed to watch the parade today? Or had she simply been doing her grocery shopping? Anna quickly told Daniel good-bye then hurried down to the street to find out.

"Clara." Anna felt slightly breathless. "Did you enjoy the parade?"

"No. I didn't see it." Clara kept her eyes downward, still scurrying along.

"So how are you doing?" Anna asked as she kept pace with her.

"Not very well."

"Why?"

"Albert has not encouraged our friendship, Anna. He's forbidden me to see you."

"Forbidden you?" Anna demanded. "You're a grown woman, Clara. This is a free country. He has no right to—"

"He's my husband. I have to obey him."

"Clara, this is the twentieth century. Women have the vote. Albert does not own you. You're not a—"

"I'm sorry, Anna." Clara walked even faster. "But I need to get back to the shop. Lots of tourists in town. We'll be busy all day."

"But we're friends," Anna reminded her. "I want to help you."

"No, thank you."

"Clara." Anna's tone grew firm. "If Albert has threatened you in any manner, you should consider getting away from him. Like I told you, we can put you and the kids up at our house and—"

"Good day!" Clara was practically running.

Anna stopped chasing her and then glanced around, curious as to whether Albert was watching. That would certainly explain Clara's frosty change of temperament. But the street was so crowded with parade-goers, both townsfolk and tourists, that Anna couldn't spot him. Still, she knew that Albert must've said or done something awful to put this kind of fear into his wife. The dirty rat!

As Anna walked home, she felt a mixture of disturbing feelings. Fierce anger at Albert, real fear for Clara's welfare, maternal worry over Katy's possible involvement with AJ, and an unsettling concern for tonight's activities. It was one thing to talk about playing spies at the dance—but what if they really uncovered something terrible? Would they be putting themselves in danger?

CHAPTER 23

A nna and Jim had agreed to meet at the seaside park and enter the dance as a "couple" around eight. That way Katy and Anna could go together in Mac's Runabout. Naturally, Katy was the driver, but as she pulled into the lot near the seaside park, Anna informed her that someday she wanted Katy to teach her to drive. "In Portland, I was comfortable with public transportation, but I feel rather helpless depending on others for transportation here."

"Driving is so easy, Mother." Katy turned off the engine. "I'm sure you'll get the hang of it." As they got out of the car, Katy started giving her tips, promising to take her out to practice the next weekend.

"Hello, ladies." Jim came over to the car. Dressed in a nice dark suit, he looked unusually handsome. So much so that Anna felt slightly nervous as she introduced him to Katy. "Like I told you, we're here to cover a story," Anna reminded her daughter.

"If you say so." Katy sounded doubtful.

"That's the plan." Anna forced her smile to stay confident.

"But keep it under your hat," Jim warned.

"Mum's the word." Katy giggled and pointed across the

crowd. "And if you'll excuse me, I see the kids I'm meeting here."

Anna glanced over to see AJ and Ellen, as well as some other young people, all dressed in party clothes and eagerly waving toward Katy. "Have fun," Anna told her. "But remember what I said."

"I won't leave the park grounds," Katy assured her.

As Jim and Anna entered the park, the band was already situated in the gazebo and playing a lively ragtime song. "It looks like a good evening for fireworks." Anna glanced upward. "The sky is fairly clear." She peered out over the ocean to see clouds gathered on the horizon. "Looks like we'll have a nice sunset in a few minutes."

"I don't see any of our suspects here yet," Jim whispered. "But that's not surprising. Want to get some punch and sit for a bit?"

Anna agreed, and soon they were settled at a table alongside the dance area, visiting pleasantly and watching as some of the younger folks trotted and hopped to a ragtime number. Naturally, Katy was right there with them. After all, she was a good dancer and well versed in the latest steps. But to Anna's relief, she was not dancing with AJ tonight. Perhaps she'd taken Anna's warning to heart. Or maybe Albert had come down on AJ the same way he'd come down on his wife.

Anna and Jim sat opposite each other in a way that allowed them both a wide vantage point across both ends of the park. "I see the mayor coming," Anna told him after thirty minutes or so. She smiled in a way to suggest they were simply having a friendly conversation. "He's got his usual entourage with him."

Jim quietly listed them by last name, including Krauss and Kempton.

"No," Anna declared. "Wesley is *not* with them." She quickly explained the squabble she'd witnessed at the parade. "I have a feeling Wesley's not welcome in the mayor's elite group now."

"Interesting. Did you overhear anything?"

"No. I was too far away."

"So how do Calvin and his cohorts appear?"

"Well, if I'm not mistaken, the boys have been imbibing," she told him. "Flushed cheeks, silly grins, shiny eyes. Already some of them are heading for the dance floor."

"Then, I suggest we join them. Ready for some turkey trot?"

"Sounds more like a fox-trot song to me."

As they danced, Jim made sure to get them close enough to various suspects that Anna could almost see into their jackets, watching for suspiciously bulging pockets or flasks strapped to ankles. But, other than being somewhat lit up, all of them appeared to be traveling light. As the sun began to set, more lanterns were illuminated, and the dance floor grew more crowded. If this wasn't about espionage, Anna could imagine having a wonderful evening.

But Anna was distracted with curiosity about Albert. Not because he was dancing with a flashy young woman—that was nothing new—but because of the way he was talking to her. The way his eyes were narrowed and he was looking around, it seemed as if he was disclosing a secret. And then he began edging his partner toward the sidelines.

Anna gave Jim a nudge, directing him toward the sidelines too. As they danced, she watched Albert lead the woman away from the lamplight and into the shadows. They were obviously heading for the outskirts of the park, or perhaps down to the beach. Whatever was going on, he was up to no good, and Anna would like nothing more than to see him get caught.

"I need to check my dance card." Anna paused to make a quick note. Then Jim, following her cue, danced them over to where they'd already spotted the plainclothes detective, loitering by the punch table. Anna slipped the note to Wade Brooks as she took a cup of punch. Then after she drank it, she and Jim began to dance to the next song. But to her dismay, Albert was already back on the dance floor—with a different woman this time. That man was so slippery...he was slimy!

But then he did the exact same thing again, leading the second woman away from the dance area, out of the light and into the shadows. Whatever was going on back there, she hoped that Chief Rollins was getting his men gathered and ready to find out. It would make a great headline for the newspaper. She could just imagine going into the office and yelling: *Stop the presses!*

Rand walked over and tapped Jim's shoulder. "Excuse me, but—"

"Perfect timing." Jim nodded politely as he handed Anna over. Then as Anna danced with Rand, Jim disappeared into the shadows on the sidelines too.

"I do hope he'll be careful," she told Rand.

"Trouble brewing?" he asked with a discreet smile.

"I think so." She tried not to be obvious as she peered about the dance floor, noticing that several others—names on their suspect list and some who were not—seemed to be pulling a similar disappearing act.

After a couple dances with Rand, Daniel made an appearance, and she danced with him. But it still bothered her that Jim wasn't back. What if he'd stepped into a rat's nest? Bootleggers and rumrunners were a rough crowd. They wouldn't take kindly to a newsman snooping about.

Anna jumped as the music suddenly stopped, and Mayor Snyder stepped up to the gazebo with the megaphone, shouting out a loud "Hello!" She felt certain something was terribly wrong, but then he simply made a welcome speech, which sounded more like another impromptu campaign speech. The crowd politely clapped and then he announced it was time for the fireworks to begin.

"Make yourselves comfortable," he boomed, "and we will dim the dance floor lights then start the show. After the last of the fireworks, the band will play a final song, and we'll all call it a night. Happy Independence Day, everyone!"

As the band played "Yankee Doodle," the lamps were darkened, and people found places to sit, either at the tables or on chairs that were lined up along the bluff or on blankets in the sand. Flanked by Daniel and Rand, Anna sat on one of the white chairs and tried not to worry about Jim. Instead, she prayed a quick, silent prayer for his safety.

Then suddenly the dark sky over the beach lit up with blasts of sparkling, bright light and flashes of red and blue, followed by earsplitting booms and the crowd's enthusiastic oohs and aahs and enthused applause. Anna still wondered about Jim and what Chief Rollins was doing, but distracted by the beautiful display, her worrisome thoughts were momentarily pushed aside.

When the fireworks show ended, a few of the dance floor lamps were relit, and the band played one last slow song. "Since I only got one dance, I don't feel out of line asking for another," Daniel told her.

Rand just waved a hand, and Anna didn't object. As she danced with Daniel, she scanned the crowd for Katy and was relieved to see her still with the young crowd. Although

Ellen was there too, AJ appeared to be absent. Not that Anna cared particularly. Also absent, it seemed, were the mayor and Albert and a number of their questionable cohorts... and the police. Suddenly Anna was extremely curious—had arrests been made? And more importantly, was Jim okay?

She voiced her concerns to Daniel. "It feels like something is up, but I don't know how to find out."

"Well, if anyone has been injured, I might find out before the night is over." The music stopped, and they went over to where Rand was waiting.

"Maybe you should get home," Anna told Daniel. "In case someone calls you for help."

"Being that I'm on foot, it might take a bit."

"Need a ride, Doc?" Rand offered.

"Wonderful." Daniel smiled. "Thank you."

Daniel and Rand walked Anna and Katy to their car. "Will you call me at Mac's house?" Anna asked Daniel. "I mean, if you hear of anything, uh, newsworthy?"

"Sure, if you like. But it could be quite late."

"No problem," she assured him. "I'm a newswoman. And if I have to stop the presses for tomorrow's paper, I will."

"Exciting stuff." Rand sounded slightly sarcastic. "Let me know if you need any legal counsel. Don't want any libel suits."

"I'll keep that in mind." She nudged Katy. "Let's get going."

As Katy drove them home, she was naturally curious.

Without going into all the details, Anna filled her in. "I'm a bit worried about Jim," she confessed as they were going into the house. "I hope he didn't get in over his head." She turned off the gas lamp in the foyer.

"I think some of your suspicions about AJ were right," Katy whispered as they tiptoed up the stairs.

"Why's that?"

"I smelled alcohol on his breath tonight."

"Oh...I wondered about that."

"I refused to dance with him because of it."

"Good for you." Anna paused on the landing but felt dismayed to see the sadness in Katy's eyes.

"I guess. But I know I hurt his feelings. And the truth is, I feel sort of sorry for him, Mother."

"Why's that?"

"I don't know. I mean, I know he's making some bad choices. But his dad is such a bad example. It almost seems that AJ doesn't have a chance. Ellen is very worried about him too."

Anna patted Katy's shoulder. "I'm worried about Clara too. I tried to talk to her today, but Albert seems to be keeping her under his thumb."

"What a sad way to live."

"I told Clara that she and her children could come here if she needed to get away from Albert."

Katy's eyes grew wide. "Really, Mother? You told her that?"

Anna just nodded.

"You honestly think she's in that much danger?"

"I don't know. But she seems so frightened that I naturally assumed the worst."

Katy hugged her. "That was so kind of you, Mother."

"Of course, it could be tricky if that really happened—I mean, if they needed to leave Albert. I'm not sure how Mac would feel."

"Grandpa is a sweetheart," Katy declared. "He'd probably welcome them with open arms."

Anna nodded, but the truth was, she felt uncertain. Mac may have changed a lot in recent years, but she couldn't imagine him opening his home up to just anyone. She told Katy good night and hurried into her room. She wanted to stay close to the phone, and fortunately Mac had taken the incentive to have one installed up here.

Instead of getting ready for bed, Anna changed out of her pretty evening dress and into a pair of old corduroy trousers and slightly moth-chewed fisherman knit sweater that she found in the ragbag last week. She'd salvaged the clothes initially because she remembered her father wearing these very togs when she was a child. It was his Saturday outfit for playing on the beach, and she couldn't stand to see them thrown away.

So she washed them out, mended the sweater, then actually tried the items on. The sweater was surprisingly comfortable, and with a belt cinched through the trousers, they weren't a bad fit. Oh, she didn't plan to go out in public in this ensemble, but for some reason it was comforting to have them. She knew that some women wore trousers—for riding or performing tasks where skirts were impractical— but for the most part society would not accept a woman in men's clothing. It was scandalous. Perhaps that was one reason she enjoyed them. Now all she needed was a cigar to go with them. Not that she really wanted to smoke, but the idea of that image always set her giggling.

Anna jumped to the sound of the phone ringing and hurried to answer it. "Hello?"

"Anna, this is Daniel. I've got Jim here in my office and—"

"Is he hurt?" she demanded.

"Yes. But he'll be okay. He really wants to talk to you, but I can't allow him to move. He's lost some blood and—"

"I'm coming over there," she declared. "Tell Jim I'm on my way." Then without giving him a chance to question her, she hung up the receiver and hurried out of the sleeping house. It wasn't until she was on the darkened street that two concerns hit her—first of all, would she be in danger out here by herself? And secondly, she was wearing trousers!

CHAPTER 24

To Anna's relief, Daniel didn't even mention her strange attire, and Jim was in too much pain to care. Fortunately for Anna, the pain medication that Daniel had just administered hadn't kicked in and knocked Jim out yet, so he was able to give Anna the whole story. Or most of it.

Jim had discovered another celebration going on during the fireworks show. Naturally it involved alcohol. Although Jim had tried to remain an outside observer, someone had jumped him from behind...with a knife. During the scuffle, Jim received a significant gash in his shoulder, which Daniel was just about to stitch up.

"Chief Rollins and some of his boys showed up," Jim continued to tell her. "Several arrests were made."

"Anyone we know?" she asked hopefully, focusing on the notepad she'd borrowed from Daniel instead of staring at Jim's shoulder.

"I'm not sure who got taken in. Must've been a couple dozen there. Some locals, some not." He winced. "Call the chief...for more information." Jim's words were becoming a bit slurred. Probably from the medication.

"I will." She paused from writing. "Anything else I should know?"

"Ask...chief." He closed his eyes.

"He's out," Daniel told her. "I'll finish stitching him up and keep him here overnight. You can talk to him in the morning."

"Yes." She pocketed her notes. "Thanks for calling me." She stole one last glance at Jim, feeling relief that he seemed to be out of pain. "Now, I've got to go stop the presses. This will be tomorrow's front page story."

Anna hurried out and down to the newspaper office, letting herself in through the back door, which the fellows left unlocked while printing. She could hear the press going and felt a tiny bit of regret for the paper that would be wasted, but this story was too big to wait until Saturday's edition. "Stop the presses!" she shouted to be heard over the sound of the machines. "We've got a big story!"

Leroy came around a corner with a startled expression, then stared at her as if she had two heads. "What's going on?" he asked.

"I said, '*Stop the presses!*'" she yelled again. "There was a raid tonight. Jim Stafford's been stabbed. And Chief Rollins has arrested several people and—"

"Hey, Henry," Leroy shouted. "Stop the presses!"

As the machinery ground to a halt, Anna explained to the fellows about the situation. She pointed to Leroy. "Can you get one of the typesetters over here? I'll get the stories ready. And then I can help set the type."

"I can help too," Leroy assured her.

"Great. I'll be in my office." As soon as she got out the typewriter, she called Chief Rollins. Although she was disappointed to learn that the arrests had only been out-of-towners, she was glad to get real names.

"The local boys must've got a tip-off somehow," the chief told her. "By the time we got there, they'd skedaddled. But they left plenty of evidence behind."

Anna told him about the interesting things she and Jim had observed at the dance, giving him names. "I'm sure they were involved. And if I'm not mistaken, Albert Krauss is at the center of it. Unfortunately, I think his son AJ is too."

"Well, I want to do some more investigating, and I'll start bringing in folks for questioning tomorrow. I don't want to put the cart before the horse. But I wouldn't mind getting some of this wrapped up before the state police step in. I'd like you and Jim to make statements sometime tomorrow. By the way, how is Jim?"

"Dr. Hollister says he'll be okay. He's stitching him up right now." They exchanged a bit more information then Anna told him she needed to get to work. As she hung up, she knew this was going to be an long night. But she also knew it would be worth it. The good citizens of Sunset Cove needed to know what was going on behind their backs. And even though none of this reflected directly on the mayor, people could draw their own conclusions for now. Hopefully, Chief Rollins would take the case to the next level in the days to come.

The sun was just coming up when the last piece of type was set. Anna looked at her blackened fingers, remembering how she used to get teased for having "printer's ink in her blood" when she was young. Apparently it was still true.

"Ready to go," she told Leroy. "Let's get this paper out."

As she went through the building, she noticed the big clock in the editorial section. It wasn't quite six yet. If she made a quick getaway, she might make it home without being observed. Spying a man's hat hanging on the rack by the front door, she decided to borrow it—just in case. Shoving her hair into it, she scurried out and hurried toward home. The only person she saw was the milkman, and he didn't even seem to notice her as his wagon rolled down Main Street. Feeling relieved and exhausted, Anna slipped into the house and up to her room, where she nearly fell asleep in the bathtub before crawling into bed in the hopes of catching an hour or two of sleep.

When Anna woke up, it was to Katy's voice. "Mother," she exclaimed. "Look at this!" Katy held up the front page of the newspaper. "Grandpa is fit to be tied. Do you know anything about this?"

Anna tried to shake the cobwebs from her head as she pulled on her dressing gown. "Yes, of course."

"Then you better go downstairs and tell Grandpa. He's worried that someone went nuts, and the newspaper will go out of business over a libel suit."

"He doesn't need to worry," she assured Katy. "It's all true."

Anna went down to find Mac still fuming at the breakfast table. Before he could ask her what happened, she began to explain about the whole thing. His eyes grew wider and wider until she finally finished her story.

"You stopped the presses?" Mac had an astonished expression.

"Yes." She smiled. "Isn't that what you would've done?"

"Yeah." He blinked then nodded.

"You must be exhausted after working all night." Katy put a sympathetic hand on Anna's shoulder. "Maybe you should go back to bed."

Anna glanced at the clock. "I should go call Daniel and

see how Jim is doing. And then I need to go speak to Chief Rollins." She kissed Mac's cheek. "Sorry to catch you by surprise like that. But it all happened so fast."

"While we were all sleeping," Katy added.

"Yeah." Mac's eyes twinkled as he picked up a piece of toast. "It has begun."

"I just wish Chief Rollins had been able to catch some of the locals." Anna poured herself a cup of coffee to take back to her room. "But at least he's got some solid evidence now. Hopefully the other pieces will fall into place." She reached for a piece of bacon and started to go.

"You be careful," Mac warned.

"Don't worry, I will." She offered him a smile and took another step toward the door.

"My hat." Mac pointed to the derby she'd borrowed from the newspaper office, looking out of place on the sideboard. "Where did you find it?"

"You must've left it at work." She chuckled. "So I brought it home for you, Mac." She wondered what he'd say about his daughter traipsing around town in the middle of the night, wearing his discarded clothes. But some things really were better left unsaid.

After learning that Daniel had taken Jim home to rest, Anna went to speak to Chief Rollins. But the news was not good. After he'd interrogated last night's rabble-rousers, he realized that all he could pin on them was possession of alcohol and public drunkenness.

"Just some college boys, over here for a good time," he explained. "We'll fine them and keep them in the drunk-tank for a couple days."

"But can they identify the men who sold them alcohol?" Anna asked.

"They claim they didn't know them and couldn't see well enough in the dark to even describe them today."

"Do you think they're lying?"

"Hard to say. They were three sheets to the wind when we picked them up during the fireworks show. Probably the reason they didn't hightail it with the others."

"But Jim and I both feel certain Albert Krauss and his buddies were involved," Anna reminded him. "Can't you—"

"I've got them coming in for questioning this morning— separately—hoping I can get them to incriminate each other." He held up today's newspaper. "Maybe your front page will make someone nervous, make 'em think we're pulling in the dragnet...maybe someone will stumble over a statement."

"I sure hope so." Anna stood. "I'll let you get on with your work."

"Keep me posted if you learn anything new. I haven't scheduled Wesley Kempton to come in yet. I know you didn't observe him there last night, but I'll be curious to hear his response to all this."

"I plan to talk to him today." As she exited the chief's office, Anna noticed Albert Krauss waiting in the hallway. Realizing it was too late to avoid him, she decided to act nonchalant, striding toward him with a fixed smile and stiff greeting. He responded with a chilly hello.

"Give Clara my best," she said cheerfully. His narrowed eyes made her wonder if she'd rattled him. Hopefully enough to make him slip up when he spoke to the chief.

As Anna walked back to the newspaper office, she made a plan for talking to Wesley. Instead of sounding suspicious or accusatory, she would simply express her concerns...

and study his reaction. After greeting Virginia and quickly answering questions about last night's excitement, Anna went back to speak to Jeanette. "Jim won't be in today. I'm sure you've read the news by now." She tapped the paper on Jeanette's desk. "He's recovering at home and should be okay." Anna lowered her voice, instructing Jeanette to send Wesley in to see her.

Anna had just finished straightening up the office from last night's writing frenzy when Wesley cracked open her door. She welcomed him in but could see he was uneasy. "Have a seat." She tried to sound warmer than she felt.

"That was quite a front page you ran today," he said as he sat. "Impressive."

"Thank you." She sensed insincerity in his tone but forced a smile anyway.

"Hope it's not just a tempest in a teapot."

Suppressing her aggravation, she reminded herself of her goal. "I want to talk to you as a friend."

"A friend?" His brows arched with suspicion.

"My father believed in you, Wesley. That's why he invested so much of himself in you. He saw your talent, he hoped for the best for you."

"Yes...*and*?"

"And...he and I are both concerned."

"Concerned for what?" He gave her a blank look.

"For you. We know you associate with some questionable characters and, as you may have guessed, the law is preparing to come down on some illegal activities."

"That's not what I hear."

"What have you heard?" She kept her tone light and impartial.

He shrugged. "Just that Chief Rollins doesn't have a shred of real evidence."

"Interesting. I've heard just the opposite."

"Maybe you're talking to the wrong people."

"Or maybe you are." Anna was tempted to point out how she'd observed him receiving what looked like a tongue-lashing from the mayor. Instead she held up a hand. "Honestly, I don't want this to turn into an argument. I'd simply hoped to encourage you to cut ties with certain people, Wesley, before it's too late."

He pursed his lips. Was he considering her words...or getting ready for another witty comeback?

"I want to ask you something." She paused, hoping to get his full attention. "And I'd appreciate an honest answer."

"What?" He looked slightly off guard.

"There was a file in Mac's office. It's missing, and he would like it back."

Wesley's brow creased. "I don't have any of Mac's files."

"I can't believe it just vanished into thin air." She studied his response. "Perhaps it got misplaced and mixed in with some of your things during the recent moves."

"Feel free to look around if you want." His tone sounded irritated...or worried.

"No, that's not necessary." She acted unconcerned. "Mac doesn't really need the file. He obviously knows what was in it. He just didn't want it to get into the wrong hands." She watched him closely. His face was stony, but his hands were fidgeting. She knew he had it.

"Anything else?" He straightened his tie.

"No, no, I don't think so." She waited, wondering if he would inquire about their assistant editor in chief's health.

"Then I should probably get back to work." He stood.

"Right. With Jim out, we'll all have to cover for him."

"Oh...how is Jim?" He paused with a hand on the doorknob.

"He'll be all right."

"Your article didn't mention any suspects. Does Jim have any idea who attacked him...or why?"

Anna peered curiously at Wesley. Did he know something about this? "I think Jim has some suspicions, but he's been too weak to talk much. Chief Rollins is following up on some leads today. If anything comes out, I may do a story for Saturday's paper." Anna hoped he didn't see through her bluff. "By the way, what are you working on right now?"

"A story about the new grade school that's being built."

"Well, I'd like you to set that aside." She locked eyes with him. "Start working on a story about the risks and consequences of rum-running along the Oregon Coast. How it impacts local residents. Get some statistics and projections. Kind of an information piece. It will go nicely alongside any other stories that might pop up before the week is over."

"Sure, if that's what you want." He scowled. "But it's a waste of time."

"A waste of time?" She felt her hackles rising.

"Everyone knows this whole prohibition business isn't going to be around for long. At least half of the town, maybe more, oppose prohibition anyway. Why bother getting them all upset with a stupid article?"

"Because rum-running is a crime, Wesley. And we should be covering it."

"A victimless crime."

"You're entitled to your opinion. But the law is the law. And right now the law prohibits selling, buying, possessing, or imbibing in alcoholic beverages."

"So you want me to write about an unenforceable law with victimless crimes. Fine. You're the boss."

"That's right." She firmly nodded. "And take a good look

around for Mac's file. Just in case it's slipped between some of your things and been overlooked." She forced a stiff smile as he exited, but as soon as the door closed, her smile faded. Not only was that man stubborn and obnoxious, she felt certain he had that file. And he obviously knew something about what was in it.

But maybe if she kept pressing him, dropping hints, as well as reminding him of Mac's concerns and hopes for him...maybe he would come to his senses. If not, well, maybe Mac could handle it. He seemed to be getting stronger every day. And his speech had improved some. Or else she'd just gotten used to the stuttering and stammering. But really, this was his problem, not hers.

Anna worked for as long as she could, but by early afternoon, her brain felt foggy and sleep deprived. She told Jeanette to hold down the fort and then stopped by Virginia's desk to ask her to check in on Jim.

"I already did," Virginia reassured her. "He claims he's feeling better but sounded tired. I had the hotel restaurant send him over some soup and a few other things to nourish him back to health."

"Bless you." Anna clasped her hand.

"Now you go home and get some rest."

As Anna walked through town, she wondered how Chief Rollins's investigation was going. She hoped and prayed he was making progress. Otherwise, it seemed likely that the scoundrels would assume they'd outwitted the law and grow even sneakier. They'd probably go deeper underground...and become harder than ever to catch, wreaking more havoc.

As she turned toward the house, Anna questioned herself. What if they'd been too eager and jumped the gun last night? What if they'd been more patient? Perhaps Jim wouldn't have gotten hurt. She cringed to think about where Jim might be right now if he hadn't fought off his attacker. Maybe it wasn't the criminals who should be scared right now...maybe it was the folks who were trying to stop them.

CHAPTER 25

By the end of the week, Anna's enthusiasm over seeing justice win was almost completely gone. Not only had Chief Rollins's investigation grown stone cold, Oregon State Police had stepped in and, according to the chief, things would slow down even more now. But at least Jim was up and moving. And they'd gotten out a decent Saturday paper. Not with the exciting headlines she'd hoped for, but respectable just the same.

Even Wesley had produced an informative piece about the impact of illegal activities on small communities. Although he'd crossed the line into editorializing by stating that if prohibition was abolished, most of these problems would be eliminated. But Anna had simply deleted that part. Perhaps that opinion was true on some levels, but the law was the law, and unless the law changed, the newspaper would support it.

Katy was up to her eyebrows planning a festive fundraiser for Wally Morris. They'd agreed on a pie social/dance at the grange on Saturday night, and Katy had recruited everyone and anyone to help—including Ellen Krauss. Although Anna felt certain Ellen's father would disapprove, she suspected he was unaware.

But when Anna caught the two girls just heading out with an armload of freshly painted fundraiser posters, she felt concerned. "How's your mother doing?" she asked Ellen in an effort to stall her.

"I, uh, I guess she's fine." Ellen looked uncertain.

"I assume she's working at the fish shop today." Anna tried to sound nonchalant. "I suppose your father's there too?"

"No. Dad got the big boat running and went out early this morning. AJ too. They'll be out all day, might not get home until tomorrow night."

"Oh?" Anna nodded. "I think I'll go pick up some fish today. Maybe I could visit with your mother for a bit."

Ellen looked slightly hopeful. "I, uh, I think she might like that."

Anna wasn't so sure, but she was determined to try—and the timing seemed perfect. So she grabbed a shopping basket from the kitchen and hurried toward Harbor Drive, checking the docks just to be sure that the Krausses' big boat wasn't there.

"Clara." Anna smiled brightly as she entered the dimly lit fish shop. "Ellen said it might be a good time to visit you." She glanced around to see that no one else was shopping just now.

"Oh, Anna." Clara lips pressed together in a flat line, but her eyes seemed to brighten just a bit.

"Listen." Anna lowered her voice. "I know that Albert doesn't approve of you speaking with me. And if it makes you feel better, don't say another word. Just answer my questions with a nod or a shake of your head. That way if

Albert asks if you've been talking to me, you won't have to lie."

Clara nodded.

"Are you doing all right?"

Clara gave a slight shrug.

"Is Albert treating you badly?"

Clara's chin dipped slightly.

"Are you afraid of him?"

She barely nodded.

"Would he be angry to know I'm here right now?"

This time she nodded vigorously.

"Are you safe with him?"

Clara frowned, cautiously nodding.

"Have you considered my offer to help you?"

Clara pursed her lips with a furrowed brow.

Anna felt torn but knew she had to ask one more question. "Clara." She lowered her voice again. "Is Albert involved in rum-running?"

Clara's eyes were filled with fear as she slowly nodded.

"Don't worry," Anna assured her. "I won't repeat that to anyone. I felt fairly certain." She went around the counter to give Clara a hug. "I really do want to help you. I wish you'd let me. I know Ellen is frightened of Albert too. I can hear it in her voice. And Katy is worried that Albert will get angry if he learns Ellen has been helping with Wally Morris's campaign."

"Ellen is involved with that?" Clara's hand flew up to her mouth.

"Yes. And I'm sure the word will get back to him... eventually. Right now, the girls are hanging posters in town, so I'm afraid Albert is sure to hear about it."

"Oh no."

"Please, Clara, consider leaving him. For your sake and

for Ellen's. If Albert is rum-running, he must be involved with some unsavory fellows. It's likely that both you and Ellen are in real danger here."

Clara slowly nodded. "I need a little more time," she said quietly. "Some business things to attend to first."

"I understand." Anna patted her back. "Just don't wait too long."

"I won't."

Anna hugged her again. "Good."

After a relatively peaceful and restful weekend, Anna was ready to get back at it on Monday. Her new plan was to act like it was business as usual. She wouldn't bring up anything about the recent investigation and developments. Perhaps if the criminal element believed the newspaper's interest had waned, they would let their guard down again. Or maybe Anna was just tired of thinking about the whole thing. Sunset Cove was such a sweet little town, and most of the people here were the salt of the earth. Why spoil her visit here by obsessing over the criminal element?

As part of her more positive outlook, Anna decided to interview Wally Morris and write a nice long article about him. By now everyone knew that the paper was endorsing Wally—no surprise since he used to work for the paper. And in fairness, Anna knew she'd need to write an article for Calvin too. But that could come later, and naturally it would be written with candid honesty.

Jim was back at work by midweek. Although his typing was slowed down a bit by his bad shoulder, he still managed to contribute, and Anna felt relieved to have her right-hand man again. She knew that when she and Katy returned to Portland at summer's end, which was coming fast, Jim would need to step into the editor in chief's role. Perhaps it was selfish of her not to allow him to do so now, but she was enjoying her responsibilities. And she felt that Mac appreciated it too.

Anna went to interview Wally on Thursday afternoon. Her plan was to write the piece tomorrow and run it on the front page on Saturday. Convenient timing since his fundraiser was the same evening. Anna had known Wally and Thelma for as long as she could remember. In many ways, they'd been like family. But she hadn't been in their home in years.

"Come in, come in," Thelma welcomed her.

Anna glanced around. "It looks just the same."

"Well, yes, I'm not given to changing much." Thelma gave her a sheepish smile. "I guess I can be a stick in the mud. That's what Wally says sometimes." She chuckled as Wally joined them.

"I happen to love your house, and I'm glad it's the same," Anna assured her. "It takes me straight back to my childhood."

"Well, if you're a stick in the mud, you're the prettiest one around." Wally winked at Thelma. "And don't forget that you gave in to me about getting that new car." He turned to Anna. "Did you see it yet?"

She nodded. "Yes. In the Founders Day parade. Very nice."

"As soon as this fundraiser is over, Thelma and I plan to drive down the beach to California to take a gander at the old redwoods down there. You know that some of them are more than a thousand years old?"

"I've heard that."

"How about I get you some refreshments," Thelma offered, "while you two sit down and visit."

Wally led Anna to the sitting room. "I know I've told you this before, Anna, but you have raised yourself one mighty fine daughter."

"Thank you." Anna sat down and removed her notebook from her briefcase. "She's very fond of you and Thelma too."

"She's smart as a whip and pretty as can be. You must be very proud."

"Katy is a treasure." Anna pulled out her pen and grinned. "But I'm not here to talk about her."

"Just one more thing." Wally raised a finger. "It concerns me that she spends time with that Krauss boy."

Anna nodded somberly. "Katy and I have discussed that very thing. I think she's trying to avoid him."

Wally frowned. "Then you must not know she's fishing with him right now."

Anna felt a wave of concern. "Really?"

"AJ and Ellen stopped by here about an hour ago to ask her to go with them."

"Ellen was with them?"

"Yes." He nodded. "And Ellen is a good girl. But that AJ... I'm not so sure."

"I'm in agreement there." Anna sighed. "But not much we can do about it now." Hopefully this news wouldn't distract her from the interview. She opened the notebook to her pre-written questions. "Should we get started?"

She spent a good hour at the Morrises' and, although most of what she discovered wasn't news to her, she felt that the good people of Sunset Cove deserved a solid reminder of what a fine and outstanding man Wally Morris had been and still was. She would also point out that although Wally was old, he was experienced and wise and still full of life. During the recent years of his retirement, he'd been involved in his church and various volunteer activities. He was always looking for new ways to help his community. If the voters couldn't see why Wally was their best choice by far, they were simply not paying attention.

Anna thanked Wally and Thelma and gathered up her notes then headed for home. She'd told her secretary not to expect her back, but Anna knew the reason she was eager to get home was concern for Katy. She did not like hearing that Katy was out with AJ. Never mind that Ellen was with them. Anna simply did not feel that AJ was trustworthy.

On her way home, she ran into Rand on Main Street. After exchanging a brief greeting, he questioned her. "You look upset. Is something wrong?"

She confessed her worry over Katy being with AJ. "I was just wishing I'd learned to drive. Katy offered to teach me, but we just didn't get around to it."

"How would being able to drive help?" he asked.

"Then I could take Mac's Runabout down to the beach and drive up and down to see if I could spot them."

He chuckled. "And what good would that do? You'd be on land, and they'd be on water."

She frowned. "I know. But I suppose it would make me feel better."

"I know." He grinned. "I'll teach you to drive. We'll take Mac's car down to the beach, and you can have your first driving lesson."

"Really?" She brightened. "You have time to do that?"

"No more appointments today." He nodded. "Let's go."

Before long, they were down on the beach, where, with the tide out, there was plenty of space for Anna to practice driving. She became so distracted with working the clutch and brakes and throttle that she nearly forgot about Katy.

"Hey, turn to your left," Rand suddenly commanded.

"What?"

"Just veer off to the left, go to the other side of that big driftwood log, Anna. *Hurry.*"

Without questioning him, she did as told, impressed that she could actually do it without too much trouble. "What's wrong?" she asked as the car stopped.

Rand reached for the binoculars that Anna had brought along in the hopes she'd spy AJ's boat, then hopped out of the car. Standing behind the big driftwood, he peered southward down the beach. "Come here," he called to her. "You need to see this."

"What?" She joined him, looking in the same direction that he was fixed on. "That boat?"

"Yes. It's one of the Krauss boats."

"Do you see Katy?"

"No."

"AJ or Ellen?"

"No."

"You're sure?"

"All I see are three fishermen. And something even more interesting."

"What?" She reached for her binoculars. "Let me see." She pulled the boat into view in time to see it disappearing into the shore. "Where's it going?"

"That's Buckman Cove," he explained.

"I've heard of it before. Is that a good place to fish?"

"No, but it's a good place to pick up or deliver illegal goods."

"Why's that?"

"It's pretty private and almost inaccessible."

"So what do you think they're doing?" She looked at Rand.

"I think they're either picking something up or dropping something off for someone else."

"Rum-running?"

"Rum, whisky, gin…you name it, they're probably running it."

"Where do you think it's coming from?"

"Canada maybe, by way of Washington, since they're dry now. I hear Washington has been supplied by some of Canada's best liquor along the coastline up there."

"Or this could be from California," she suggested. "That's even closer."

"That's true," he agreed.

"Is there a Coast Guard station nearby?"

"Tillamook. But that's a fair distance."

"Which makes Sunset Cove ideal for rum-running."

He nodded. "Very ideal."

She lifted the binoculars again. "And you're positive that Katy wasn't on that boat? Or Ellen or AJ?"

"I didn't see them. And, think about it, Anna. Would AJ be that stupid? To take the editor's daughter out to do some rum-running? And in broad daylight too?"

"Good point." She kept looking. "That'd be incredibly dumb. Hey, the boat is coming out again. Pretty fast stop, don't you think?"

"How long does it take to deliver or, more likely, pick up goods?"

"You're right. And I can see some crates on the deck of the boat. Do you think they were there before?"

"Let me see." He reached for the binoculars. "If I were a betting man, I'd say those crates contain alcohol. And a lot of it."

"So where will they take it?" she asked.

"Right now it looks like they're heading out to sea.

Probably to pretend they've been out fishing...in case anyone happens to be watching. Then they'll probably slip back into the harbor after dark and unload."

"In the Krauss warehouse." Anna grabbed his arm. "Let's go tell Chief Rollins. He and his men could be waiting for them there."

"Good idea."

"Maybe you should drive," she suggested. "I want to get there quickly and without a crash."

He chuckled. "Good thinking."

As Rand drove up the beach, Anna began to form the news story in her head. "I've got to be there too," she told Rand. "To get the full story."

He slowed down to turn onto the access road. "I don't think that's a good idea, Anna."

"Why not?" she demanded.

"You must've covered stories about organized crime in Portland. You have to know how dangerous it is to intervene or take them by surprise."

"But I'm a reporter and—"

"And you saw what happened to Jim. He's a reporter too. And he only spied on some partygoers. He wasn't trying to apprehend a big shipment of illegal booze. Those boys on that boat are probably heavily armed—and I'm not talking knives."

"But I want to be there—" Anna suddenly stopped. "What about Katy?"

"What do you mean? What about Katy?"

"What if AJ's boat comes in around the same time as the rumrunner boat? Wally said they'd gotten a late start. It's likely they'll come in late too."

Rand pulled onto Main Street and parked. "What do you want to do?"

"I don't know. Let me think."

"I know we should inform the chief," he spoke slowly, "but your concern for Katy is justified. Anyone in the harbor during a raid like that could be in danger."

Anna bit her lip. If only Katy had heeded her warning! With so many things to admire about her daughter, her headstrong independence wasn't always one of them. "We can't tell the chief until Katy is safely home," she finally said.

Rand nodded. "Agreed."

"And another thing...I need time to tell Clara about it. I've told her that she and Ellen can stay with us if they need to. If there's any shooting at the warehouse, I don't want them there."

"Then you shouldn't waste any time in warning her. That is, if you want to see these thugs caught with the goods and put away for a while. My guess is they won't let their booze sit in one place for too long."

"I've heard that before." Still, Anna felt torn. As badly as she wanted the rumrunners caught, she didn't want any innocent bystanders to get hurt. Especially her own daughter. This called for caution.

CHAPTER 26

Anna insisted Rand wait in the car while she went into the fish shop to speak to Clara. But to Anna's surprise and dismay, Albert was lurking by the back door. And he didn't look the least pleased to see her.

"I told Mac I'd stop by on my way home from work to see if you have any salmon today." She looked into her friend's eyes, hoping that she could convey her concerns but knowing it was probably not working.

"Nope." Albert came forward, shaking his head with a suspicious look. "Haven't had much luck with salmon since early June. Probably won't see many until the September run."

"Is that unusual?"

"Nope. Salmon don't run much in midsummer." He made a harrumph sound. "Thought you'd know that. Didn't you grow up here in Sunset Cove?"

"That's right, but I was never much of a fisherman." She feigned an innocent smile. "Anyway, I hear that Ellen and Katy went out with AJ today. Maybe Katy will catch something to bring home."

Albert's brow creased as he turned to his wife. "You let the girls go out with AJ today, Clara?"

Her eyes grew wide. "I, uh, I didn't know they went out. No one told me any—"

"That figures."

"Any idea when they'll be back?" Anna directed this to Clara, trying to keep her tone even. "Should we wait dinner?"

"Guess that's up to you," Albert grumbled. "Clara, I need you in back—that is, if you're not too busy."

"Well, thank you." Anna turned and left. She was clearly not welcome here. And the news that Katy and Ellen had gone out with AJ was not welcome either—and that was concerning.

Anna told Rand what she'd discovered as he drove her home. "Now I really don't know what to do." She frowned as he parked Mac's car in the carriage house. "How can I tell the chief...until Katy is safely home?"

"Good question." Rand opened the door for her and helped her out of the car. "What if I spend some time down at the wharf? I could keep an eye on things and make sure that Katy comes directly home as soon as AJ's boat comes in."

"Oh, would you do that?"

"Sure. I'll take my camera with me and pretend to be doing some photography." He looked up. "The light's actually pretty good right now."

"Thank you so much. I'll be on pins and needles until Katy is safely home." Anna thought of something. "What if I wrote you a little note," she suggested, "that you could pass to Clara if you get the chance—would you be willing?"

"Certainly. In fact, I might even park my car down there.

Just in case Clara and Ellen feel like going for a little spin with Katy and me."

"You mean you'd help them to get out of there?" Anna dug her pen and notepad from her briefcase and quickly scribbled an urgent note to Clara.

Rand grinned. "Just like your knight in shining armor?" She chuckled, then grew sober. "Be careful though."

"Count on it."

Anna folded the note and handed it to him. "I didn't sign my name or mention your name on this. Just in case Albert gets ahold of it."

"You're a clever one, Anna McDowell."

"Thank you." She made a nervous smile. "And thank you for helping us. Now, I better go inside and see how Mac feels about sharing his home with Clara and Ellen."

As she entered the house, Anna heard the sound of Lucille's laughter coming from the front room. Fighting back her irritation, Anna decided to cut right to the chase with Mac. "I'm sorry to interrupt." She glanced about as she entered the room. "But I need to speak to Mac about something very urgent."

Mac's brows arched. "Yeah? Go ahead."

Anna glanced nervously at Lucille. She really didn't want her present for this conversation.

"Anna," Mac said slowly. "You can trust your mother."

"That's right," Lucille told her. "Despite what you may think, I can be trusted."

Anna decided to be selective about how much she revealed, simply telling Mac that Clara and Ellen might need a safe place to stay. "I told Clara they could stay with us here, but I want to be sure you don't mind."

"Stay here?" Mac frowned.

"Yes." Anna nodded. "I'll give them my room and take the little room up—"

"That's your room." Mac firmly shook his head. "Why do they need—"

"I think they could be in very serious danger," Anna declared.

"With that scoundrel husband of Clara's?" Lucille asked.

Anna turned to her in surprise. "What do you know about this?"

"My housekeeper is a bit of a gossip," Lucille confessed. "Sally has mentioned concerns about our Katy spending time with the Krauss kids. She's very suspicious about that family. She claims that Albert is a womanizer. And even though I think Ellen is a sweet girl, I've never met the mother, so I can't really say."

"Well, the mother—Clara—is a good person who is caught in a very bad marriage. Albert, besides being a bully and perhaps a philanderer, may also be a rumrunner. And I have reason to be very worried that it's about to get seriously dangerous down by the docks." Anna purposely didn't mention her concerns about Katy being with AJ right now. No sense in worrying Mac any more than necessary.

"I know!" Lucille's eyes lit up. "Clara and Ellen can stay with me. My house is quite large, and I suspect no one would ever guess they'd be there. It would be much safer than here, Anna."

"You'd do that?" Anna felt stunned.

"Of course. Ellen is Katy's good friend. Clara is your friend. It would be like taking in family." She smiled. "In fact, it might be rather fun. It's a bit lonely in that big old house. Just Sally and me."

"That would be wonderful." Anna was so touched by

Lucille's generosity that she felt close to tears. "That is so kind of you."

Lucille waved a dismissive hand as she stood. "Well, I better get home and let Sally know that we might be having guests." She turned to Anna. "Do you have any idea when they might arrive?"

"Not exactly, but I hope sometime this afternoon or evening."

"We'll be ready for them," Lucille promised as she gathered her parasol and purse. "Perhaps you could give me a ring on the telephone when you know. Mac has my number." She blew Mac a kiss and hurried out.

"That was unexpected," Anna told Mac.

He still looked slightly stunned. "What is going on?"

Anna sat down and filled him in on what she and Rand had observed from the beach and how they felt certain it was contraband.

"Call Harvey," Mac demanded. "Right now!"

Anna grimaced. "I can't call the chief until Katy gets home."

"Where is Katy?" He looked confused.

"With AJ and Ellen...fishing."

Mac placed his hand over his forehead with a groan.

She placed a comforting hand on his shoulder. "Rand will be keeping watch at the docks. He'll help Katy get safely home. And maybe he'll help Clara and Ellen too, if he gets the chance." She hoped this was the best way to handle this.

"Then you'll call Harvey?"

"Yes, of course. I would call the chief right now if I knew everyone was safe. But we can't endanger Katy or Clara and Ellen."

Mac let out a long sigh. "Yeah...you're right."

Anna could tell that Mac was now as worried as she

felt. To distract him, she told him about her interview with Wally. "But now I'm not sure I'll have time to write that article in time for Saturday's edition."

"I'll write it." He reached for his cane and pushed himself to his feet.

"Can you?"

"I type faster than I speak," he said slowly. "Even with one hand."

She was already digging the notes from her briefcase. "You may not need these, Mac. I mean, since you've known Wally for most of your life."

He took them. "This will help."

"I'll go tell Bernice to wait dinner a bit, until Katy gets home." She tried to sound more confident than she felt, but as she headed for the kitchen, she sent up a silent prayer for Katy's safety...and for Clara and Ellen's.

Bernice was immediately suspicious. "What's wrong with you, Anna?" she asked after agreeing to wait dinner. "I can tell you're upset about something. Is it because Lucille was here when you got home?"

"No, not at all." Anna smiled. "In fact, I'm growing fonder of Lucille."

Bernice looked surprised.

"I know I can trust you, but I don't want to worry you."

Bernice pointed to the kitchen table. "Sit down while I pour you a cup of coffee. Then you better start talking."

Anna knew she had no choice, and as she relayed a short version of today's events, she got an idea. "I'd really like to get word to Rand that he should take Clara and Ellen to Lucille's house. I mean if he gets the chance to help them. Do you think Mickey could wander down that way?"

"Sure, he could. I often send him down there to get fish. And not from Krauss's either. He has a couple friends with boats that he's been buying from lately. Better selection of fish than Sunset Fish Company."

"That's no surprise." Anna sipped her coffee. "I think Albert Krauss has spent more time rum-running than fishing lately."

"I think you're right." Bernice opened the back door, called for her husband, then, once he arrived, quickly told him of his assignment. "But you need to make it look like a casual encounter," she explained. "And be sure and bring home some good fish too. See if anyone has crabs or maybe some mussels. We'll have a seafood dinner tomorrow."

Mickey agreed, wasting no time as he grabbed his hat and shopping basket and, once again, Anna prayed a silent prayer for his safety...and for Rand's too. But she still felt uneasy about keeping this news from Chief Rollins. After all, he was a smart man. He would understand her concerns for the safety of innocent bystanders. Maybe the prudent thing was to give him a warning. She glanced at the kitchen clock, realizing that he'd still be at the station. But this needed to be a face-to-face conversation—she needed to look into his eyes and know he understood the dangers involved.

"I'm going to run into town," she told Bernice. "I won't be gone long. If Katy gets home, don't let her leave again."

Bernice nodded. "You can count on it."

As Anna hurried toward the police station, she decided to make this visit appear to be newspaper related...just in case any of the less trustworthy officers were around. She told the receptionist that she needed to ask the chief for some quotes for Saturday's paper then went on back to his office.

"Anna." He looked up in surprise as she closed the door behind her. "To what do I owe this—"

"I have urgent news." She pulled a chair close to his desk. "And I can only tell you if you promise to proceed with great caution."

"What is it?"

She quickly told him the whole story, giving specific details as well as her suspicions about the Sunset Fish Company. "The reason I didn't come directly to you is because I want Katy and Clara and Ellen safely out of there before you or anyone else goes in there. I lived in Portland, and I know how dangerous a situation like this can get. Do you understand me?"

He nodded somberly. "Of course."

"I would never assume to tell you how to run your force, but I'm worried about my daughter...and our friends. And I know the state police are still crawling around town."

"Just getting in the way, if you ask me." He grimly shook his head. "And barking up the wrong tree too."

"Which is just one more reason I want to be sure Katy and the others are safely out before someone blows it all wide open."

The chief pursed his lips. "But I do think I'll send Brooks in—in plainclothes. He can dress like a fisherman and blend in with the dock crowd. Then I'll get my most trustworthy officers ready for action." He frowned. "I wish I could say they're all trustworthy, but I've got my eye on a couple of them."

"I know." She remembered Clint Collins watching her closely as she came into the station just now. "I do too."

"I'll issue search warrants and get my ducks in a row here, Anna. And you promise to call me the minute your daughter and friends are out of harm's way."

"Will you be here at the station?"

"Yes. I'll make up some excuse to stay late." He pointed

to his telephone. "You have my direct line number, don't you?"

"I do."

"When you call, use some kind of code—in case the switchboard is listening."

"What should I say?"

His brow creased. "Just say you're calling for Mac. To remind me about our chess game. If it's late, ask why I'm not there yet. That'll work."

Anna was pacing the floor when Katy finally burst through the door at half past seven. "Mother?" she cried. "What is going on? Are you okay? Is Grandpa okay?"

"Yes, of course." Anna grabbed her and hugged her. "I'm so glad you're all right." She held Katy at arm's length. "You were supposed to tell me when you go fishing!"

"But what is wrong? Rand said there was an emergency at home when he met me on the dock. I assumed it was—"

"The emergency isn't at home. Tell me, where did Ellen go?"

"I don't know." Katy frowned. "Probably home. Why do you—"

"Where is Rand?"

"I don't know." Katy looked rattled. "He just dumped me here and drove off like he was heading for a fire or something."

"Just you? No one else was with him?"

"No. Just me."

"Oh dear."

"What is it?" Katy demanded. "What's going on?"

Anna led Katy to the dining room. "Go tell Bernice you're

here. She waited dinner for you. I'll tell Mac." Despite Katy's protests and questions, Anna hurried to get Mac, and before long, they were seated for dinner.

"Will someone please tell me what's going on?" Katy asked as Bernice served the soup.

"How was your fishing expedition?" Anna asked pointedly. "Catch anything?"

"Not really. I mean, I caught some that had to be thrown back, and Ellen caught a bass, but—"

"Did anything unusual happen on the boat?" Anna asked. "Anything besides fishing? Did AJ stop anywhere?"

Katy frowned. "Well, he did stop to drop some crab pots—"

"Crab pots?" Mac questioned. "On the ocean?"

"Yes." Katy nodded.

"In July?" Mac shook his head.

"Don't people crab in July?" Anna asked him.

"Not the ocean...not in July." Mac's eyes narrowed with what seemed to be suspicion.

"Did he pull in any crabs?" Anna asked Katy.

Katy's mouth twisted to one side. "AJ never went back to get them. I figured he was leaving them overnight."

"Did you actually *see* the crab pots?" Anna pressed. "I mean, when he put them in the water, were you watching?"

"No. Ellen and I were handling the boat for him. We were in front. He was in back."

"I assume there were buoy markers on the lines...so he could get them later?"

"Of course."

"Where do you think you were when he dropped the crab pots?"

"I don't know exactly. A couple miles from shore. Maybe

four or five miles south of town." Katy was clearly perplexed. "Mother, please, tell me what this is all about."

"Well, I could be wrong, but I suspect you and Ellen assisted AJ in rum-running today. I'm guessing he took you girls out there as a cover."

Katy's eyes grew wide. "You can't be serious."

Anna just nodded. "I'm afraid I am." She checked her watch to see that nearly twenty minutes had passed since Katy had come home. Enough time for Rand to have gone back for Ellen and Clara, if that's what he'd planned on doing.

"Big news story," Mac said wryly. "Girl rumrunners."

"But we didn't know—"

"Excuse me." Anna stood. "I need to check something." But first she sternly warned Katy not to leave the house or speak to anyone on the phone. "And *I mean it*." She used her I-mean-business look then slipped out the back door, gathered up the small bundle she'd left back there, and hurried along the cliff-side path down to Lucille's house, where she rapped on the back door until the housekeeper answered with a curious expression. Anna greeted her and asked to see Lucille.

"She's in the living room with her guests," Sally told her.

"The Krauss women?" Anna asked hopefully.

"And a fellow too."

Anna stashed her bundle then hurried through the kitchen to see Rand, Clara, Ellen, and Lucille all in the living room. "Oh, you made it safely here." Anna hurried to Lucille's telephone. "Mind if I use this?" she asked.

"Not at all."

First Anna called the chief's number. "Mac is expecting you for chess," she crisply told him. "Any time now." Next she called Jim's number. After a quick inquiry about his shoulder, she quietly informed him that a story would soon break. "I just thought you'd like to know."

"Where?" he asked eagerly. "When?"

"Down by the docks, but hard to say when. Probably sometime tonight. I'll let you know how it goes—"

"I want to cover it!"

"But what about your—"

"That's why I need to cover this, Anna. I've earned this. Don't try to stop me either."

Anna understood. No reporter worth his salt wanted to be pushed out of a story. And neither did she. As she hung up, she noticed the others all staring curiously at her. But she simply smiled. "I'm so glad you made it safely here," she told Clara and Ellen. "I know it can't be easy for you. And it was very brave of you to leave like that. But I'm sure you'll be relieved...eventually."

"Rand explained some of the situation to us." Clara's voice trembled slightly. "But, Anna, do you honestly believe the police will raid the warehouse tonight?"

"I really can't say." Anna knew they'd all remain safer if ignorant of the details. "But I want to warn you to remain indoors with doors locked until you hear from me or Rand or Chief Rollins." She glanced to the front window, relieved to see the drapes were already closed. "And if the phone rings, only Lucille should answer." She looked at Lucille for confirmation. "And don't reveal their whereabouts or anything."

"Of course not." Lucille nodded knowingly.

Anna turned to Rand. "Where's your car?"

"In the carriage house," he told her. "Lucille kindly left it open for me."

"Did anyone see you on your way here?" Anna asked him.

"Albert had just taken the big boat out," Clara told Anna. "With a full crew. He said they'd probably be out all night. The boat was out of the harbor when Rand came to the door."

"What perfect timing. But what about AJ?"

"He jumped aboard Dad's boat just before they left," Ellen told them.

"Well, I'm glad you're both safely here," Anna told them. "We'll all know more about what's going on by tomorrow." She nudged Rand. "Mind giving me a ride?"

"Not at all." He grinned. "Where are we going?"

"You'll see." She turned to Lucille. "Thank you again for opening your home up like this. It was very generous."

Lucille smiled brightly. "I'm happy to help."

Anna led Rand through the kitchen, retrieving her bundle on the back porch. Then they both sneaked through the backyard to the carriage house. "You wait out here a couple of minutes." She went inside the carriage house and quickly changed into Mac's old corduroy trousers and fisherman knit sweater. "Okay. You can come in now."

"What's going—" Rand stared at her in wonder. "Anna McDowell, what on earth are you—"

"I don't want to stand out down on the docks." She shoved her curls into Mac's old hat.

"On the docks?"

"How else will I know what's going on?" As Rand drove toward the harbor, Anna explained her plan to continue covering this story.

"But you're a woman...a mother...you can't just—"

"This is my job. I'm a reporter. This is what we do."

"But it's too dangerous," he insisted.

"I'll understand if you're worried about getting hurt, Rand. Just drop me off, and you can go on home."

"Right. I'm going to just leave you down—"

"Jim will be there. And Chief Rollins and his men. It's not as if I'll be alone. And I know how to lay low. I'm only there to observe. Please, just drop me off near the docks, and you can go—"

"Are you kidding? I don't want to miss out on this." He chuckled. "Besides, someone might be looking for a good attorney before the night is over."

"I sure hope so." She scowled. "Not that I think they deserve it."

"According to the law, they do. The presumption of innocence applies to rumrunners too."

"Just promise not to represent Albert Krauss."

"Well, he wouldn't be my first choice...but you never can tell."

Anna sincerely hoped that Albert and his cohorts would all be safely locked up by morning. Hopefully with enough evidence to convict and send them to the state penitentiary for a good, long while. Well, with some legal representation, of course.

CHAPTER 27

As Rand cruised down Harbor Drive, Anna wasn't too surprised to see that Jim was already there. Dressed casually in dungarees and a tartan wool shirt, he was strolling down the dockside walk, swinging a fishing creel in his good hand.

"Rand!" Anna turned to look at him. "You'll stick out like a sore thumb down here in that business suit."

He frowned. "You're right."

"And so will this car."

"I'll run the car home, change into my play clothes, and be right back."

"Did you have any dinner yet?" she asked.

"Nope. How about you?"

"I left after just a bite of soup." She opened the door and hopped out.

"I'll bring us something."

Anna tipped her head then strode purposefully down the stairs toward the docks, hoping she looked like a young man about to hop a fishing boat. When she caught up with Jim, he didn't recognize her at first. "I guess you didn't notice my disguise on July Fourth," she said. "You were a little distracted while Daniel was stitching you up."

"What are you doing down here?" Jim demanded. "This is my story."

"It's my story too," she reminded him. "And don't forget I'm your boss."

"Don't remind me," he growled.

"Chief Rollins has got a man down here too," she said quietly.

"Yeah, I just saw Wade Brooks. He was talking to the captain of *Lady Luck*." Jim stopped at a bench splattered with white seagull droppings, set down his creel, and pulled a bag of tobacco from his shirt pocket.

"I didn't know you smoked." Anna watched as he rolled a cigarette.

"I don't smoke much. But it makes for a good cover." He glanced at her. "Want one?"

She tried not to giggle.

"For your disguise," he clarified as he lit the cigarette. "Just pretend to smoke it. Gives us a reason to just stand around and take it all in." He handed her the cigarette. "And makes you look tough. Just don't inhale, or you'll have a coughing fit and really draw some attention."

She tried to act natural as she pretended to puff on the cigarette. Yet she couldn't help but wonder what Mac would say if he could see her now. She tried not to appear obvious as she glanced up and down the docks and out across the harbor and finally to the mouth that opened into the ocean. "Pretty quiet tonight."

"At least for now."

"Here comes Wade." She tried to act discrete. "Wanna offer him a smoke?"

"You're getting good at this." Jim looked amused as he pulled out his bag again.

Soon all three of them huddled there together, like three fishermen exchanging fish stories. "I forgot to mention something important to the chief," Anna told Wade. "My daughter may have witnessed AJ Krauss dropping some suspicious crab pots." She described the location. "They have buoy markers, so you could probably find them."

"My guess is they've been picked up by now." Wade frowned. "A state detective mentioned that's been done up north. A way to make a discrete drop. One boat puts them down, and another one picks them up. But apparently the Coast Guard up north is catching on."

"You'd think if OSP was aware of that practice, they'd be doing some looking around out on the ocean."

"Aw, they're too busy reinventing the wheel. The chief told them about our leads, but they're doing it their own way." His eyes darted up the dock. "Haven't seen a single one of them around tonight. Probably a good thing though. They might just mess it up for everyone."

"I noticed something I forgot to mention too," Jim told them. "Might interest Anna more than you, since it has to do with one of the reporters from the newspaper."

"What?" Anna asked.

"Well, as you may know, Wesley lives in my boardinghouse. Anyway, I happened to notice him out back, having a conversation with Albert Krauss—just last night. Got pretty interesting too."

"Interesting how?"

"I couldn't hear what they were saying, but Albert looked angry. Seemed like he was trying to intimidate Wesley by shaking his fist in his face. Then just before he left, Albert grabbed Wesley by the shirt collar, gave him a hard shake, and threw him to the ground."

"That is interesting." Now Anna relayed what she and Daniel had seen during the Independence Day parade. "Looked like the mayor was pretty vexed at him too."

"Sounds like Kempton has made some enemies." Wade rubbed his chin.

"I wonder what's going on." Anna feigned a puff on the cigarette.

"Doesn't make sense," Jim added. "Wesley has never hidden the fact that he opposes prohibition, and we all know he drinks like a fish and is pretty friendly with the likes of Albert and his buddies. Plus he's always been on good terms with the mayor."

"Who's that?" Wade asked as a lone figure strolled down the dock toward them.

Anna peered at the man as he passed under a gas lantern. "Oh, that's just Rand Douglas."

"So did you think we'd need an attorney tonight?" Jim asked.

"No, he just wanted to see the action." Anna waved to him, and he came over to join them.

"Didn't know you were a smoker." Rand looked genuinely concerned. "You're just full of surprises, Anna."

"It's part of my disguise," she told him.

Rand had just exchanged greetings with Jim and Wade when Anna noticed what appeared to be running lights on a good-sized boat coming into the harbor. "Is that Krauss's boat?" she quietly asked the guys.

Wade casually glanced over his shoulder. "Yep." He dropped his cigarette and ground it with the heel of his boot. "I'll see you two around. Keep a safe distance and, whatever you do, don't get in the way." He tossed a warning look to Anna. "It's one thing to cover the news, something else to *make* the news." Then he strode down the dock and headed straight for the Krauss building.

Anna could only imagine what was about to unfold, but she didn't want to miss it.

"What now?" She watched nervously as the Krauss boat slowly chugged into the harbor. It probably looked innocent and ordinary to a casual observer, as if it had just come in from a long day of fishing. Although she knew it had only been out a few hours.

"Over there." Jim nodded toward a midsized fishing boat. "Wade said the captain of the *Lady Luck* is a good guy. We'll have a safe vantage point from his boat."

Captain Rex was very accommodating—and curious. Jim explained they were Sunset Cove reporters, trying to scoop a rumrunner story—without getting killed.

"Well, I've had my suspicions about the Krauss outfit for several months," the captain confided. "But I try to mind my own business."

Anna kept her eyes on the boat's lights as it slowed down, maneuvering up to its normal spot on the dock, right next to the fish company. Although there were some lights on the boat, it was too dark to see anything more than a few shadowy figures moving around on the bow, throwing ropes and tying it down. She peered across the docks and around the dark warehouse building nearby, wondering where Chief Rollins and his men were lurking. Hopefully they were in place by now, although she hadn't noticed anyone earlier.

"They're unloading," she whispered, although from this distance she knew they couldn't be heard.

"And you don't think they got fish in them crates?" Captain Rex chuckled. "This I gotta see."

By the light of the gas lamp next to the fish shop, they could see the men moving crates through an open side door and into the building.

"Where're the coppers?" Captain Rex asked.

Before anyone could answer, they heard voices shouting, followed by an exchange of gunfire. The men on the dock began scrambling, some of them jumping into a nearby, smaller fishing boat. As the motor roared into action, there was more shouting and more gunshots.

Anna's fingers tightened on the rail she clung to as she prayed that the chief and his men would be safe.

Almost as quickly as it started, it seemed to be over. The area grew quiet except for an occasional shout. But it appeared that the fishermen, at least the ones who didn't get away, were being rounded up.

"I see the chief." Anna felt a rush of relief. "It looks like he and his men are handcuffing the fishermen."

"You mean rumrunners," Captain Rex corrected her.

"I'm going over to see." Jim jumped onto the gangway and ran down the dock.

"I'm going too." Rand headed for the gangway.

Anna started to follow, but Rand stopped her with a raised hand.

"No!" he insisted. "You stay here until we know it's safe."

"But I'm—"

"Captain Rex," Rand called out. "Mind keeping her here for a while? Until I'm certain it's safe over there?"

The bulky captain stepped in front of Anna, blocking the gangway. "Sorry, ma'am, but I agree with your friend. That's no place for a lady." He chuckled. "Even though you don't look much like a lady right now, I can tell you are. So just sit tight until your buddies give you the go-ahead."

"Fine," Anna growled, returning to her position on

the stern and watching as what appeared to be officers holding lanterns boarded the big Krauss boat. Probably searching for more evidence. "If I have to stay here, maybe I'll interview you, Captain Rex. You mentioned suspicions about the Krauss boats. Can you go into any details as to why that is?"

"Will this go in the newspaper?"

"It could. But if you like, I can simply list you as an anonymous source."

"A what?"

"I'll keep your name out of it."

"Okay. Well, I noticed last spring that the Krauss boats were spending a lot of time close to shore. That didn't make sense. And lately they've been crabbing on the ocean, and everyone knows the best crabs are in the harbor right now. Couldn't figure why they'd waste time dropping pots out there. And at odd times of the day too. And, of course, everyone on the docks knows that Albert Krauss sells booze from the fish shop. You put two and two together, and it adds up to trouble. About time those boys got caught."

"I'm surprised to hear a fisherman say that. I don't like to generalize, but there's an assumption that most fishermen enjoy a drink now and then." And, she felt, that was putting it lightly.

"Can't argue with you there. But I gave up whiskey more'n ten years ago, when my wife told me it was the bottle or her." He shook his head. "But I've had to let men go because their drinking got out of control. Some men can hold their liquor...some can't." He nodded toward the dock. "Looks like your lawyer friend is waving to you."

Anna stood. "Thanks, Captain Rex."

"You be careful now, little lady. Don't you forget that

some of them boys got away in that boat, and they're probably madder than hornets by now."

"I'll keep that in mind." She hopped onto the gangway and hurried down to meet Rand. "What'd you find out?"

"They only rounded up five guys. And a lot of booze. Unfortunately, Albert and two others got away. Well, the police assume it's Albert. Naturally, his buddies aren't talking. Not yet anyway."

"Was anyone shot?" Anna asked.

"A couple of Albert's boys caught some bullets. And one policeman was wounded. Nothing life threatening."

"That's a relief."

"I'm going to ride with the criminals to the jail. Just in case any of them want legal counsel."

"That's very kind of you."

"Well, I figure if I can get them to talk…maybe turn over some evidence…it might go better for them on down the line. Plus, their information could lead to future arrests. Maybe bring in some bigger fish."

"Good thinking."

Anna found Jim talking to the officer who was holding a gun on a couple of handcuffed suspects. Anna went over to listen in.

"From what I heard, the state police weren't called in to help," the policeman was telling Jim. "Seems they've been more interested in the roadhouse up north. Too bad. We could've used a few more hands tonight."

"I heard a policeman was injured," Anna said. "Is it serious?"

"Sergeant Arnold got shot in the leg and is already being transported to Dr. Hollister's for care. I'm not sure how serious it is, but he was bleeding pretty bad."

"Come on," Chief Rollins was calling out. "Load 'em up in the wagon and get 'em out of here."

"'Scuse me." The officer grabbed the cuffed men and shoved them toward the stairs that led to the street, where several wagons and vehicles were waiting.

Anna stepped back, watching as the other captives were taken up. Judging by the bandages, someone had attended to their wounds, but she guessed Daniel would be seeing them later. She turned to the chief. "I heard Albert and a couple others got away."

"Yep, we took some shots at the boat, and we know Albert was with them." He grimly shook his head. "But they got away. For a little boat, it has a big engine. But I got one of my boys calling the Coast Guard. Although it's unlikely they'll find them tonight."

"The boat's clean now," one of the policemen told the chief. "We removed six more crates of booze, but I think we got it all."

"Make sure Roberts disables the engine," the chief told him. "On all the Krauss boats."

"Was AJ arrested too?" Anna asked the chief.

"No. Are you certain he was out with his dad tonight?"

"According to Ellen, he jumped aboard just as they left."

"Then he must be one of the other men that escaped with Albert."

Chief Rollins called out commands to his other men, assigning them an all-night search and watch on all the Krauss properties. Anna asked him a few more questions then, not wanting to get in his way, excused herself.

"I appreciate your help," he told her. "Without your tip tonight, we wouldn't have gotten them. Thank you."

"I just wish you'd gotten Albert." She shook her head.

"Well, Albert can't very well come home now." The chief

grinned. "Not without getting hauled off to the hoosegow to join his friends."

Anna wondered how Albert and AJ were feeling right now, out on the ocean with the knowledge that their friends were being taken in, or worse, and that they would never be able to come home again...as free men. More concerning than Albert and AJ, she wondered how Clara and Ellen would respond to this news. As much as Anna had longed to see justice served, she felt badly for the Krauss family. What a sad, sorry mess.

CHAPTER 28

Although it was close to midnight by the time Rand dropped Anna at home, Katy was still up. "Mother," she whispered as she followed her up the stairs, "I've been so worried. What is going on? Where were you?"

"Katy, you should be in bed."

"How could I sleep knowing my only mother was out there doing goodness knows what?" Katy paused on the landing, staring at Anna's outfit with wide eyes. "And what on earth—why are you dressed like that?"

"It's a long story...and I'm very tired."

"But what happened tonight?"

"I'll tell you all about it in the morning." Anna kissed Katy's cheek. "Just be assured that all is well, and your only mother is safely home. Now go to bed."

Katy didn't argue, but when Anna finally got into bed, she was wide awake. She felt concerned for Clara and Ellen, wondering how they would react to the news about Albert and AJ. Anna knew it was up to her to break it to them. First thing in the morning. In the meantime, all she could do was to pray for them—all the Krausses—and hopefully get some sleep. Because tomorrow would be a busy day.

Anna woke early, quickly getting dressed for a day at work. When she got downstairs, Bernice was already in the kitchen. Like Katy, she was full of questions.

"I'll tell you all about it," Anna assured her. "As soon as I get back from Lucille's."

"Why are you going to Lucille's?" Bernice scowled.

"Believe it or not, Lucille has shown me a new side." Anna smiled. "I may have been somewhat wrong about her."

"Well, this I gotta hear."

"Later," Anna promised as she slipped out the backdoor. Once again, she took the back trail to Lucille's house. With Albert and AJ still on the lam, one couldn't be too cautious. Sally let her into the house, informing her that Clara was already up and in the living room. "And she's been pacing back and forth," Sally confided. "I think she's upset."

Anna nodded. "I'll go to her."

"Anna," Clara exclaimed, "I'm so glad to see you! Please, tell me everything."

"Sit down." Anna kept her voice calm. And then, with Clara listening with teary eyes, followed by tears, Anna relayed the whole story.

"So they are out on the ocean right now?" Clara asked.

"I don't know. They escaped on one of the smaller boats. One with a big engine."

"That's AJ's boat."

"But shots were fired at them," Anna clarified. "There's a chance the boat could've been damaged."

"Or AJ...or Albert."

"No one knew for sure."

"So they really were smuggling liquor." Clara scowled. "I had my suspicions, but each time I asked, well, Albert got so angry.... It was scary. Easier just to ignore it. Like those silly monkeys. Hear no evil, see no evil, speak no evil."

"Well, the police gathered enough evidence to ensure that Albert will be arrested at the first opportunity. If he sets foot in Sunset Cove, the police will be sure to nab him."

"And AJ too?"

"I'm afraid so." Anna sighed. "Although the court will go easier on him because he's only seventeen. And they might take into account that his father influenced him onto a wrong path. It really seems like your boy didn't have much of a chance. In fact, I wonder if my good friend Rand Douglas would consider representing him."

"I have money," Clara exclaimed. "I would gladly pay Mr. Douglas—whatever he needed."

Anna felt uncertain. "Is this money from the rum-running operation?"

"Oh, no." Clara firmly shook her head. "It's from the items I made myself and sold at the fish shop. Just little things like huckleberry jam or knitted fisherman hats and whatnot. Also I've done sewing for years. But I've always kept my funds separate." She grimaced as if worried. "I hid my earnings under a loose floorboard in the kitchen. Over the years, it's added up."

"Well, good for you." Anna could hear someone moving upstairs. "I'll let you tell Ellen and Lucille the news. But I must insist that all three of you remain behind locked doors. You must be on high alert until Albert is apprehended. Can you do that?"

"Of course. Gladly."

"And I promise to let you know if I learn anything new today."

"Yes. Please do." She sighed. "I'm not concerned about what happens to Albert. Oh, I don't wish him dead, but if he goes to jail for a good long time, I won't care. But AJ...oh dear...do you really think there's still hope for him?"

"There must be." Anna squeezed her hand. "This whole ordeal might be exactly what he needs to shake him up and bring him to his senses."

"I hope and pray it does."

Anna decided that Saturday's edition of the *Sunset Times* needed to go out as soon as possible. So everyone in the office worked extra hard all day and by Friday afternoon, the paper was delivered...and devoured by locals and tourists. The papers flew out so quickly that the pressmen had to do an extra printing to supply the demand.

"This is a first," Mac admitted at dinner after Anna told him the good news. "First second printing ever." He held up the newspaper with a proud smile. "Good work, Anna."

"I liked your article about Wally Morris too," Anna told him. "Sorry it only made page four."

"That's because the first four pages were packed with all those big news stories," Katy said. "Made it seem like Sunset Cove was a big city."

"That wasn't exactly my intention," Anna told her. "I just wanted to make sure the story was honestly and thoroughly told."

"Any news about Albert and AJ?" Mac asked.

"No one has seen or heard from them."

"I talked to Clara and Ellen earlier." Katy sighed. "They're both so sad and worried for AJ. They were both blaming themselves, saying they should've done this or that differently. Or that Albert should've been a better father." Her brow furrowed. "Do you know what I told them?"

"I don't have the slightest idea," Anna admitted.

Katy looked uncertain. "I hope it was okay, Mother."

"I can't imagine you'd say anything that wasn't okay." Anna reached for the butter.

"Lucille heard it too." Katy glanced at Mac. "I hope you don't mind."

Anna felt confused. "What do you mean? What did you say?"

"Well, I told them that my father was a criminal and that—"

"What?" Anna dropped the butter knife with a clang.

"I told them that my father was a convicted criminal who got locked up in a state penitentiary and—"

"Why on earth did you—"

"I was only trying to point out that my father's mistakes haven't done any great damage to me, so I think it's just plain silly for everyone to blame someone else for what AJ has or has not done. Don't you think that's true, Mother?"

Anna didn't know what to say. That had been such a carefully guarded secret in Portland—originally for Anna's sake and then for Katy's. She could hardly believe that Katy had willingly shared it. And did that mean all of Sunset Cove would soon know?

"What I mean is that AJ made his own choices," Katy continued. "He has only himself to blame. Oh, sure, his father had an influence on him. But look at Ellen. She has the exact same father. And yet she's made different choices. She thinks differently than AJ. So, you see, I think it's senseless to blame anyone except for the person who did it. And that's exactly what I told them." She turned to Mac. "Don't you think so too, Grandpa?"

He looked somewhat surprised, but simply nodded. "Yeah, I agree."

"Well." Anna retrieved her butter knife. "You make an excellent point, Katy."

To Anna's relief, Mac didn't seem inclined to further pursue this conversation, so she decided to reroute them by inquiring about tomorrow night's fundraiser for Wally. "Do you have everything all organized?" she asked Katy, knowing full well that her efficient daughter probably had it under control by now.

"I think so." She began describing all the plans in enthusiastic detail. "But I did want to ask Grandmother and Clara and Ellen to make some extra pies. Bernice and I are going to make six more pies tonight. We don't want to run out. And I suspect lots of folks will be coming." She giggled as she wiped her mouth. "Today's newspaper won't garner Mayor Snyder new votes. And although you never said as much, Mother, I'm guessing you just helped Wally Morris slip onto the winner's podium."

After Katy excused herself to go call Lucille about the extra pies, Anna turned to her father. "I hope you don't mind that Katy has gone public with our dirty linen, Mac."

He waved a hand, but his eyes looked sad.

"I know you've always protected your reputation. I don't want to bring shame on you."

"No shame. You and Katy...you both make me proud."

"Thanks, Mac." She got out of her chair to hug him. "I'm actually glad Katy told Clara and Ellen about it. It feels good not to have secrets."

"Too many secrets in this town." He glumly shook his head.

She studied him for a moment. Something about his countenance suggested he wasn't referring to the recently exposed rum-running secrets. Did he mean there were some closer to home? "I'm confused," she admitted. "Are you saying you have secrets too?"

He simply nodded. "Yeah."

Anna didn't know what to say. Should she press him to tell her about his secrets...or wait until he was ready to disclose something?

"Hard to talk for long," he said quietly. "Words still get jumbled."

"I know, but your speech has really improved since we first got here, Mac. Most people can understand you quite well now."

"Tongue ties...speech slow." He sighed. "I have something. By my typewriter, Anna. Go read it."

"You've typed up something? You want me to read it?"

He somberly nodded.

Anna went to his den, and next to his typewriter was a manila folder. She opened it and saw the front page was blank except for the word LUCILLE. She flipped to the next page and began reading a detailed account of what had happened between her parents and why they eventually parted.

It was a painfully honest retelling of two young people who'd fallen in love and married too quickly. The young man brought his bride home only to receive his mother's shock and dire disapproval. Nothing about Lucille amounted to what Mac's mother considered to be a good wife. In fact, she did not even like her. Anna's grandmother considered Lucille to be a spoiled child. It did not help that they all lived together under the same roof. According to Mac, his mother treated his wife like a "useless piece of fluff that had to be tolerated." It seemed that Lucille was even disparaged by her mother-in-law in public. Before long the whole community was against Mac's young bride. So much so that Lucille could never make real friends or find her place. She was treated like a joke.

When Anna was born, Lucille was pushed aside by her

mother-in-law. Deciding that Lucille was a sad excuse of a mother, Grandmother stepped in and, with Bernice's help, took over caring for Anna. Consequently, Lucille felt even more useless and frivolous. Eventually Lucille and the mother-in-law locked horns so horribly that Lucille gave her husband an ultimatum. Mac had to choose—Lucille or his mother. They couldn't keep living under the same roof. When Mac refused to choose, Lucille left. End of story.

For the first time in her life, Anna understood. Mac was partially to blame. Like Katy had so energetically declared tonight, people needed to take responsibility for their own actions and choices. True, but as a reporter, Anna knew there was always more to a story. More layers. More pieces to the puzzle. More questions to ask. She slid the typewritten pages back in their folder and went to find Mac in his private sitting room with a very troubled expression.

"Thank you." She went over to kiss his cheek. "You don't know how much it means for me to know about that. Thank you for telling me the rest of the story, Mac."

"I am to blame." He looked down at his hands in his lap.

"Only partly," she clarified. "I can see there was a lot going on. More than I ever knew. Grandmother played a role. You played a role. So did Lucille. But my childish perspective was skewed." She pointed to him. "You were always the hero of my childhood story. And Grandmother too. Lucille was the villain. Now I can see it differently. You wanted to be the hero, Mac. And Grandmother wanted to do her best to take care of me. And Lucille, well, I think she just wanted to be loved." She smiled. "Maybe it's not too late."

"Maybe...." His lopsided face curved into a charming half-smile.

To the delight of her daughter, the pie social/dance was a huge hit. It seemed like most of the town showed up and, as the pie slices grew skinnier, Anna hoped they wouldn't run short. Meanwhile, the music was lively, and the young folks danced energetically into the night. Midway through the festivities, Wally's speech had been upbeat and encouraging, and the applause that followed was thunderous. Anna suspected that Katy was right about Wally's chances for winning this election. It seemed the tide had turned. And, not surprisingly, Mayor Snyder and his shady cohorts were nowhere to be seen all evening.

Anna hoped the happy celebration had provided Clara and Ellen with a good distraction from yesterday's troubling news. Katy had made sure to keep them busy. But Anna couldn't help but notice the sadness in Clara's eyes as they worked to clean up the grange hall afterward. Anna felt certain Clara was worrying about her son. And she was relieved when Rand insisted on driving the Krauss women and Lucille safely home.

"Thank you for your help," Katy called out as they left.

"You sure you don't want me to stay?" Ellen asked.

"No. Mother and I can handle this. We're almost done."

"That's right," Anna confirmed. "We've got this under control."

The grange hall seemed strangely quiet after the last stragglers left. If not for the elderly grange member who'd supervised the use of the building, Anna might've felt nervous about being here with Katy at this hour of night. But Mr. Griffin cheerfully chattered at them as they finished up.

Anna felt uneasy to know that Albert, AJ, and the third unidentified man were still on the run. No one had seen any sign of them, but Chief Rollins seemed certain they were long gone by now. The Coast Guard had sent down a cruiser to search the coastline, and the state police were combing nearby towns. Even the local fishermen had been on the lookout. But Anna suspected that each passing day diminished the hopes of capture. And maybe that was for the best. Maybe they'd gone down to Mexico to restart their lives. Hopefully on a better track.

As Anna wiped down the last table, Katy came over to give her a big hug. "Thanks so much for your help tonight, Mother."

"You pulled off a very successful evening." Anna dropped the rag back into the bucket of soapy water. "Congratulations on being a great campaign manager."

Katy beamed at her. "I really believe Wally is going to win the election in the fall. Won't it be wonderful for Sunset Cove to have an honest mayor?"

"It will be just what this town needs." Anna removed the work apron she'd been wearing to protect her pretty silk dress and sighed. "I think we can honestly say that we'll be leaving this place even better than we found it, Katy. That makes me very happy."

"So we really are going back to Portland?" Katy dumped out the soapy water into the oversized sink.

"You made me promise, Katy. You insisted you had to return to your school and your friends in late August. Remember?" Anna wondered if Katy might be changing her mind about going home to Portland.

"Of course I remember. But I wasn't sure about you, Mother. I thought perhaps you were getting attached to this place. And I mean, seeing you here tonight...why, you were the belle of the ball."

"Belle of the ball?" Anna couldn't help but laugh as she gathered her purse and gloves and evening wrap.

"Goodness, yes. You had a string of beaux waiting to dance with you." Katy slipped on her driving gloves and a lightweight car coat that looked rather silly over her pretty pink gown.

"My dear, you are exaggerating." Anna waited as Mr. Griffin opened the back door for them.

"I am not. There was Dr. Hollister, Rand Douglas, and your reporter friend Mr. Stafford. Honestly, Mother, your dance card was full. Clara even mentioned it."

"They're just my good friends," Anna explained as they went outside. She turned to Mr. Griffin and thanked him for his help.

"You girls be safe on the road." He bolted the door.

"Don't worry," Katy assured him. "I'm an excellent driver."

"I expect you are." He chuckled. "But it's foggy tonight. Best to go slow on the beach road."

Katy assured him she would be cautious, and then they bade him good night. As Anna got into the passenger seat, she wished her own driving skills were more polished so that she could drive, but she knew that Katy was capable. "I really was very proud of you tonight," she told Katy as they went down the bumpy road leading back into town. "So were both your grandparents. Honestly, Katy, you accomplished something that most adults would've been challenged by. And, goodness, you should've heard Wally and Thelma singing your high—"

"*Mother!*" Katy hit the brakes so hard that Anna nearly

slid onto the floorboards. "Look! There's someone out there."

Anna peered through the fog to see what appeared to be a man in the middle of the road. "Get a little closer," she told Katy, "so we can see better."

"He's limping, Mother. And he's filthy."

"Maybe he was hit by a car."

"Mother! It's AJ."

"Goodness gracious!" Anna felt her chest tighten with fear. What did this mean? Why was AJ out here like this? Had Albert sent him out to be a decoy—a trap? Were they about to be ambushed? "Dear God," Anna prayed aloud in a trembling voice, "please, please, help us!"

CHAPTER 29

We have to help him," Katy declared as she drove the car right up to AJ.

"Help him?" Anna felt sick inside. Where were Albert and the other man? She peered through the fog to the blackberry bushes growing alongside the road. "Just keep driving, Katy. Go to town, and we'll send someone back for—"

"No, Mother." Katy set the brake and, before Anna could stop her, leaped out of the car. "AJ," she cried. "It's me—Katy." She ran up to him in time to catch him as he fell toward her. "Mother!" she screamed. "Help me get him into the car."

"But Katy." Anna jumped out of the car. "Wait—"

"Hurry, Mother, he's too heavy for me."

Anna ran to them and, supporting AJ's on either side, they stumbled back to the car and somehow managed to load him into the rumble seat of the little Runabout. "Drive fast," Anna commanded as Katy slipped behind the wheel. "As fast as you feel is safe—and don't stop for anyone."

"Yes." Katy stepped on the accelerator. "I wonder how he got here."

Anna gripped the dashboard, watching the road with wide eyes, expecting Albert and the other man to leap out at them. "Go straight to the police station," Anna told Katy as they reached the outskirts of town.

"But he's hurt, Mother. He needs medical help."

"He'll get help," Anna assured her. "After we turn him in to the police, we'll go find Daniel and ask him to care for him."

"But they'll throw him in jail."

"Of course they will." Anna felt alarmed. "That's where he belongs."

"But he's only seventeen, Mother."

"I'm aware of that. But he did the crimes of an adult man."

Katy slowed down on Main Street, but her expression was grim. She clearly didn't like the idea of turning AJ in to the authorities. But what else could they do?

"Katy," Anna said gently. "I'm glad you care about AJ. And I do too. I already talked to Rand about the possibility of representing AJ in court. That's the most anyone can offer him right now."

When Katy pulled up in front of the station, Anna insisted that Katy go inside and ask for help. "Tell them it's an emergency," Anna told her. "I'll stay here with AJ." As Katy ran inside, Anna turned to see that AJ was slumped over and not moving. As Anna silently prayed that he would be all right, a pair of officers came out and began to extract him from the rumble seat.

"Be careful with him," Anna warned them. "He's only seventeen, and he's been injured."

"We got him from here on out," an officer called back with confidence.

"I'm calling Dr. Hollister to come check on him,"

she informed them. "And Mr. Douglas will be his legal representation. So take good care of that boy, or you'll be hearing from Chief Rollins about it." Anna and Katy followed behind them as they half-carried, half-dragged AJ into the building.

"Thanks for warning those policemen, Mother." Katy hugged her once they got inside. "That was good for them to know."

"Now I'll borrow their phone and call Daniel and Rand," Anna told Katy.

Before long, both of Anna's good friends were on their way to the station, and Katy and Anna were on their way home. But first they stopped by Lucille's house and, seeing that the lights were still on, lightly tapped on the door. Although the women were in various stages of getting ready for bed, all of them rejoiced to hear that AJ had been found. Katy enthusiastically told the story of rescuing him on the road, and Anna assured them that AJ would be well looked after with Dr. Hollister and Rand Douglas by his side. She didn't go into any details regarding AJ's condition. The truth was, she did not really know.

"Thank you both." Clara used her hanky to blot her tears. "I think I'll be able to sleep tonight."

"Me too," Ellen declared happily. "AJ might be a heel, but he's still my brother."

"Just be sure to remain on your guard and keep your doors locked," Anna reminded them. "More so now than ever."

AJ was in much worse shape than anyone had imagined. Besides an infected gunshot wound in the thigh, he'd suffered from exposure and pneumonia and had a head injury. Because he'd been unconscious and in critical condition, the chief had allowed him to be transported to the private room in Daniel's medical office. There, Daniel and his nurse, as well as Clara and Ellen, had been taking turns to care for him round the clock, and the whole while an armed policeman had been posted by the door.

"He's finally regained consciousness," Daniel informed Anna more than a week later. They'd met for tea at the hotel on Monday afternoon. "But he's as weak as a newborn kitten."

"Still, Clara must be so relieved."

"She's with him now, with instructions just to sit quietly. He's not ready to engage with anyone yet."

"Do you think he'll fully recover?" She stirred sugar into her tea.

"I think he's turned a corner. He's not out of the woods yet, but at least he won't lose his leg."

"Do the police know he's conscious?" she asked quietly.

"No." Daniel glanced around. "And for the boy's sake, I'd like to keep it like that."

"I understand."

"An interrogation could seriously set him back."

"It's strange...I used to barely tolerate that surly kid," Anna admitted. "Now I honestly feel sorry for him. I've been praying for him daily."

"Well, he owes you and Katy a great deal of thanks for rescuing him that night. I doubt he would've survived otherwise."

"I'm just so curious as to how he got there. And even more curious about the whereabouts of Albert and the other man."

"Did you hear that the boat was found?"

"No." She set down her teacup. "Are you certain?"

"I don't like to eavesdrop, but this morning during the changing of the guard—"

"What?"

"You know, the policemen outside AJ's door. I overheard the replacement cop telling the other one that they found the missing Krauss boat at low tide this morning. Or what was left of it. They think it sank just outside of the harbor. Parts of it washed up onto the beach. On the south end of town."

"Do you think that means that Albert and the other man may have drowned—and that somehow AJ made it to safety?"

"I have no idea." He frowned.

"Or...is it possible that Albert and the other guy are around here somewhere...hiding out?" She felt a shiver go through her.

"I guess that's possible."

"I'm sure the police will be even more eager to question AJ now." For that matter, Anna was eager too. Not just because it would make a great story for the paper, but if two dangerous men were at large, it seemed the press's responsibility to inform the public and engage their help.

"And that is precisely why I think I should cut our visit short, Anna. I don't want anyone bursting in on that boy, hoping to extract information. Not until he's stronger." Daniel laid money on the table. "So, please excuse me."

"Of course." She held her teacup up to him. "I appreciate your devotion to your patient."

Anna was just finishing her tea when Rand entered the restaurant. Waving at her, he came to her table. "I thought I saw you and Daniel coming in here." He glanced around. "Where is the good doctor?"

"He needed to check on his patient."

"May I?" Rand pointed to the chair.

"Certainly." She smiled.

"You mean he's checking on AJ?"

She just nodded. "Did you hear the news?"

"What news?"

"About AJ's boat washing ashore this morning?"

"Really?"

"That's why Daniel hurried back. He's worried the police will want to interrogate AJ now."

"But isn't he unconscious?"

"He's awake."

Rand suddenly stood. "Then I need to see him."

"May I go with you?"

"Why not? After all, you and Katy are the only reason he's not dead right now."

"What are you going to do there?" she asked as they exited the hotel.

"First of all, I need to ensure that the police don't question AJ. Not without his lawyer present."

"Daniel doesn't want them to speak to him at all. Not yet anyway."

"That works for me." As they hurried down to Daniel's office, Rand confided to her that he hoped to get a statement from AJ before the police got involved. "I think I'll have an easier time getting the truth out of him without their intervention. The police might come across as the enemy. He might clam up. But I need him to be honest with me. That's his best chance at getting less time."

"Meaning you think he'll be sentenced?"

"It's likely. First he'll be charged and arraigned. But I think the court will be lenient if they see him cooperating. At least that's my hope."

When they got to AJ's bedside, they were surprised to see him sitting up in bed and appearing fairly coherent. "He ate most of this." Clara held up a bowl of unfinished soup. "Dr. Hollister says he's improving."

"Have the police tried to question him?" Rand asked her.

"Not yet. The doctor is holding them back."

"Good." Rand pulled a chair up next to the bed. "I don't want them talking to him unless I'm here." He looked into AJ's face. "I'm your attorney." He stuck out a hand. "And, believe me, buddy, you're going to need one."

AJ frowned as he shook Rand's hand.

"Do you feel up to talking a little? Or do you need to rest?"

AJ glanced around the room, his eyes settling on his mother. "You should go," he told her. Clara looked slightly hurt but didn't argue as she slipped out. Now AJ frowned at Anna. "What's she here for?" he asked Rand.

"You may not remember this, but Anna and Katy are the ones who saved your life. And Anna got Dr. Hollister to help you, and she asked me to be your legal representation. You owe her a world of gratitude, son."

AJ's brow creased. "I do remember you and Katy...that night. Thanks."

"I'll go if you want." Anna moved for the door.

"I'd like Anna to stay and take notes, if you don't mind, AJ. While we talk. Kind of like my legal secretary. She can be trusted."

He shrugged. "Okay."

So Anna sat in the chair by the window, removed her notepad and pencil from her briefcase, and quietly listened as Rand made friendly small talk with AJ. He was obviously trying to win his trust. And then Rand put on his lawyer hat and informed AJ that he was in very serious trouble, explaining how the law might go more gently with him if he disclosed everything.

"Everything?" AJ questioned.

"I mean everything." Rand nodded. "You need to understand that your other friends, the ones that were caught the night of the raid, are already cooperating with the police. Several of them have given full confessions in hope of leniency. So the law knows exactly what your dad's involvement has been in running rum. What they don't know is where he is right now...and what happened after you guys got away...and who your dad is connected with. Stuff like that." Rand leaned back in the chair, folding his hands behind his head. "So if you feel like talking, now is the time, AJ. Before the police burst in here and attempt to shake you down."

"I don't know." AJ let out a sigh. "You could be tricking me."

Anna couldn't remain quiet. "AJ," she spoke gently. "Mr. Douglas is your attorney. That means he's on *your* side. He has nothing to gain by tricking you. He's just trying to make sure the police don't come in here and get you to say something you'll regret. Their goal is to put you away—for a long time. Mr. Douglas's goal is to see you are treated fairly—by the police and by the court."

"It's your choice," Rand told him. "Trust me...or leave yourself in the hands of the police." He stood, acting like he was going to leave.

"I'll trust you," AJ said sullenly. "What do you want to know?"

"Where's your dad?"

"I don't know." AJ's eyes narrowed.

"Do you know if he's alive?"

"Yeah. He's alive." AJ slowly relayed the story of how his

boat started taking in water from a gunshot hole, how they had to swim for shore. "My leg was bleeding and hurting real bad. Ralph was trying to help me."

"Ralph Greeley?"

"Yeah." AJ's eyes grew sad.

"Where was your dad then?" Rand questioned.

"He swam ahead. But Ralph was helping me. Then he started cramping up, and he kept going down. I could tell he wasn't going to make it. I yelled at Dad to help us, but he...he just kept swimming for shore." AJ looked close to tears. "I had to leave Ralph behind. Barely made it myself."

"And your dad? Did he help you on the beach?"

"By the time I made land, Dad wasn't there."

"You didn't see him at all?"

"I tried to follow his tracks in the sand, but I passed out in the bushes...it was the next day when I came to. Dad was long gone."

"Do you have any idea where he went?"

AJ just shook his head. "But he was real mad. When we were on the boat and it was starting to sink, he claimed he knew who to blame."

"Who to blame for what?"

"For the raid. He said he was gonna get the squealer."

Anna cringed inwardly but kept her expression composed. Did Albert know she was the "squealer"? Did he plan to get her?

"Do you think your dad is still nearby?" Rand calmly asked. "Somewhere near town?"

"I don't know." AJ scowled.

"Did he have any place where he'd try to hide out?"

AJ rubbed the bandage on his head with a pained expression.

Anna came over to stand by the bed. "I think that's

enough, Rand. AJ needs rest. Let him get better before you question him further."

"You're probably right." He placed a hand on AJ's shoulder. "Good job, AJ. You keep cooperating with me, and I'll do everything I can to help you. And don't tell the police anything unless I'm here with you. Understand?"

"Yeah." AJ looked up at Anna with sad eyes. "Please...tell Katy I'm sorry."

"Sorry?" she asked.

"She told me to stay out of it. She warned me. I wish I'd listened."

"I'll tell Katy," Anna promised. "You just keep getting well, AJ. I have a feeling life will get better for you in time."

He leaned back with a doubtful expression. "I don't know." He closed his eyes with a weary sigh. "I think I've sealed my fate."

After they left AJ's room, Rand spoke to the policeman guarding the door, convincing him that AJ was still too tired to talk much. "I'll let the chief know what's going on," he assured him. "But we need to give the boy a day or two. The doctor can tell you more about his condition."

As she waited for Rand, Anna's heart went out to AJ. With a father like Albert, why would anyone be surprised that he'd fallen into such a mess? What kind of man would leave his wounded son and friend behind to drown? And what about his vendetta plans? Did Albert really know who was responsible for his downfall? And what if he came after Anna—or worse, her family? She knew she had to do something, but she wasn't sure what.

CHAPTER 30

Before leaving Daniel's office, Anna borrowed the phone to call home. When Bernice answered, Anna told her—in no uncertain terms—that Katy was to be kept to the confines of the house. "And keep the doors and windows all locked." She quickly explained the possibility of Albert still being in town...and dangerous. "I'll ask Chief Rollins to send out a man to keep an eye on things."

"But Katy is down at Lucille's." Bernice's voice was heavy with concern.

"Well, that's probably even better. Just the same, keep the doors locked and be on your guard. If anything suspicious happens, call the police immediately. And I'll call Lucille's and let Katy know to stay put until I get home."

Finally reassured that her loved ones were as safe as possible, Anna went with Rand to the police station, where she immediately asked the chief to send a man out to keep an eye on the house. Then she and Rand took turns relaying the significant portions of AJ's confession to Chief Rollins. The chief expressed his gratitude, and Anna prepared to leave.

"I've always believed in the power of the pen." Anna

gathered her things. "And I feel an urgent responsibility to run a front-page story that will warn our neighbors that Albert could be hiding anywhere right now. He's a desperate outlaw, and we all need to be on the lookout for him. The sooner he's caught, the safer we'll all be."

"Especially Anna." Rand reminded the chief about Albert's threat to get the "squealer." "I think we need to take that seriously."

"And I really appreciate you sending someone to guard our house and Lucille's too," Anna told the chief. "Hopefully it's not necessary."

"You really don't think Albert *knows* it was you?" Chief Rollins pressed her.

"I honestly don't see how he could know."

"So you're not terribly concerned?"

She shrugged. "Of course I'm concerned. But not just for me. I'm concerned for everyone. Albert is a desperate man. I have no doubt he's dangerous." She stood, gathering up her things. "But, if you'll excuse me, I have a newspaper to get out."

Her bravado may have been a good act, but Anna was no fool and, as she walked the short distance to the newspaper office, she kept her eyes wide open.

Back at the office, she stopped by Virginia's desk. "Any word from Wesley yet?" she asked as she picked up the mail. He'd been absent from their morning meeting. "Did he call in sick or anything?"

"Not a word. I even called his boardinghouse to check on him." Virginia frowned. "Mrs. Halverson told me she hasn't seen him. Not in days."

"In days?"

"That's what she said."

"Interesting." Anna went to Jim's office and asked if he'd seen Wesley during the weekend.

Jim's brow creased. "Come to think of it, I don't recall seeing him at all. Not since Friday afternoon."

"Is that unusual? I know you're not friends, but you do live in the same building. Don't your paths normally cross?"

"Sure. Whether I like it or not." He grinned. "What's up?"

"I don't know. But I think I'll ask Mrs. Halverson to check on him. Maybe he's sick. He might need help."

Anna went to her office to call the boardinghouse, waiting on the phone while Mrs. Halverson went to check on him. After a few minutes, she came back to the phone. "I can't make heads or tails of it." Mrs. Halverson sounded perplexed. "He wasn't in his room. And, according to the elderly man with a room next door, he hasn't heard a peep out of him in days. And, believe you me, these walls are paper thin."

"Did it look like he'd moved out? Or perhaps he took a weekend trip?"

"His bed was made up, and his clothes were in the closet. Even his shaving things and hairbrush were on the dresser, and his suitcase still under the bed. I'm used to looking for these sorts of clues—sometimes tenants skip out on me—but Wesley's rent was paid through the end of August. I can't figure where he's disappeared to, but I must say it looks suspicious."

Anna thanked her then called Chief Rollins with this concerning information. "And there are a few other things you should probably know." She relayed how she and Daniel had witnessed Wesley in a confrontation with Mayor Snyder. "And then Jim observed Wesley in a heated argument with Albert Krauss not long before the dustup down at the docks."

"Interesting. I thought Wesley was on good terms with both of them."

"That's why it caught our attention," she confided.

"So Wesley somehow got on their bad side."

"At the time, I'd hoped it was because Wesley had come to his senses and stood up to them," she confessed. "I actually tried to talk to him...reminded him about Mac's hopes for him, tried to get him to listen. Not that it did any good." Now she told the chief about Mac's missing file and how she felt certain that Wesley had taken it. "Mac can't remember what was in the file, but we're pretty sure it had some incriminating stuff. Maybe it was regarding the mayor or Albert."

"That wouldn't be surprising. Mac certainly had his suspicions about their operations."

Anna suddenly got an idea. "Do you think Wesley might've attempted to use that information against them somehow?"

"You mean like blackmail?"

"I don't know about that. But I do know Wesley loves power. He's exhibited that to me more than once here at the newspaper. Maybe he wanted to get the upper hand with them for some reason."

"Interesting theory."

"Well, I just thought you should know that Wesley is missing."

"And I wanted to let you know that, besides sending a man to watch Mac's house, I also sent some men and hounds out to poke around the nearby coastline. It occurred to me there are plenty of places to hide out along our beach and around the cove. With any luck, they'll unearth Albert's hideout and haul him in. Then everyone can sleep well again."

"I'd sure appreciate that, Chief." As Anna hung up the phone, she prayed a quick prayer for Albert to be captured, then turned to her typewriter. She had a vital story to write—something to get everyone on the lookout for Albert Krauss. Too bad they didn't have a reward to offer.

Everyone in Sunset Cove seemed to be on high alert after the midweek paper came out, informing everyone that Albert Krauss could be hiding anywhere nearby. But Anna was probably more on edge than anyone. "Sunset Cove used to be such a sweet, peaceful place," she said absently. She was having tea with Lucille and Clara. Ellen and Katy were upstairs, working on a sewing project. In many ways, all seemed peaceful and well.

"I know just what you mean," Lucille agreed. "But now it feels so sinister and dangerous. It's as if I'm a captive in my own home."

"And all because of Albert." Clara fretted with her napkin. "I'm so sorry."

"It's not your fault," Anna assured her. "I'm sorry I even brought it up."

"I just wish they could find him." Clara twisted the napkin into a tight ball. "I wish they would nab him and lock him up and throw away the key." She glanced at Lucille. "Does that make me a terrible person?"

"Not at all, dear." Lucille patted her hand.

"Do you have any idea where he might be hiding?" Anna asked Clara...not for the first time. "Any place you might've forgotten about?"

"Like I told you and Chief Rollins...I honestly don't know where he could be. Albert was always out and about on his boats—only the good Lord knows where. Besides that, there are so many places to hide right on our own property—the warehouse, the boats, our home, and the outbuildings—but according to the chief, his men are checking those places off and on every day."

Anna suddenly thought of something. "What about looking inside your little fish shop, Clara? Do you think the police have done careful checks in there?"

"I assume they go through all the buildings." Clara shook her head.

"It's just that I recall that first time when I visited you in the shop. Do you remember that day, Clara?"

"Yes, sort of."

"Remember how Albert seemed to pop out of nowhere? It nearly scared me to death, because he just seemed to appear."

"Oh yes. He'd been in the storage closet."

"But there was no door," Anna reminded her.

"Yes." Clara nodded eagerly. "You're right. It's a secret closet that Albert designed because he was afraid we'd get robbed and—" Clara stood up with wide eyes. "Do you think?"

"What if he's hiding there?" Anna pointed to the phone. "Call the chief, Clara. Tell him all about it."

"Yes," Lucille urged her. "Call him at once."

They both listened as Clara explained the secret closet to Chief Rollins, describing exactly where it was, how big it was, and how Albert could be ducking into it when the police came around. "Albert would have access to food in the shop," she continued. "And the closet is big enough for a man to sleep in and stay warm. And the shop has running water and everything." She gave a few more details then hung up the phone. "Chief Rollins is going to go check on it today," she told Anna and Lucille. "Wouldn't it be wonderful if—"

"Here we come," Katy announced as she and Ellen came down the stairs, wearing pretty dresses. "What do you think of these?"

Anna looked at the pair of stylish girls. "You both look lovely. Did you sew those yourselves?" She got up to inspect the workmanship more closely. Though Katy was clever with designing, occasionally her patience wasn't quite as developed and her sewing would get sloppy. But these garments looked very professional.

"Mama did most of the sewing," Ellen told Anna. "But Katy is the designer."

"These are beautifully made." Anna fingered a seam as Lucille came over to examine them.

"Very, very nice," Lucille confirmed. "I do believe you ladies could open your own dress shop, if you were so inclined."

"Oh, wouldn't that be a dream come true?" Ellen exclaimed. "Katy could be the designer, and Mama could be the seamstress, and I suppose I could sweep the floors."

"No. You could do the finish work," Katy told Ellen. "You're a whiz with the needle, Ellen."

"Wouldn't that be fun?" Ellen sighed dreamily. "Our own dress shop." She laughed. "As if that could ever happen."

"I don't see why it couldn't." Lucille grinned. "You ladies have the talent...I have the funds...all we need is a building."

Suddenly they were all musing about the possibilities of starting up a small dress shop business in town, even discussing properties that might be available. Although Clara had a small amount of money saved up, much of it was promised to AJ's legal defense, and she still wasn't sure if the fish company was going to be confiscated by the law.

But Lucille's offer to help finance a small business seemed entirely sincere.

"You would really do that for us, Grandmother?" Katy asked hopefully.

"Well, if I thought my granddaughter was going to remain here in Sunset Cove..." Lucille's words seemed laced with enticement. "I'm not so sure about my involvement if my granddaughter returns to Portland."

Katy looked torn.

"Well, it's certainly something to consider," Anna told them. "But it'll be dinnertime soon, and I promised Bernice we wouldn't be late. Perhaps we can all discuss this—" Her words were cut off by the shrill ringing of the telephone. They all stopped talking, waiting as Lucille answered it.

"Yes, Chief Rollins, Clara and Ellen are still here with me. Anna and Katy are here as well." She paused to listen, her pale brows arching with interest. "You don't say. Well, that is very good news. Yes, I will let them know." She smiled at the women. "And, yes, I will tell them that too." She thanked him and hung up. "Well, ladies, we have some happy news. Happy for us anyway." She chuckled. "Albert Krauss was apprehended at the fish shop—hiding in the secret closet, just like you had suspected. And the chief thanks you, Clara, for the helpful tip."

"Dad has been arrested?" Ellen looked slightly upset.

"Yes, dear." Clara went over to hug her. "You know, it's really for the best."

Ellen blinked back tears. "I know. And I'm very relieved, Mama. But a little sad too." She sighed. "And embarrassed."

"Embarrassed?" Lucille frowned. "Whatever for, dear girl?"

"Oh, you know...my father is a crook."

Katy slipped an arm around Ellen. "Well, you're in good company, friend. I already told you about my father."

Lucille held up a finger. "And, my darlings, if it makes you feel any better, my father was a good-for-nothing too." Suddenly they were all laughing...and crying...but mostly in relief.

CHAPTER 31

For Saturday's paper, Anna's editorial column focused on what some people, including the missing Wesley Kempton, liked to call "a victimless crime." She listed all the people—some by name and some by innuendo—who had been hurt by the blatant disregard of state prohibition laws. She detailed how individuals had suffered and what it had cost the community, in general as well as financially. She also voiced her concerns that this battle was not yet over. She pointed out that, living in a free democracy, it was up to the citizens to make and support the law of the land. And she essentially called the good people of Sunset Cove to a higher level of accountability—and encouraged them to vote with their conscience in the upcoming fall election. Although, to be honest, she felt relatively certain that Wally had it won.

Anna did not allude to the fact that this piece was, in essence, her Sunset Cove swan song. But she knew that since it was late August, it was decision-making time. And, believing that much of her work here in Sunset Cove was done, she didn't feel too guilty about leaving. It did bother her that Wesley was still missing, but there was nothing she could do about it. And Jim had agreed to take over as editor in chief, with Mac operating from home in an advisory role.

Anna actually had some excitement about returning to Portland. Especially after her recent exchange of telegrams with the editor in chief at the *Oregonian*. She'd been pleasantly surprised to discover that a good editorial job awaited her there, combined with the satisfaction that she'd actually been missed and that her previous boss had been let go.

Did that mean she wanted to go back to Portland for good? She wasn't really sure and even wondered if she might only stay long enough for Katy to finish her education. Of course, there were activities she enjoyed in a metropolitan city...but there were things she loved about Sunset Cove as well. It didn't help matters that Katy had been unusually quiet and hard to read of late. In some ways, Katy seemed just as torn as Anna on the subject of *home*. Finally, Anna decided she would let her daughter make the decision. It seemed only fair.

"Grandmother has invited us all to a big dinner party on Tuesday night," Katy told Anna. It was one of those perfect summer afternoons—sunny with no wind—and Anna and Katy were having lemonade out on the terrace overlooking the ocean. "I think it's to say good-bye."

"So you told her we're going home to Portland?" Anna asked hesitantly.

"Well, this is the last week of August." Katy's tone was a bit sharp. "My friends have written to me about parties and social activities. All sorts of picnics and dances are scheduled during Labor Day weekend. I'd hate to miss out on all the fun. Not a good way to start a new school year."

"Of course." Anna nodded resolutely.

"And you've got your job at the *Oregonian* back, so it seems only—"

"What's this?" Mac stepped out from his sitting room, hobbling toward them with the help of his cane. "What did you say?"

"Lemonade?" Anna offered, hoping to change the subject.

"What's this job?" he demanded as he sat down next to Anna.

"Mother has been offered an editorial job at the *Oregonian*," Katy informed him.

As Anna filled a glass of lemonade, she wished she'd kept that bit of information from her daughter. At least for the time being. She'd hoped to break it gently to Mac...after they were certain.

"You *already* have a job," Mac declared.

Anna attempted a meek smile as she handed him the glass. "I know, Mac. And I've really enjoyed working at the *Sunset Times*, and it's been—"

"But you're leaving?" His voice cracked with emotion.

Anna glanced at Katy. "Well, Katy has her school and her friends...I promised her we'd go home after summer—"

"*This* is home," he insisted.

"Yes," she agreed. "Sunset Cove will always be home. I expect that Katy and I will be coming back here every chance we get, and—"

"No." He slammed his glass down onto the side table so hard that the pitcher of lemonade rattled. "You can't go. I won't let you."

"Mac." Anna placed a hand on his shoulder. "Let's just be thankful that we got reconnected this summer. That is worth so—"

"No!" he declared loudly. "This is your home, Anna. And

your home, Katy." He turned to Anna with glistening eyes. "Please, please, *don't go.*"

Anna felt her heart twisting painfully as tears slid down his cheeks. "Oh, Mac. I don't want to go, it's just that—"

"I don't want to go either!" Katy exclaimed.

"But your school? Your friends?" Anna asked her.

"I can go to school right here. I have friends here."

"That's right!" Mac declared.

"You would be happy here?" Anna asked Katy. "Honestly?"

"Yes." Katy nodded eagerly. "I want to stay, Mother. I love being around my grandparents. I love being near the ocean. And there's Ellen and Clara. And we want to start our dress shop and—"

"You really want to stay?" Anna asked again. "You're not just saying that for me?"

"I *want* to stay, Mother. But I was afraid that you wanted to go back to Portland—and then you got that telegram from the *Oregonian*, and—"

"Then it's settled." Mac stuck out a hand to Anna. "You will stay here. You will run the *Sunset Times.*"

She shook his hand. "Yes. If that's what you want. What Katy wants."

"It's what we all want, Mother." Katy threw her arms around both of them, hugging them tightly and kissing both of them on the cheek. "I'm going over to Grandmother's to tell them our good news." She stood happily. "I'll tell her that her dinner party can be a celebration—that we are staying!"

"Thank you, Anna." Mac blotted his tears with his handkerchief as Katy hurried away.

"You're welcome," she told him. "But I should be thanking *you.* Thanks for insisting that we stay, Mac. Both

Katy and I were having such a hard time deciding. I guess we both wanted to give each other what we thought the other needed."

He looked into her eyes. "I need you, Anna. I need both of you. Thank you for staying."

Lucille had been glad to change her farewell dinner party to a happy celebration over the news that her daughter and granddaughter had decided to make Sunset Cove their permanent home. In her enthusiasm, she invited so many of their friends that she had to beg Mac to relocate the party to his much more spacious house. Mac assured her that he was delighted to play co-host. And it was plain to see that he was in his element as he and Lucille welcomed friends of all ages into his home. The older folks, including Wally and Thelma and several other couples, were happily visiting in the living room. Meanwhile, the younger ones, Katy and Ellen and their friends, were enjoying Mac's billiard table downstairs.

Anna was enjoying the companionship of her friends out on the terrace. It was fun to see Clara dressed prettily—thanks to Katy's efforts. Rand was reassuring her that AJ was going to be given an option to serve time in a juvenile facility until he turned eighteen, with the understanding he would then enlist in the military, which was something he'd wanted to do anyway.

"And his leg is healing up so nicely that I don't think he'll have any problems with the physical," Daniel confirmed to Clara.

"If AJ agrees, I'd like to run an article about that," Anna told Clara. "I mean when the time comes. I just think the public would enjoy hearing a happy ending to a difficult tale."

"That's a wonderful idea." Clara's eyes shone with gratitude.

Anna turned to Jim. "Maybe you'd like to write it."

"You bet." He nodded. "And just for the record, I'm glad I don't have to act as editor in chief after all."

"Really?" She was relieved but slightly surprised.

"Oh yeah. I'd much rather write than manage," he admitted. Then he started to tell them about a novel he was working on. "It's about a small town trying to enforce prohibition." He laughed. "If you can imagine that." He was just starting to describe the opening scene when Anna noticed that Chief Rollins was waving to her.

She excused herself and went over to say hello.

"Can we talk privately?" he asked with a furrowed brow.

"Of course." She led him around the house to the back porch. "What's going on?"

"Well, I didn't want to tell the others. I especially don't want Mac to know. Not yet."

"What is it?"

"It's Wesley Kempton." He grimly shook his head. "We found him."

"Is he—"

"Dead," he answered quietly.

Anna felt a lump in her throat. "Oh dear."

"It looks like murder, and I suspect that Albert Krauss or his cronies are involved, but I haven't begun to interrogate yet."

"Poor Wesley." Anna retrieved a handkerchief from her dress pocket. "Mac will be so sad to hear this."

"I know." He nodded somberly. "The only reason I'm

telling you this tonight is because you'd been asking about him. I felt you should know."

"Yes, I appreciate that. I just wish it'd had a better outcome."

"So do I."

"Wesley made his mistakes, but he didn't deserve this." She dabbed her tears.

"I agree. I'm sure you'll want to do a piece for the paper, Anna. And I know you'll handle it fairly...and responsibly. But the public deserves your honesty."

"Yes, of course."

"The fact is that Wesley got involved with a bad crowd, and I'm afraid it caught up with him."

"I just wish he'd listened to me...I tried to warn him." She sadly shook her head. "I remember Wesley's claim that rum-running was a victimless crime."

"Until he became the victim."

For a long moment, neither of them spoke. There was just the sound of the waves hitting the rocks down below them.

"Thank you for not telling Mac about this tonight," she finally told him.

"I didn't want to ruin his evening. And I sure hope I didn't spoil the party for you. I just felt you deserved to know."

"I appreciate that. And don't worry, I'll be fine," she assured him. "After all, I'm a newspaperwoman. I'm used to this sort of thing." She stood straighter as she pocketed her handkerchief. "Remember, I worked in Portland for many years. I heard and saw a lot during that time." She knew her words expressed more confidence than she felt.

He reached out to shake her hand. "I'm sure glad you're sticking around Sunset Cove, Anna. You're a strong woman and a real asset here. And we need you at the helm of the newspaper. More than ever right now. Especially with the upcoming election...and everything else that's going on around town." His smile was slightly grim. "Mac should be very proud of you."

Anna thanked him again. Then, with a contrasting mix of emotions rumbling inside of her, she returned to her friends on the terrace, and the chief went to visit with Mac and the others in the living room. Both of them acting as if everything was perfectly fine and normal.

And what she'd said was true—Anna was used to tragedies like this, and she was a newspaperwoman. Still, she was human too. Pasting on a smile wasn't easy, but it seemed necessary. And as the evening continued, she did her best to visit with everyone, maintaining her party face until she finally began to relax again. Chief Rollins's words had begun to resonate within her. She believed she really was here in Sunset Cove for a reason...and her work here was far from done. And, really, she didn't expect it to be easy. She didn't even *want* it to be easy. She'd always welcomed challenges...and she knew there were plenty on the road up ahead.

But her life here in Sunset Cove wouldn't only be about problems. Anna smiled at the three interesting and attractive men now vying for her attention and the right to escort her into the dining room. Now this was a pleasant sort of problem—and something she'd never imagined while living back in the city! Another good reminder that her life shouldn't be limited to career goals alone. That was a luxury she could never afford as a single mother working hard to provide for her child.

As much as Anna had enjoyed being a newswoman, she now looked forward to simply being a woman...with a real life. And seeing her two parents, smiling happily as they sat down at opposite ends of the long dining room table... and watching as her daughter with her new young friends took their places...and seeing herself surrounded by happy friends and family, Anna felt certain that—perhaps for the first time ever—she was truly home.

OTHER BOOKS BY MELODY CARLSON

THE MULLIGAN SISTERS
I'll Be Seeing You
As Time Goes By
String of Pearls
We'll Meet Again

DEAR DAPHNE
Home, Hearth, and the Holidays
A Will, a Way, and a Wedding

SECOND CHANCES
Heartland Skies
Built with Love
Shades of Light
Thursday's Child
Looking for Cassandra Jane
Armando's Treasure

WHISPERING PINES
A Place to Come Home To
Everything I Long For
Looking for You All My Life
Someone to Belong To